SIBERIAN
TRANSFER

Also by Hans Herlin

Grishin
The Last Spring in Paris
Solo Run
Which Way the Wind
Commemorations

Hans Herlin

Translated from the German by John Brownjohn

St. Martin's Press   New York

This novel is a work of fiction. All of the events, characters, names, and places depicted in this novel are entirely fictitious or are used fictitiously. No representation that any statement made in this novel is true, or that any incident depicted in this novel actually occurred, is intended or should be inferred by the reader.

Originally published as SIBIRIEN TRANSFER
© 1988 Hans Herlin.

Design by Judith Christensen

Library of Congress Cataloging-in-Publication Data

Herlin, Hans
    Siberian transfer / Hans Herlin.
        p. cm.
    ISBN 0-312-07803-X
     1. Soviet Union—History—Revolution, 1917–1921—Fiction.
  I. Title.
PR9105.9.H45S5   1992
813'.54—dc20   90-27502
                                                      CIP
                                                      r92

First Edition: July 1992

10 9 8 7 6 5 4 3 2 1

SIBERIAN
TRANSFER

PART ONE

PART ONE

THE SENTINEL

"*AKULA! Prokliataya akula! Poluchai eto!*"

Although he had almost certainly killed the Englishman with his first shot, Nikulin went on cursing and firing until the magazine was empty. He didn't put his last few rounds into the figure on the ground. They ripped dry bark from the surrounding trees and, when he aimed still higher, lacerated the leaves overhead. Little patches of blue showed through.

The clear, cloudless sky and the thought of the airplane brought him to his senses. He held his breath and froze until the reverberations grew fainter and died away. Long shafts of sunlight slanted down through the trees. The air was warm and heavy with the scent of pine resin. The forest was alive with bees.

All was as peaceful as before, but to Nikulin the hush seemed to have taken on a different character—a hostile, conspiratorial quality. He dismissed the impression but recharged his magazine.

The Englishman was lying among some tall ferns at the forest's edge, face down on a thick carpet of moss, one hand clawing the ground. Nikulin couldn't see the point of entry, but the blood that had discolored the man's jacket was still oozing into the forest floor. He bent down to roll him over on his back. One cuff was protruding from his sleeve, and something shiny caught the Russian's eye: a heavy, chunky gold cuff link in the shape of a four-leaf clover.

Nikulin straightened up and stepped back. His anger revived.

"*Akula!*" he swore. "You earned that, you goddamned shark!"

Then he noticed the anthill and saw the first of its big, black denizens making for the body.

"I ought to leave you lying there till they chew you down to your bones."

The airplane ruled that out, he knew. He struggled to regain his composure. It helped to remind himself of who and where he was: Fyodor Nikulin, commander of the Blue Train, cut off behind enemy lines. He'd been alone in the mountains, watching and waiting, for five long weeks. He should have taken it for granted that the consignment would attract sharks. The scent was too strong, too alluring.

"Thanks for the warning."

Nikulin turned the Englishman on his back. The dead face, which was heavily tanned, might have been cast in bronze. Only the vivid blue of the eyes suggested that this had been a living, breathing human being just moments ago.

Nikulin suddenly found the eyes unnerving. He put out a hand and thumbed the eyelids shut. Blood began to ooze once more from the wound near the heart as he dragged the body out of the sunlight and into the trees.

The Englishman's corpse was crawling with ants by the time Nikulin returned an hour later, carrying a pick and shovel. Unhurriedly he dug a hole in the forest floor and rolled the body into it. The other cuff link was missing, but there was no sign of it in the vicinity.

"You'll have to get by with one," Nikulin said aloud.

He shoveled soil back into the grave, trod it flat, and scattered the residue. He'd only just finished when he heard the drone of the airplane. It turned up every day, at precisely the same time. Two hours before sunset it overflew Two Brothers Pass and headed for Karmel along the northern arm of the Trans-Siberian Railroad, which traversed the Urals. After circling the Karmel area for half an hour it flew back the way it had come.

The machine was a two-seater biplane of British design. Nikulin had seen it more than once at very close range, skimming the treetops so low that he could make out the pilot and, seated behind him, an observer with a camera. He'd grown accustomed to the airplane and found the sight of it reassuring because its reconnaissance flights seemed to indicate that nothing had yet been detected. Today was different from that angle too: he didn't feel so sure anymore.

He stayed where he was until the airplane disappeared. As soon as the roar of the engine had faded and died he set off for his cabin.

His route took him through a dense pine forest of soaring gray trunks. It hadn't rained for weeks and the carpet of needles underfoot was tinder-dry. The long spell of fine weather, an alpine Indian summer, had simplified his life in the mountains till now.

The trees thinned and the rising ground became stonier. Nikulin was feeling hungry and yearned for a cigarette, but he pressed on. Though not a big man, he moved in a way that betokened toughness and stamina. His face, lean with broad cheekbones, was set in a look of unflagging determination.

He paused only once, and that was when he reached a point on the old pass road known locally as the Horses' Graveyard. The air felt thinner and colder here, but not only because of the altitude and the setting sun. The wind had veered. It was now blowing from the northeast in strong, chill gusts. Nikulin shivered in his sweat-sodden clothes.

He turned. From here he had a panoramic view of the whole Karmel area, the crests and valleys of the Urals, chain after chain of thickly wooded hills, and, rising above the timberline in the northeast, massive walls of bare rock and one or two rugged, isolated peaks. He couldn't see Karmel itself. At night the town's location was betrayed by a glow in the sky, but by day it was hidden from view behind one of the wooded crests. All that could be seen was the railroad station on the edge of the plain, and the settlement of the mine workers. His face seemed to get even leaner.

He would never see Moura again now. Not to be able to talk with her anymore would leave his life more empty than even he could bear. He put no great hope in the future, but he had lately discovered how much it helped to remember. And Moura Toumanova was such an important part of his past. . . .

He turned his gaze to the horizon. Clouds were gathering on the distant skyline, but the plain was bathed in the light peculiar to these mountains just before sunset, a glow that infused the air with singular clarity and transparency. Nothing was stirring on the plain, not even a plume of dust, but again Nikulin sensed a change: he seemed to detect movement everywhere. The sharks were converging on Karmel in droves, not singly like the Englishman. They could smell blood.

Nothing definable had really changed, but to Nikulin everything felt different.

"*Akula! Prokliataya akula!*"

He growled the words again and turned away, only to stop short after a couple of steps and look back. He peered again at the densely wooded hills around Karmel.

There were deciduous trees growing among the spruces and pines on the lower slopes. He noticed for the first time that their leaves had begun to turn.

Fyodor Nikulin smiled grimly to himself. They were just the color of gold ingots. . . .

1

QUINN should have been feeling good. He was not a man prone to melancholic introspection, and here, in the outdoors, his life, despite certain memories, seemed to him just as it should be: an adventure as limitless as the vast Siberian steppe.

The day had gotten off to a promising start. The bulrushes were encrusted with dry, white hoarfrost and the dawn light was clear and crystalline. The Irtysh flooded here every fall, creating a marshy lakeland many miles wide: countless channels separated by islands overgrown with reeds. A wafer-thin film of fresh ice broke up on either side of the boat as it glided along. The ice fractured with a high-pitched, metallic sound that pierced the frosty air like the note of a tuning fork. In the east, on the far side of the river, the sun was rising. A pale disk shrouded in early morning mist, it would never, so it seemed, develop strength enough to illuminate the whole vast expanse.

"If it goes on freezing like this," Sednev had predicted, "there'll be plenty of duck." They'd left Omsk at midnight, reached the old Russian hunter's cabin outside Boloto before sunup, and embarked as soon as their simple breakfast was over.

Oliver Quinn had spent most of his life outdoors, and it showed. He was forty-two, with graying but luxuriant hair. Everything about him radiated health and strength. He had a narrow face and eyes so deep set that the intensity of their gaze was not immediately apparent; a once kind and open face that time and weather had carved into something sterner. No one would have put him down as a man prone to self-doubt.

Sednev, seated on the thwart behind him, shipped the pole he'd been using to propel them along. The flat-bottomed, puntlike boat glided on for a couple of lengths and came to rest, half-hidden by reeds, alongside one of the countless islets. The current was stronger here, so no ice had formed. Some feathers drifted past on the gunmetal surface—freshly shed feathers, from the way they rode high in the water. Sednev pointed in silence, but Quinn had already spotted them. "You were right," he said.

"Ready, *Anglichanin?*"

Sednev couldn't pronounce the name Quinn. Quinn had invited the old hunter to use his first name, but it wasn't in his nature to do it. Sednev felt that anyone who paid good money for his services had purchased his respect and deference as well, so he left it at plain *Anglichanin*, Englishman.

Quinn heard another whisper behind his back and reached for the double-barreled shotgun. "What's the matter with me?" he wondered aloud. He usually forgot his cares in the wild. Hunting blocked out all thoughts of anything else.

"Ready? He'll fly straight at you."

Sednev cupped his hands together and put them to his mouth. Quinn cocked both hammers and peered ahead. From behind him, skillfully imitated, came the call of a duck. It sounded so soft and seductive that Quinn himself was momentarily deceived.

There was a blur of movement above the reeds. All at once the airborne shape rocketed skyward and banked away steeply, wings whirring. Quinn, who had hesitated for an instant, failed to get off a shot. The drake glided away and splashed down somewhere out of sight. Quinn's brief glimpse of the bird's glossy green head and white neck ring told him that it was a large mallard. He felt annoyed with himself.

"I'd only have winged him."

"He'll be back," Sednev whispered. "You wait and see. He won't be able to resist." He cupped his hands again.

Quinn knelt down in the bow. The boat was rocking with the current, too narrow and light to provide a secure footing. The breeze had died, and Sednev's mating call floated across the water like thistledown. Remote surroundings, natural beauty, the hunter's thrill of anticipation—these things never failed in their effect on Quinn, always soothed his restless soul, and he told himself that this morning would be no exception. He breathed more evenly through parted lips. The air was so cold it seemed to freeze in his mouth. His hands tightened on the shotgun.

Again he heard a sudden flurry of wingbeats. The reeds flexed and swayed as the bird got up. This time he fired without delay. The mallard lurched in midair and began to climb, then plummeted, followed by a comet's tail of purplish-brown breast feathers.

The old hunter picked up the pole and thrust it into the bank. The craft floated clear, and he punted it over to where the bird was drifting with outspread wings.

They'd shot a dozen assorted ducks and four snipes. The sun blazed down out of a cloudless sky but the day was cold enough to keep the mosquitoes at bay. On the way back to the cabin they made a detour, and Sednev caught some grayling for their evening meal.

Quinn had achieved the physical exhaustion that was one of his keys to a sense of well-being. He was beginning to forget Omsk. They would spend the night out here and go duck hunting again at dawn tomorrow. The arrangement with Captain Balayev still stood: the Russian pilot would fly over from Omsk and ferry them to the Aissary Mountains in two days' time.

Anyone wishing to hunt in peace had to put a considerable distance between himself and Omsk, the White Army's Siberian headquarters. The officers stationed there had plenty of time on their hands, so they went hunting en masse, mowing down small game with machine guns and fishing with hand grenades. Game was now scarce in the immediate neighborhood of the city, but Sednev had managed to persuade the governor to issue them a special permit for two stags and one bear. They planned to spend a whole week hunting in the highlands. Quinn would then decide whether to quit his job at Omsk and return to England.

They hadn't wasted time on settling into their bivouac that morning, so they remedied the omission now. The cabin, a primitive wooden shack thatched with reeds, stood at the head of one of the river's minor tributaries. Quinn went inside to pull off his waterlogged boots while Sednev proceeded to rebuild the fireplace, which had collapsed during the summer. "Couldn't resist," Sednev sang to himself, "he couldn't resist, just couldn't resist the temptation. . . ."

It was Sednev's habit to muse and reminisce in song. When the old Kirghiz spoke normally—and he spoke as little as possible—you could be sure he had something important on his mind. This was a case in point. Quinn, still inside the cabin, heard his singsong voice die away.

"*Anglichanin*, here a minute!"

Quinn emerged into the open. On the far side of an expanse of peat bog the ground rose to form an embankment with a narrow track running along the top. A car was parked there, and beside it stood a man in uniform. He waved energetically.

"Captain Quinn? Hello, Captain Quinn!"

He was no more than a hundred yards away, but the long shadows cast by the setting sun played tricks with perspective. Seen against the immensity of the landscape beyond them, man and car looked toylike.

"Captain Quinn, sir, may I have a word? Captain Quinn!"

"That was a short hunting trip, *Anglichanin*." Sednev's nut-brown face was threaded with furrows and fissures, like ancient leather. They made him look even older than his years.

"Ignore him." Quinn turned back toward the cabin as if sheer inattention could dematerialize the man and the car.

"Quinn, the major wants to see you!"

Quinn tried to disregard the intrusive voice. "How's supper coming along?" he asked Sednev.

There was no escaping these people, even for a day. The irritation of recent weeks came back in an instant. The decision to accept the Russian assignment had been his, so he couldn't complain. Still, Fitzmaurice was the last person he wanted to see just now.

Quinn surveyed the scenery as if it might lend him some inner support. He looked out across the flooded river and the reed-fringed islands—out across the vast, deserted steppe that stretched away to the horizon. Wide open spaces had always fascinated him. Half of his forty-two years had been spent in the wilds, twenty of them, on and off, prospecting for gold in Canada. It was nostalgia for those days that had prompted him to exchange London for Siberia. He had been in Siberia once before, ten years ago. Now, as he surveyed the desolate terrain in the strange half-light of evening, its bleak expanse seemed suggestive of an alien planet.

He turned to Sednev. "I'll be back by dawn tomorrow," he said. "Or the day after at the latest, with Balayev."

"I'll wait," Sednev replied. The furrows in his cheeks deepened to the intimation of a smile. "A pity to waste that hunting permit."

Quinn was grateful to the old hunter for pretending to accept what neither of them really believed.

2

THE drive from Boloto to Omsk was tedious at the best of times. To Quinn in his present mood it seemed to take forever. The track meandered aimlessly across the parched gray grassland of the Siberian steppe. Last night's frost had thawed and dried, so they now trailed a thick plume of dust. In September, when it rained in torrents every day, the cabin was quite inaccessible, but the September rains had petered out three weeks ago.

The driver of the Ford groped for something under his seat. His hand reappeared holding a flat bottle labeled GENUINE NAVY RUM. As if guessing that Quinn would refuse, he raised the bottle to his lips and took a long pull. He threw his passenger a sidelong glance.

"I'm off duty, sir, in a manner of speaking."

The man's nasal voice made him sound as if he had a cold. His uniform was tight. Thirty or so, he had pale, colorless eyes and a fleshy face whose expression conveyed that he cherished few illusions and sought only one thing in life: as easy a ride as possible. He'd introduced himself as Sergeant Rice. Quinn couldn't recall having come across him before, but the British Military Mission at Omsk had many such misfits on its staff.

"You work for Fitzmaurice?"

"Yes, sir. Have done for years."

"Why does he want to see me?"

Rice broke into a kind of pidgin English. "Me only humble Indian bearer. Bring message from great white sahib."

"Any new crises at headquarters?"

Rice eyed Quinn. "There are sahibs and bearers," he said. "That's life. To change the subject, sir, what about those birds? Got any plans for them?"

12

Sednev had divided up their bag, and Quinn's share of the duck and snipe was stowed on the Ford's back seat.

"I could make you a good offer for them."

"They aren't for sale."

"I'll pay you in rum—genuine stuff from Navy stores. What would you say to a bottle a bird?"

"I don't drink rum."

"Soap, then? Genuine French soap—three bars apiece?"

Quinn felt disinclined to pursue conversation with the man. Perhaps Rice really didn't know why Fitzmaurice had sent for him. Then, to his surprise, the sergeant volunteered a crumb of information.

"Someone's been killed, that's all I know."

"Someone?"

"An agent—one of ours . . . I only heard by chance." Rice proffered the bottle. "Sure you won't have a drop?"

Quinn waved it away without a word. Major John Fitzmaurice headed the Secret Service outstation in Russia, but Quinn's work for him was unconnected with his network of agents. He'd been given the temporary rank of captain and sent to Siberia as an expert on mineral resources. When offering him the job six months ago the man from the War Office had represented it as a fascinating adventure, a mission worthy of Lawrence of Arabia, and reminded him of his patriotic duty. "You're a rich man, Quinn. Getting richer—is that really your only interest in life? Is it fulfilling enough for a man of your age? You're genuinely needed out there."

He'd spent most of his time in England behind a desk. That was just where his problem lay: the surplus pounds he was carrying around were mute testimony to what was wrong with his way of life. Overweight, indifferent to what he ate, sloppy in his dress, and obsessed with an overwhelming desire for physical activity, Quinn had never managed to resist his natural inclinations for long.

* * *

The road was more precipitous now that they'd left the plain behind them. Darkness was falling fast, and Quinn could already see the lights of the city glimmering in the dusk.

Omsk, which styled itself the capital of the Siberian steppe, was currently undergoing promotion to the seat of an anti-Bolshevik government headed by a new "Supreme Ruler," Admiral Kolchak. For the first time in this civil war between the Whites and the Reds it seemed that agreement on a unified high command had been reached by the leaders of the various White Russian armies: General Denikin in the Don area, General Yudenich outside Petrograd, and Admiral Kolchak in Siberia. Likewise for the first time, military successes had been scored against the Reds. The disconnected battlefronts were welding themselves into a ring around Moscow, and the ring was steadily tightening.

As Quinn saw it, however, Omsk was less a capital city than a temporary expedient. The single-story timber buildings stood huddled together on both sides of the river, their featureless appearance little enhanced by a dozen or more churches with squat, gilded onion domes, a few white stone mansions, and some drab gray government buildings and barracks. The whole place was permanently enveloped in swirling clouds of fine steppe sand carried there by the incessant east wind, which dumped them on the city as if it were an eyesore to be buried as soon as possible.

They had to cross the Om, whose waters were almost obscured by row upon row of river craft moored cheek by jowl: old barges laden with rotting timber and steamers that had once plied between Omsk and Irtysh but now served as floating hotels. Omsk's population, which numbered forty thousand in normal times, had been trebled by an influx of military personnel and, more especially, by refugees fleeing there from areas under Bolshevik occupation.

14

The far end of the bridge over the Om was guarded by a machine-gun post and walls of sandbags just far enough apart to allow the Ford to pass. The sentries wore British army uniforms and steel helmets in the colors of the Intervention Forces, black with a white star.

Most of them were older men unfit for combat duty. Responsible for internal security, they guarded the depots around the railroad station and patrolled the streets at night. The sentry who barred their path was no exception. He was an overage corporal with four wound stripes on his sleeve and a face to match, haggard and hollow-cheeked. His expression, clearly discernible in the glare of the lights strung across the bridge, was sour and suspicious.

"Papers?" His tone was studiously brusque. Then, recognizing Rice, he wearily waved them on. "You took your bloody time, didn't you? They've been asking for you—twice."

"We stopped to change a tire."

The sentry had spotted the birds in the back of the open car.

"Sell me a couple?"

"Why? Getting sick of bully beef?" Rice said.

"They say you'd sell your own grandmother if the price was right."

Rice laughed, let in the clutch, and drove on. The streets, crowded with refugees by day, were utterly deserted. The only sign of life was an occasional four-man patrol in black helmets.

Their destination lay on the other side of the city. Quinn briefly debated whether to tell the sergeant to stop at his billet and wait while he changed, but that would have seemed an admission that he'd abandoned hope of returning to Boloto the same night, so he said nothing.

As they passed the last of the low, timber-framed houses on the southern outskirts, an almost preternatural glow in the sky signaled that they were approaching the headquarters of the Allied Military Mission. Dozens of railroad cars—whole trains of them—stood arrayed on the tracks.

Arc lights powered by the mission's own generating plant blazed down on the sidings from tall poles. The "Golden Ghetto," as this enclave had been christened, was symbolic. Its lights seemed to proclaim that the Bolsheviks were doomed to defeat.

The compound was enclosed by towering coils of barbed wire erected in two parallel rows. The main entrance, a wooden gateway, boasted an arch adorned with the flags of the four powers that had sided with the Whites against Reds: the Union Jack, the Stars and Stripes, the French tricolor, and the dominion flag of Canada.

There were machine-gun posts here too, but the sentries were snappy young military policemen who insisted on checking Rice's papers and silently ignored his foul-mouthed protests.

As soon as the Ford was inside the compound Quinn told the sergeant to pull up.

"Thanks, I'll walk the rest of the way."

"What about those birds? I could run to . . . a bottle of rum and a bar of soap apiece."

"Give them to Ivory," Quinn told him curtly. Ivory was Fitzmaurice's Indian cook. Rice looked astonished, but he refused to give up.

"A quart bottle of genuine Navy rum and two bars of soap—that's my final offer."

"To Ivory. Now." Quinn walked away. Behind him, Rice's voice made itself heard once more.

"*Two* bottles and two bars of soap . . ."

3

QUINN walked slowly, taking his time, making the most of this opportunity to stretch his legs. It had been three weeks since his last visit to the compound. That day had been a torrid one; the air was humming with insects. Tarpaulins had been suspended above the railroad cars to shield them from the scorching sun. These had since been removed and replaced with wooden roofs in readiness for the snowfalls to come.

He skirted a row of freight cars and picked his way across a maze of tracks. There was rolling stock everywhere, sometimes in twos or threes, sometimes forming whole trains complete with locomotives. Fitzmaurice's staff was housed in several first-class cars, one of which was brightly illuminated and had a tall radio antenna projecting from the roof.

Trains were extremely important in Russia, and not only because they provided the only means of transportation in a country whose roads were often axle-deep in mud for months on end. Since the start of the civil war, they had connected far-flung battlefronts with the rear echelon, preserved whole armies from starvation, and reinforced the troops' morale. In addition to the creature comforts they offered, they also conferred authority. The higher an officer's rank or the greater an official's self-esteem, the more eagerly he strove to requisition a splendrous parlor car for himself.

Fitzmaurice's palatial car had once belonged to the czar's mother, Empress Maria Fyodorovna. He'd commandeered it as a matter of course, partly because self-effacement was foreign to his nature and partly because his many years' service in India had accustomed him to a certain degree of luxury. His private quarters comprised the empress's former dining saloon, now his office, a drawing room, a magnificently appointed bedroom, Ivory's kitchen, and three smaller sections equipped with twin bunks for junior members of his staff.

Two MPs stood guard outside this handsome blue car, and a powerful arc light hung directly overhead. The other cars were standing alongside on a parallel track. In one of them a window had been lowered, and through it drifted the strains of a phonograph. The record was so worn and the phonograph so inadequately wound that the tune was almost unrecognizable. Quinn went up to the open window.

"Hollis?"

A man's face appeared, half obscured by a haze of smoke from the cigarette in his mouth. It was Fraser, one of Fitzmaurice's staff.

"Oh, it's y-you. Hello, Quinn."

"Where's Hollis?" Hollis was Fitzmaurice's deputy.

"He went into town—just left. D-didn't you see him?"

"What's up?"

Fraser removed the cigarette from his lips. He had curiously colorless hair, almost like an albino. "He's g-gone to get drunk," he said. "You know Hollis. Once the sun g-goes down . . ."

"Any special reason?" Quinn broke in.

"Take your pick," Fraser replied, gesturing with both hands. "It's this b-bloody compound, this b-bloody town, this whole b-bloody country. Christ, what are we d-doing here anyhow?" He flicked his butt away. "I thought you were out after d-duck. I suppose the Russkis have slaughtered them all?"

Quinn indicated the Pullman car. "Why does the major want to see me? Did Hollis say?"

"No. He was in a hurry to g-get to town—more of a hurry than usual. Fitzmaurice is in a b-bloody b-bad mood, that's all I can tell you."

Fraser withdrew his head and disappeared from view. Quinn heard him crank up the phonograph and put on the

18

"Decca" again. It was a tango that had taken London by storm.

One of the MPs asked Quinn for his papers, checked them in silence, handed them back. "Mind the steps, sir," he warned, "they're on the steep side." Carpenters had constructed a flight of four steps to enable Major Fitzmaurice to enter his quarters in greater style.

John Neville Fitzmaurice was a small man, not that this was the impression he gave at first sight. The uncharitable whispered that he wore a corset. Whatever the truth, he held himself so poker-backed that it seemed to add three inches to his height. His head enhanced this optical illusion. Quinn, who sat down facing him, had it directly in his line of sight: a bullet-head planted on a squat bull neck and thatched with short hair parted in the middle.

"Comfortable there?" he inquired. "Had any dinner? There's some roast beef and Yorkshire pudding left."

"No, thanks." If Fitzmaurice was in a bad mood, it didn't show. But Quinn knew from experience that his affable manner meant nothing.

"You won't say no to some tea, though?"

"Tea would be fine." Quinn was feeling constricted in his three-quarter-length sheepskin coat. Fitzmaurice hadn't invited him to take it off.

He looked around. The light from the desk lamp was all that relieved the gloom. The paneling was gilded, like the furniture, and the floor thickly carpeted. The windows were draped with curtains made of some plush material. The decor had clearly been chosen by a woman of extravagant tastes. But it was Fitzmaurice himself, lean as a jockey in his immaculately tailored uniform, who lent the empress's dining saloon a phantasmagoric appearance. Quinn involuntarily pictured him lying in her ornate four-poster.

Fitzmaurice smiled as if he'd read his thoughts. "I haven't changed a thing. The old dear wants her toy back, by the way. She's been moving heaven and earth to get it since she heard it was here in Omsk."

"How does one say no to an empress?" asked Quinn.

"She's down in the Crimea; we're up here in Siberia with the Reds in between. I don't foresee any immediate change in the situation." Fitzmaurice brushed an invisible speck of dust off the uniform he continued to affect in spite of his Secret Service status. "If we British had waged our wars like these Whites we wouldn't have an empire at all."

Fitzmaurice was a professional soldier, an army man from an army family that had supplied the British Empire with distinguished military commanders for generations. He himself had served first in China, where he saw action in the Boxer Rebellion, and then in India. His military career had been cut short by ill health—chronic asthma and a nearly fatal attack of amebic dysentery. Such was the official version, but rumor had it otherwise. It was said that he'd taken a maharaja's daughter as his mistress, and that the scandal had been hushed up. At all events, his reasons for joining the Secret Service were shrouded in obscurity.

There was a knock on the rear door of the saloon and Ivory entered, a lean, swarthy Indian in a starched white jacket. He deposited the tea things on the desk and withdrew. At the door he turned and said, "Many thanks for the birds, Captain Quinn. A welcome change from our usual fare."

"So your luck was in," Fitzmaurice said when Ivory had gone.

"While it lasted."

"I've never known such a war. Our only successes are achieved with fishing rod and gun."

He seemed in no hurry. Producing a silver snuffbox from his pocket, he offered it to Quinn. "Help yourself." The snuffbox contained fine flakes of gold leaf. Fitzmaurice made a habit of sprinkling them on Scotch, tea, even consommé. An Indian guru had recommended this practice and he swore by it.

Quinn took a pinch of gold leaf without troubling to disguise what he thought of the major's fad. He was stifling in his sheepskin coat and thoroughly nonplussed by Fitzmaurice's manner. The heavy drapes muffled the few sounds that drifted in from outside: the tramp of the sentries' boots as they paced up and down, the strains of Fraser's worn-out phonograph record.

At last Fitzmaurice laid his cup aside. "You're looking a bit down in the mouth today, Quinn. Not enjoying your work? You've turned in some first-class reports."

"Have you ever read one of them?"

"I'm no expert. London has repeatedly assured me what an excellent job you're doing, that's good enough for me. It seems our backroom boys are gloating over those assays of yours. Gold, platinum—who knows what else besides? You make our presence here worthwhile. Nowadays wars are fought for the sake of export markets and mineral resources. Perhaps they always were. You're indispensable, irreplaceable—doesn't that tickle your vanity?"

"Did you haul me back here just to tell me that?"

Fitzmaurice didn't reply at once. Then he said, "Are you thinking of quitting?"

Quinn wondered how Fitzmaurice had guessed. He hadn't discussed it with anyone. Prevarication now seemed pointless. "That was why I took this week off," he said, "to think things over."

"Well, what conclusion did you come to?"

"I haven't decided—you didn't give me enough time. But I find the idea of boarding a train to Vladivostock very tempting."

"How would you describe yourself, Quinn?"

"I'm sorry?"

21

"Professionally, I mean."

"I'm a geologist."

Fitzmaurice fell silent, as if surprised by the answer. Then he continued. "You're also a wealthy man, I'm told."

"I'm a man of simple tastes," he said, looking around the car. "But yes, I've got more money than I can ever spend, if that's what you mean."

"And you made your millions in gold. Midas, isn't that what they call you on the London bullion market?"

"Midas just touched something and it turned to gold. It took me fifteen years to find a place with 'good rock,' as we call it."

"You're the owner of the biggest gold mine in Canada and a member of the London gold cartel. . . . How rich are you really? Could you put a figure on it?"

This time Quinn laughed aloud. "Is this really how you spend your time, Fitzmaurice?—sitting around in a commandeered imperial boudoir, speculating about other men's money?"

Fitzmaurice leaned back in his chair. "I'm trying to figure you out. Look at yourself from an outsider's point of view. You're a rich man who could sit back and enjoy life. You know the right people, belong to the right London clubs. You're a widower, forty-two, good-looking. And yet . . . when you're offered this job in Siberia you absolutely jump at it. Intriguing, don't you agree?"

Quinn's urge to unbutton his coat had become almost irresistible, but he restrained himself.

"You can do me a favor before you pack your bags. I'd like you to make a little trip on my behalf."

Quinn recalled what Sergeant Rice had told him. "Become an agent of yours, you mean?"

Fitzmaurice didn't even blink. "How much do you know about my network?"

"Next to nothing."

"You're a friend of Hollis's. Haven't you ever discussed the subject with him?"

"The last thing Hollis needs is a friend who talks shop."

"Why don't you take that coat off?"

Quinn ignored the invitation. Noticing that he'd instinctively undone a few buttons, he did them up again. Enduring his present discomfort had somehow become a matter of pride.

"The Service used to have a first-class Russian network," Fitzmaurice said, "but the Revolution changed that overnight. More tea while it's still hot?"

"No, thanks."

Fitzmaurice refilled his own cup and sprinkled it with another pinch of gold leaf. He took a sip and put it down.

"When I took over this job the Service had all but ceased to exist in Russia. The Bolsheviks subscribe to different methods and rules of war, they are not, shall we say, delicate people. We lost one agent after another. Some of them managed to escape and a few went underground. I had to start again from nothing."

He rose. There was a map on the wall behind him, the only alien feature in the entire saloon. Stuck in the map was a handful of pins with black heads. He pointed to them.

"Those, to use your own jargon, are my 'claims.' I go after any nugget, however small. We're at the level where even when we only manage to derail a train, blow up a bridge, or put a munitions factory out of action for a week, we feel like celebrating." He indicated a pin in the southern reaches of the Urals. "Sometimes I cheat to keep my spirits up. For instance, this pin shouldn't really be there anymore." He removed it, resumed his seat, and deposited the pin on a sheet of paper. Then he looked up. "That was one of my agents. His name was Tom Cutter."

The words transfixed Quinn, resurrecting something he'd thought long dead. As if it were yesterday, he saw the steep downhill run from the Duo Mine, slick with frozen rain, the shattered remains of the overturned sled jammed between two tree trunks. *Catherine* . . .

Catherine, the girl he'd loved and married, the girl who'd resembled him in so many ways—in her vitality, her curiosity, her urge to explore and discover. She had been everything to him—his partner, his confidante. Their love affair had not yet been consummated but was in every other aspect complete on the day Tom Cutter had talked her into making the trip: a day away from the university where she was studying geology, a respite from the books Cutter despised so much, an excursion to Lake Superior, where the ice was already thick enough for skating.

And it was Cutter, his best friend and closest competitor, who had sent the telegram. Catherine had still been alive then, but so badly injured that she never regained consciousness. Quinn had been up north, examining some assays. By the time the news reached him and he got to the hospital at Hemlo she was dead. . . .

He was revisited by the same visions, the same agony of mind that had afflicted him then. From that day forward he'd never exchanged another word with Cutter. As he saw it, Cutter was to blame for his young wife's death.

"You knew him, didn't you?"

Fitzmaurice's voice seemed to come from very far away. Perhaps because of its very remoteness, Quinn made a surprising discovery: it sounded almost imploring.

"You and Cutter were partners, weren't you?"

Fitzmaurice spoke as if everything depended on Quinn's answer.

"You were in Canada together. They called you the Golden Duo."

To Quinn there were two Cutters, one before the accident and one after it. The latter he'd erased from his life; the former, who still occupied a place in it, he could speak of.

24

"We each had the same idea at the same time. We met on board a ship at Liverpool—stowaways, both of us. I was seventeen, Cutter a year younger."

"And you both went looking for gold?"

"He got the bug first. I caught it from him."

"You know," said Fitzmaurice, "when I asked him the same question I asked you—about his profession, I mean—he called himself a forty-niner."

"Cutter always laughed at my academic approach. He relied on his nose. He could smell gold, and all he cared about was finding the stuff. It was an insatiable itch."

"You fell out with him?"

"We split up ten years ago," Quinn said impassively.

"For business reasons?"

"No. Cutter outclassed me when it came to spotting a potential deposit. He had only to look at a river, an outcrop of volcanic rock, a watercourse. If he pointed to a place you could be sure there was good rock somewhere down there." Quinn paused. "Ninety percent of all the gold mined is discovered by men like Cutter."

"But only ten percent of them get rich on it?"

"You have to acquire the mineral rights—preferably those of the surrounding claims as well. Mineral rights cost money. Then there are the trial borings—that entails raising more capital. You form a company, float a loan. . . . Cutter found such things tedious—they weren't in his nature. He was a prospector pure and simple. He had this love of buried treasure and was always on the lookout for another strike. He didn't have a thought for anything else."

"That matches my own impression of him."

"How did he come to be working for you?"

"I ran into him in Vladivostock—he'd been prospecting in the Kolyma area. I recruited him, talked him into joining us. Mark you, I could foresee problems with a temperament like his. Loners like Cutter don't make good Service material as a rule. But I still think my decision was sound. He spoke highly of you, that's why I got in touch with you, though I didn't tell you that at the time."

"It doesn't seem at all like Cutter to work for an outfit like yours."

Fitzmaurice looked down at the black-headed pin. "Cutter did an excellent job for nearly two months. Then his luck ran out. We don't know exactly what happened. Maybe we never will. You know how the Reds handle their executions: no witnesses. Their victims vanish without trace."

He waited for some reaction, but in vain. Cutter's death—if that's what it was—had left Quinn quite unmoved. As far as he was concerned, Cutter had been dead for years. Yet he caught himself yielding to a sudden surge of curiosity.

"What's this favor you mentioned?"

"You know Karmel, I believe."

Quinn glanced at the spot on the map where the pin had been. "Is that where he went missing?"

"We presume so. Tell me what you know about the place."

"Karmel? Wealthy Muscovites used to go there to ski or vacation in summer."

"That's not what I meant," Fitzmaurice said impatiently. "Didn't you carry out a geological survey there for Prince Diatsaro?"

"For his mother, Princess Xenia, to be precise. That was ten years ago."

"In connection with a gold mine?"

"Yes. It was losing money in spite of all the dirt-cheap labor available. Xenia Diatsaro wanted me to produce a report—a favorable one, naturally." Quinn gave a reminiscent smile. "A gold mine in the Urals! European investors jumped at such projects in those palmy days before the war. The Diatsaros intended to float the stock in Paris and London, guaranteeing an annual return of ten percent in gold rubles."

"Well?"

26

"The family was honest enough to drop the plan when my survey found that its mine wasn't worth exploiting on an industrial scale." Quinn leaned forward. "But really, Fitzmaurice, what is all this? Surely you don't see me as a replacement for Cutter?"

"A replacement for Cutter?" Fitzmaurice paused as if the question had surprised him. "No, what I have in mind is something far less spectacular. I was going to ask you to escort someone back from there. A woman." He picked up the sheet of paper in front of him and passed it across the desk. The pin rolled off as he did so. "This was his last signal."

Someone had gummed a strip of gray paper to the sheet. It bore two lines of typescript so faint that Quinn could barely decipher them: IF ANYTHING HAPPENS TO ME TAKE CARE OF MOURA TOUMANOVA STOP MESSAGE ENDS. There was no signature.

Quinn raised his eyebrows. "A Russian woman?" he asked. "She was his agent?"

Fitzmaurice smiled. "That was Cutter's big plus—it was easy for him to win women over. For his work—and for his bed."

Quinn stared fixedly at the sheet of paper in his hand. The name meant nothing to him, yet it moved him somehow. He handed the radio message back to Fitzmaurice. "That's why you sent for me?"

"I'm aware of my reputation," Fitzmaurice said. "They claim I drive my agents too hard and demand the impossible of them. The fact is, I've always looked after those who work for me. This signal is Cutter's last will and testament, so to speak. Whatever his reasons, he wanted Moura Toumanova brought to safety."

"There must be other suitable candidates for the job."

Fitzmaurice might not have heard him. "Go and get her, Quinn. We'll fix her up with new papers, a new identity if she wants—you can assure her of that. If she wants to leave the country, we'll help her with that, too. Financially, I mean. Let me have your answer by noon tomorrow. That's all for now."

Fitzmaurice lingered at his desk for a long time after Quinn had gone, pondering what he had discovered.

Not too concerned about the impression he makes . . . That was more than could be said for himself: he remained a Fitzmaurice at all times, as if permanently subjected to the scrutiny of all his Fitzmaurice ancestors.

Not afraid to speak his mind . . . That, of course, came of having money.

Not a man to be bought or bribed . . . so did that.

Not easily intimidated . . . An additional asset, like his experience as a geologist, which would enable him to assess the situation on the spot with greater accuracy.

Fitzmaurice stared at the sheet of paper on his desk. Should he have come out with the whole truth? Quinn would be risking his neck, after all, just as Cutter had done.

Suddenly his breathing became labored. He gasped and wheezed, terrified by the thought of impending asphyxia, pinned to his chair by a kind of paralysis. Reason told him that these bouts of asthma soon passed, but his fear of them never diminished.

At last he managed to stand up and open a window. When his breathing slowed and steadied, his sense of relief was so profound he almost wept.

He returned to his desk and took out another sheet of paper. It bore the complete text of Cutter's last signal:

AGREEMENT IMMINENT STOP ARRANGE SIBERIAN TRANSFER STOP.

Then came the wording Quinn had been allowed to see:

IF ANYTHING HAPPENS TO ME TAKE CARE OF MOURA TOUMANOVA STOP MESSAGE ENDS.

If things went according to plan and Quinn embarked on

this mission he would have to follow it through—he wouldn't be able to help himself.

Fitzmaurice rose and went over to the map, pin in hand. He replaced it in its original location, Karmel in the Urals.

4

T H E Russian did his best to dissuade Quinn from going in. He stood outside the door and spread his arms, a puny little man with drooping shoulders. "I know this one," he said imploringly. "He gets violent. Why not let him sleep it off?"

Quinn thrust the proprietor of the "Divan" impatiently aside. He strode into the room and shut the door, muffling the gamblers' hectic voices and the music from the bar.

The only light in the low-ceilinged room came from a window in the background, through which a pallid moon could be seen gliding across a sky filled with broken cloud. The mattress on the floor in the corner was shrouded in a mosquito net suspended from a hook. Although the recumbent form inside was only dimly visible, its dimensions confirmed that Quinn had come to the right place.

Cloudesley Hollis, Fitzmaurice's deputy, was a giant of a man who draped the doorways of his railroad car with towels to remind him to duck. Dapper little Fitzmaurice and his gigantic sidekick made such an ill-assorted pair that their subordinates couldn't fail to find them a source of secret amusement.

Quinn drew the muslin net aside. Hollis was lying on his back, breathing stertorously, his handsome face, neck, and hairy chest bathed in sweat.

"Hollis!" Quinn took hold of his arm and shook him. "Get up, I'm taking you home."

Hollis sat up with a jerk. His upper body was swaying, but he put his fists up like a boxer. "Wanna try me?" He lashed out so suddenly that Quinn only just evaded the blow. "C'mon, let's have at it!" He scrambled to his feet and lunged at Quinn, but Quinn was too quick for him. His fist caught Hollis full on the mouth. Hollis swayed and slumped back on the mattress.

Quinn strode from the room. He ran to the window at the end of the passage and wrenched it open. The feeble light over the entrance dimly illuminated a narrow street flanked by mean houses. Fraser had climbed out of the Ford and was standing beside it. The passersby gave him a wide berth, but he'd drawn his service revolver just in case. Quinn could tell, even from above, how apprehensive he was. He jumped when he heard his name.

"Fraser, come up here!"

Fraser stepped back and looked up. "What about the c-car? I c-can't afford to leave it unattended."

"I'm telling you to leave it. I need you up here."

Quinn managed to get Hollis dressed with Fraser's help. Although the big man continued to struggle, they each grabbed an arm and hustled him downstairs.

The proprietor was anxiously awaiting them below, but the patrons barely glanced at them. A dozen couples were dancing in the bar while a number of unattached girls, mostly Chinese, Mongols, and Eurasians in flimsy silk dresses, sat on the cushions that lined the walls, waiting for customers. The gaming room beyond was so packed that nothing could be seen but the backs of the gamblers clustered around the tables.

Quinn found the chill night air a relief after the heavy, sweetish odor of perfume and perspiration. They half-carried Hollis to the Ford and bundled him into the back. Quinn got in beside him while Fraser took the wheel. A Chinese pimp sidled up and tried to sell them some pornographic postcards. That apart, they aroused as little attention here as they had inside the "Divan."

"Get going," said Quinn. He himself had spent enough time

in the "Divan" that he knew not to take Hollis's condition too seriously.

Fraser looked around. "Where to? If Fitzmaurice sees him like this he'll pop an artery."

"I'll put him up at my place."

The wind had risen and dispersed the clouds. Stars were visible in the sky. There were no street lights, so Fraser drove gingerly. The neighborhood in which the "Divan" stood was a slum, a labyrinth of dingy little streets. It was home to the poorest of the poor, but Omsk's richest citizens made fortunes out of its countless nightclubs, brothels, and gambling joints.

Prostitution, gambling, and black-marketeering—those, Quinn reflected, were Omsk's only means of sneering at the Revolution and the civil war. The actual fighting was in progress far away. Eight hundred miles from the nearest battlefront, Omsk declined to acknowledge the existence of any military threat and cherished an ambition to become the brand-new capital of the old bourgeoisie.

Most of the recent arrivals were merchants and industrialists deprived of their sawmills and textile factories, or aristocrats who had fled their mansions and country estates. Some were still wealthy and lived luxuriously while ordinary folk starved. They suppressed their mounting fear that there were irreversible changes going on, that they would never return to their former homes, that Omsk was just another step on the road to eventual emigration—that all they could expect from the future was bare survival.

The Ford pulled up at a roadblock. They showed their papers, drove on, and emerged into a well-lighted thoroughfare. After such a maze of gloomy little streets the contrast was jarring. Even the sky above the roofs glowed with reflected light.

31

The boulevard was deserted. By day thousands of refugees thronged Omsk's streets and squares exchanging news and rumors, discussing black-market prices, or pursuing the possibility of obtaining—for a horrendously extortionate sum—a seat on the Trans-Siberian Express and a passage aboard some ship outward bound from Vladivostock. When darkness fell they disappeared—probably, thought Quinn, into the very limbo from which he and the other two had just emerged. They were the kind of people who danced the night away at the "Divan" or jostled each other at the gaming tables in the hope that the next spin of the wheel, the next throw of the dice, would win them enough to finance their flight east.

The Ford slowed. Set back from the street behind some tall iron railings was a two-storied stone building whose tiers of identical windows made it look more like a prison than the girls' school it used to be, now requisitioned for the use of British army personnel.

They drove into the forecourt and pulled up outside the main entrance. This, too, was protected by the ubiquitous walls of sandbags. The man on guard beside the door, a private, emerged from his sentry box. He recognized the two men with the drunk between them and waved them on, shivering.

"Friend of yours, sir? Does he know how lucky he is, sir?" He waved them on and called after them, "In this hellhole God knows you need friends."

Booze and gambling had always been the rule in prospectors' camps. Quinn had sat in on games in which whole fortunes hung on the turn of a card, but gambling had never really appealed to him; his travels put enough risks in his life already. That was another respect in which he differed from Tom Cutter: Cutter had always counted on winning, and never looked back.

As with gambling, so with hard liquor. Quinn hated being

32

out of control and seldom touched it, not even as an antidote to cold, exhaustion, or pain, though it was hard to resist out here. He didn't relish the company of drunks, and when Fraser had departed, leaving him alone with Hollis, he almost regretted having taken him back to his quarters.

They'd borrowed a cot and dumped Hollis on it. His cut lower lip had stopped bleeding, but he was sweating all over and twitching convulsively. By the time Quinn awoke in the morning he was sleeping placidly.

All was still quiet in the former school. Quinn got up and made his way to the washroom at the end of the corridor, where he showered, shaved, and dressed.

The kitchen was down in the basement. The Russian kitchen staff were already breakfasting at a table laden with big white loaves and cans of bully beef. All Russian employees were searched before they left the building, but it was an unwritten rule that they could eat as much as they liked on the premises.

Quinn filled two mugs with strong tea and carried them upstairs. Hollis was sitting bolt upright on the edge of the cot when he returned. He gazed at Quinn with the bemused, pathetic solemnity of a man suffering from alcoholic amnesia.

"Here, I've brought you some tea." Quinn pulled a chair up to the cot and deposited one of the mugs on the floor beside it.

Hollis's face was so out of keeping with his massive frame that it often made Quinn chuckle. His snub nose, rosebud mouth, and friendly eyes were a perpetual reminder of what the newspapers had christened this much-decorated flier: "the Boy Hero." Lieutenant Cloudesley Hollis of the Royal Flying Corps had shot down twenty-six German planes before forfeiting his aviator's status by striking a superior officer during a binge. He'd since been drafted into Military Intelligence as a captain in the Royal Engineers, a corps whose officers were famed for their eccentricities.

Quinn sat down facing him and sipped his tea in silence. Hollis gingerly felt his lip. "Did you do that?" he asked.

"It was your lip or mine."

"How did you find me?"

"Fraser knows your favorite places for prayer and meditation."

"You shouldn't have bothered. I'm usually fine by the morning."

"I'd have left you in peace, but I've got a couple of questions to ask you. Fitzmaurice sent Rice to Boloto to fetch me. You knew that, no?"

"Sometimes he tells me things, sometimes he doesn't. He thinks I'm just a buffoon, don't forget."

"Why didn't you come yourself?"

"Because I wasn't asked." Hollis struggled to get up, lost his balance, flopped back on the bed. "Don't let's talk about Fitzmaurice or my job. My wonderful job, in which any lie is better than the truth, and the most prized talent is the ability to deceive."

"Hollis. Self-pity in a man your size?"

"Sure you don't have a bottle tucked away somewhere?"

"Listen, I've got only a couple of questions. The sooner you answer the sooner you can partake of the healing waters again. Now look. Fitzmaurice has asked me to go to Karmel for him. He showed me a signal from one of his agents."

"Isn't it preposterous?" Hollis broke in. "I told him you'd never take the job."

"I wondered what you thought. I'm considering taking it."

"Good God, Oliver, the situation there is hopeless! All the Whites care about is money or escape or both. They're too yellow to fight, even though they know they're all through if the Reds win. Hop a train and head for home—forget about Karmel."

Quinn drew his chair closer. "Tell me about the place."

"It's just some godforsaken dump in the Urals."

34

"The Whites have captured it. I had a chat with Fraser last night," Quinn said. "According to him it was captured by the Whites in a major military operation employing fresh, well-equipped troops."

"Amazing," Hollis drawled.

"The attack was launched from Tobolsk in a westerly direction. The Whites advanced with exceptional speed. Fraser says they captured a town or a village a day for twenty-eight days in a row."

Hollis looked unimpressed. "That's the way this war is being fought. Both sides march fast on empty bellies—they have to loot the next village or starve."

"They kept going that fast until they got to Karmel. Since then they haven't budged. Now, why do you suppose that is?"

"They're Czech troops," Hollis said. "The chap in command is that child prodigy, General Wajda. He's a law unto himself."

"And his law says Karmel, a 'godforsaken dump in the Urals,' is a nice place to settle down. Raise your kids, maybe. Build a retirement cottage."

"How should I know, Oliver? The Czechs have spent four years fighting and dying for an Austrian emperor they hate—a foreigner who refuses to grant them a country of their own. They deserted in droves at the first opportunity. The Whites have promised them independence. Help us to defeat the Reds, they say, and we'll ship you home from Vladivostock. Well, maybe the Czechs are simply sick of risking their necks for other people."

"The Czech Legion is the only decent fighting force the Whites can muster," Quinn said. "They were busy capturing Karmel while Kazan was at stake, and Kazan's a strategically important place. If the Whites can get across the Volga there'll be nothing between them and Moscow. If they lose Kazan they'll have lost their last chance of taking Moscow this year. Every day counts. Everything depends on fresh reinforcements, but the Whites' reserves—the only ones that matter—aren't available because they're occupying a heaven-on-earth they found in delightful Siberia."

Hollis looked up. "What do you want me to say?"

"Fitzmaurice is keeping something from me. I want to know what it is."

"He's secretive by nature. People tend to think he's hiding something when there's nothing to hide. More than that I can't say."

"Tell me about Cutter—what was his job?"

"Gathering intelligence behind the lines for the Czech Legion. If so required, he also engaged in sabotage."

Hollis had answered without faltering. Quinn asked, "How was he inserted?"

"By air. Another pilot flew him in, a man named Katov." Hollis gave a wry smile. "Not me. I've forgotten what it's like up there."

"Did Cutter handle his own communications?"

"He had a wireless operator with him named Frank Davis."

"Is Davis still alive?"

"As far as I'm aware."

"Alive and in Karmel?"

"Yes, damn it, alive and well in Karmel! For Christ sake, Oliver! Who the hell are you, the Grand Inquisitor? Listen to yourself!"

Fitzmaurice hadn't mentioned Davis, Quinn reflected. He hadn't lied to him. He'd simply chosen to suppress an important fact. That was worse. "You met Cutter, I take it?"

"Only briefly." Hollis looked grim.

"Did he mention me?"

"No. You weren't here—you were away on one of your field trips."

"What was your personal impression of him?"

"I drove him and Davis to the airfield." He looked up and stared intently at Quinn. At last he went on. "That's all.

36

Cutter was Fitzmaurice's baby. Nobody asked me to form an opinion of him. Now the man's dead. I'd rather not discuss him."

"You didn't like him?"

He sighed. "Not exactly." Hollis groped for words. "He had the sort of exaggerated self-confidence that gets up my nose. Not to mention a lot of lady friends. One even turned up at the airfield to see him off—he'd fixed it with her, which was strictly against orders. He wasn't here long, but long enough to get half a dozen women drooling over him. . . . You know I hate any man who's had more luck with the ladies than me."

Quinn made no comment. The memory of Catherine's death revived, and it surprised him yet again that an event so deeply buried in the past should still have the power to hurt him. He strove to dismiss the thought and concentrate.

"What do you know about this woman in Karmel—the one Cutter mentioned in his last signal?"

"Discounting the fact that her name is Moura Toumanova, not much."

"Was she working for him?"

"He may have been using her. Or vice versa."

"How do you mean?"

"Maybe she wanted to get out of Russia. The best way of doing that is to marry a Britisher. There's a regular marriage market here in Omsk. Whites with pretty daughters will pay the earth to provide them with foreign husbands. We have nothing in the files on her, if that's what you mean. That last radio transmission was the first time her name turned up."

Quinn thought for a moment. Then he said, "Something's missing. I knew Tom Cutter well. I've no idea what he'd been doing these last ten years, but men like him don't change. He never felt anything for a woman. He took his pleasure where he found it, but he was never prepared to give back anything of himself. And another thing: he wasn't agent material. Fitz-

37

maurice must have realized that, so why did he take him on?"

"Strange bedfellows aren't uncommon in our trade."

"No, Hollis. Cutter would never have accepted the assignment—not the one you just described." Quinn broke off: the thought had come to him like a revelation. "But if Fitzmaurice had put him on the track of something else . . ."

Hollis wiped his mouth on the back of his hand as if his cut lip had started bleeding again. "I don't know what you're getting at."

Quinn gave him a skeptical look. "What was Cutter's real mission?" he asked.

"I can't tell you any more than Fitzmaurice did," Hollis replied. His blank expression persisted.

Quinn wondered briefly if his imagination was running away with him. But the more he thought about it the more convinced he became that Fitzmaurice and Hollis were holding out on him. Their story didn't tally with the ore samples he'd seen.

"Hate to be a skeptic. But I also hate to be a fool-tool. What should I believe, Hollis?"

"Cutter's dead," said Hollis. "That much you can believe."

The light in the room had changed with the coming of the day. Quinn glanced at the window. Raindrops lashed against the window in short, sharp bursts.

"Fitzmaurice wants my answer by noon."

Hollis's smile was faintly apologetic. "I always expect other people to turn Fitzmaurice down. Personally, I've never been able to. Damn it all, Oliver . . ." He got up off the cot. "I never even asked you how your duck shoot went."

"It was going fine till Sergeant Rice turned up," Quinn said. "Sednev has a permit to shoot bear in the Aissary highlands. Why not come with us?"

"Are you flying there?"

"That was our intention."

"Do it—go off to the mountains with Sednev," Hollis said

38

with another limp, weary, superficial smile. He made his way across the room. His coat was hanging from a hook on the door. He pulled it on and departed without a backward glance.

5

CLOUDS hung low in the sky. The rain, which was still streaming down, had turned the road beside the railroad tracks into a quagmire indistinguishable from the fields around. Quinn's only guide to its lateral extent were the telegraph poles on either side. The road forked. Quinn bore right to the airfield. The flat roofs of the hangars were distantly visible through a curtain of rain.

He drove past some rolling stock guarded by sentries, flatcars laden with aircraft whose wings had been dismantled and lashed to the sides of each fuselage. More planes were dispersed in bays on the edge of the airfield, enclosed by banks of earth. These too were guarded by sentries stationed in the open and exposed to the driving rain.

Quinn wondered why the authorities bothered to guard them at all. The British had bequeathed the Whites their oldest planes. Some were so decrepit you could kill yourself in them without ever meeting an enemy in the air. The Russians who flew them seemed to regard their sorties as a game of chance, a kind of aerial Russian roulette.

He parked as close as possible to one of the hangars. A bedraggled pennant hung from the flagpole on top. Inside stood a two-seater RE8, which the Russians used for bombing and reconnaissance. The tail fin was adorned with the death-head emblem of their group.

The RE8's engine was turning over, and the hangar was filled with the black smoke belching from the exhaust behind the cockpit. A mechanic was lying on his back beneath the machine, a pair of feet the only visible sign of his presence. The concrete floor was streaked with oil.

Quinn tried to attract the man's attention. "Katov?" he yelled above the roar of the engine.

The mechanic heard him at last. He crawled out from beneath the nose, raised his head, and pointed to the far end of the hangar.

Quinn made his way to a door half-obstructed by drums of lubricating oil and gasoline. Outside, some planks had been laid on the muddy ground to form a causeway between the hangar and a corrugated-iron shed. Quinn opened another door and found himself in a sizable room lined with wooden racks holding spare parts. A mechanic had just drawn one from the storeman and was signing for it in a ledger.

Quinn repeated his question. The storeman shook his head. "He's busy."

"I won't keep him long."

The storeman pointed to a passage lined with more racks. The passage, which was dark and windowless, led to another room. A man was seated at a desk by the light of a naked bulb suspended from the ceiling. He was wearing a leather flying jacket adorned with a remarkable assortment of badges, ribbons, and medals. He was writing.

Quinn cleared his throat.

Alexander Katov looked up. "Hello, Quinn." His eyes twinkled, his face remained totally impassive. It was a moon face with prominent cheekbones rendered still more conspicuous by the harsh glare of the bulb overhead. "I suppose you're looking for Balayev."

"Is he here?"

"Your trip's off, I'm afraid. We can't repair his machine— no spare parts available. All Balayev's prayers to St. Nicholas have been in vain." There was a Pekingese perched on the desk, a young dog with snow-white fur. Katov fondled it.

"It was you I wanted a word with," Quinn said.

Katov stopped stroking the dog's long, silky coat. The Pekingese seemed to resent this, because it yapped indignantly. Katov began fondling it again.

Quinn noted the diamond ring on the little finger of the Russian's left hand. It was almost as if he meant to create a misleading impression. Alexander Katov had been a celebrated ace in the Czar's air force. Just like Hollis in the Royal Flying Corps, his score amounted to nineteen German planes, some of which he was reputed to have rammed when his ammunition ran out or his guns jammed. After the Revolution he was compelled to join the Red air force. When he heard what a premium the British were offering—ten thousand gold rubles per pilot complete with plane—he deserted to the Whites.

"Can you spare me five minutes?" Quinn asked.

"Of course."

Quinn had forgotten to ask Hollis what names Cutter and Davis had assumed, so he merely said, "Two British agents, remember? You landed them behind the Red lines."

Katov ran his fingers through his hair. It was dark and wavy but tinged with gray, and the eyes in his deeply tanned face were weary. "Look at this desk of mine," he said evasively. "A paper war, that's all I'm fighting these days."

"It was early in September, two months ago. Two agents, both British. I presume they parachuted in."

"Yes, I remember. One of them was airsick all the way, poor fellow. These machines aren't designed for passengers with weak stomachs."

"That must have been Davis."

"I was never told their names."

"Where did you put them down?"

"East of Kazan in the neighborhood of Yelabuga."

"Anyone there to meet them?"

Katov shook his head. "The whole operation was very rushed."

"Can you remember how they were equipped? They had a wireless set with them, I know. Anything else? Explosives? Dynamite?"

"I didn't see any." Katov paused, still fondling the Pekingese. He leaned over the desk with a sudden glint in his eyes. "The other one was wearing a pair of gold cuff links," he said briskly, "in the shape of a four-leaf clover. A man dressed like a Russian peasant wearing gold cuff links, I ask you! They didn't match his disguise. I pointed that out and offered to buy them from him. . . ." He paused again. Rain was still drumming on the corrugated iron overhead. "He wouldn't part with them, though. I suppose they were a kind of lucky charm."

"Any idea what their assignment was?" Quinn asked it without much hope.

"I never heard—they didn't talk about it. I landed them the best place I could. There was only an hour of daylight left, so I took off again as soon as possible. I've no objection to risking my neck occasionally, but the Reds have upped the price on my head to fifty thousand rubles—in gold. How's that for inflation? Did they make it?"

"Only one."

"I can guess which one didn't: the poor fellow who nearly died of fright on the way."

"No, Davis is still alive," Quinn said. "It was the other man who didn't make it."

Katov ran a hand through his hair. "So he might as well have sold me his cuff links."

Another silence fell. Katov continued to fondle the Pekingese, which snuffled contentedly. The rain continued to drum down on the roof.

"Ever been to Karmel? Karmel in the Urals?" It was just an idle question on Quinn's part. He'd already said all there was to say, but something made him linger. Katov's only response was to swivel around in his chair. Quinn, following the direc-

42

tion of his gaze, saw a much-enlarged photograph on the wall, apparently showing a mass of dark clouds. He discovered when he went over to it that it was an aerial photograph taken from a considerable altitude. The cloud formations turned out to be ranges of wooded hills interspersed with valleys and isolated peaks. He couldn't at first be sure that the photograph was of the Karmel area because he'd never seen it from the air. Then he identified the pass, the railroad track, the station, and the branch line leading to the derelict mine.

"Imagine," he said laconically. "To someone that's home sweet home."

Katov came out from behind his desk. The Pekingese promptly let out a series of high-pitched barks. He turned and picked it up. With the dog clasped to his chest he joined Quinn in front of the photograph and gazed at it, lost in thought.

"I'm worth ten thousand rubles alive and fifty thousand dead," he said in a flat voice. "Sometimes I don't know which side I should be on."

Quinn looked at him. The Russian's aura of resignation was so strong that he recoiled, as if Katov were suffering from some infectious disease.

"Who took these photographs? I assume there are others."

"They were taken while our group was still based at Tyumen."

"Where did they go for evaluation—to Major Fitzmaurice?"

"Why ask if you already know?"

"Everybody does seem to love Karmel. I'd say it's found some new irresistible charm it didn't have ten years ago."

"All he asked for was a mosaic of the district—in the first instance, some shots of the railroad station." Katov indicated a spot on the print. "It doesn't appear in this one, but there was a train standing in the station. I counted fourteen cars, two locomotives, a Pullman car, and a diner."

"Don't you have a print of it?"

"We had to surrender the entire set complete with negatives. This is the only one I kept."

"I suppose there are still some planes based at Tyumen?"

"Yes, one squadron."

"And they're maintaining their reconnaissance flights over Karmel?"

"While the weather holds." Katov's face darkened. "We'll be grounded when the weather really sets in. . . . I'm sorry about your trip to the mountains."

"Do me a favor," Quinn said, slapping his shoulder. "Let Balayev know."

"That it's postponed, or that it's off altogether?"

Quinn was absolved from answering by the sound of approaching footsteps. Into view came the filthy dungarees and oil-stained face of the mechanic he'd seen at work on the machine in the hangar. Katov turned to the man and said, "Well, so what's wrong with it?"

6

OMSK'S railroad station, which lay well beyond the outskirts of town, was in almost total darkness. Several of the poles that supported the overhead power cables had been felled by the storm that afternoon, and the buildings were without electricity. The two men crossing the tracks had nothing to guide them but the red lights at the rear of the train.

Quinn had taken up his post at Omsk as a supernumerary captain in the Royal Engineers, like Hollis, but he'd felt a fraud in his brand-new uniform and abandoned it after the first few days. He was now wearing the outfit in which he felt most at home, a worn old jacket and breeches and lace-up boots. The only army-issue items he'd retained were the knee-length sheepskin coat and a cloth money belt, and his only baggage consisted of a battered leather suitcase.

He was wearing the money belt next to his skin. It felt good somehow, less because of the dollars and sterling Fitzmaurice had given him for the trip than because it compelled him to stiffen his back and walk tall. Or was it because it reminded him of the Canadian gold fields? That was where he'd last worn such a belt.

The train, ringed by a double cordon of sentries, was in a siding some way from the main building. Hollis, who had issued the necessary papers, snapped at the noncom in charge when asked to produce them for inspection. His mood since picking up Quinn at his quarters had been tetchy in the extreme.

They made their way across another set of tracks to the train. First came a flatcar with sandbags piled along the sides. As they passed them Quinn made out the sandbag embrasures that had been left for the convenience of machine-gunners.

Some ramshackle freight cars came next. The decrepit locomotive at the head of the train was burning wood, to judge by the smell of the fumes issuing from the smokestack, and the noises it made had an asthmatic sound. The paintwork of the only passenger car had flaked off in places and the underlying metal was leprous with rust.

One section had a sheet of white paper gummed to the window. Hollis paused outside the door and looked around. A slim, dark-haired man in U.S. Army uniform emerged from the gloom carrying a lantern. He raised the lantern for a closer look at the newcomers, then shone it on the window. The sheet of paper read "Reserved."

"This is your man's section, Hollis," he said. He spoke English with a strong Italian accent. "It's clean and the windows are in one piece. That's the best I could do."

"I'm sure it'll do me fine," said Quinn.

The American nodded approvingly. "Mike Catania's my

name. I'm the RTO responsible for this box of tricks." He gripped the door handle as if expecting it to resist, depressed it, and wrenched the door open. *"Ecco!"* he said, stepping aside.

"Are you coming too?" Quinn asked.

"No, but don't worry. You won't starve, and you'll get some hot tea whenever the loco stops to take on wood and water." So saying he turned on his heel and walked off.

Quinn hoisted his old leather suitcase aboard. The section was flanked by two crude wooden bench seats, but they seemed clean enough and one of them was piled high with woolen blankets.

Hollis groped in his pockets for a pack of cigarettes and eventually found one. "Got a light?"

Quinn struck a match. Hollis's expression was so thunderous that he said, "I wasn't expecting to travel first-class. How long will the train take to get there?"

Hollis took a quick pull at his cigarette. "Ask me something simple."

"All right. When will it leave?"

"You never know. Why didn't you ask Catania?"

Hollis looked along the train. Russian laborers were still busy loading the freight cars—toting bales and boxes to the open doors and stowing them inside under the sentries' supervision. The bulk of the freight seemed to consist of food and clothing, but there were also some machine parts in crates. Every pair of toiling Russians was supervised by the shadowy figure of an armed guard.

Hollis tossed away his cigarette almost unsmoked. "You've no idea the racketeering that goes on here," he said. "The locals are greenhorns compared to the Yanks that run this railroad. They're just a bunch of crooks. Mafiosi, all of them. The entire railroad network is in their hands. They divert whole trainloads of gasoline, pump the tank cars dry, and sell it off for a fortune. The trains simply vanish into thin air."

Quinn smiled. "Are you trying to undermine my morale?"

Hollis had another look around. He wandered off, only to return a moment later. "Why isn't he here, goddammit?"

"Expecting someone?"

"Fitzmaurice."

"Why? We said our good-byes this afternoon."

Hollis peered along the train again. "It must be the weather—his asthma. . . . Got another match?"

Quinn handed him the box. "I never expected Fitzmaurice to have a last-minute change of heart and come clean with me."

"Fitzmaurice is a bastard." Hollis struck three matches in succession because the first two were damp. He got his cigarette going and took a couple of long drags.

Quinn produced a small leather jewel case from his pocket and opened it. "Know what these are?" Embedded in the blue velvet was a pair of gold cuff links in the shape of four-leaf clovers.

"Fitzmaurice?" said Hollis.

Quinn nodded. "Do all Fitzmaurice's agents get a pair for conversion into cash in case of accidents?"

"Only if he thinks they're accident-prone, I imagine." Hollis's tone was sarcastic.

"Well, they're hardly my style," Quinn said, shutting the case with a snap. "Do me a favor. Give them to Katov. He tried to buy Cutter's."

Hollis looked up in alarm. "You spoke to Katov?"

Quinn thrust the case into Hollis's hand. "Just see that he gets them." He patted the big man on the arm. "Thanks for the lift. You'd better go now."

Hollis pocketed the case. "All right," he said. Brusquely, as if issuing an order, he added, "Don't forget to send that telegram when you get there."

He turned abruptly and strode off without looking back. Quinn watched him go, then climbed aboard and slammed the

47

door. He lifted his suitcase onto the rack, draped one of the seats in a couple of blankets, improvised a pillow out of his sheepskin coat, and removed his shoes before wrapping himself in more blankets and stretching out full length.

He was feeling better by the minute now that Hollis had left. For a while he lay there listening to the sounds from outside: men's voices, the murmur of the wind, the locomotive's asthmatic wheezing. They became more and more blurred until he finally ceased to distinguish between them.

Pervaded by a growing sense of well-being, he recalled the long-forgotten day when he and Cutter had found gold. The images were too vivid to be a dream—even a daydream: the remote surroundings, the rocky gorge, the river's fast-flowing waters turned milky-white by melted snow from the mountains above. Making their way upstream with shovels and pans, one on either bank, they began to wash the sand and fine gravel. . . .

The door of the section swung open. "Want some tea before you . . ." It was Catania's voice.

Quinn didn't move or open his eyes when the lantern light fell on his face. The door slammed shut again.

The image returned, and with it the thrill of excitement that had overwhelmed him at the sight of those specks of gold in the residue of sand at the bottom of the pan. When he straightened up to show off his find, he saw Tom Cutter wading toward him through the icy water. Cutter came to a halt beside him, unspeaking, eyes shining. With a cursory glance at his partner's pan, he extended a clenched fist. His fingers opened. "You ain't seen nothing, pal. Take a look at this . . ."

He hadn't relived that day in years.

The train gave a jolt and the wooden slats beneath him started to vibrate, but Quinn never noticed that they were pulling out of the station: nothing could have broken the spell of the moment.

48

PART TWO

THE SENTINEL

A fine drizzle had been falling since dawn. Mist hung low between the trees, but Fyodor Nikulin's vantage point, which overlooked a wooded defile, enabled him to keep watch on the former posthouse and a short stretch of the old road leading to the pass.

He wiped the lenses of his binoculars and looked again. The building swam into view. No sign of life. Nothing had changed since yesterday—or had it? He peered more closely at the window to the right of the door. The shutters were closed.

"*Akula! Prokliataya. Akula!*" he swore loudly.

He'd severed all contact with Karmel since the Englishman's death. His communications with Govorov were limited to three simple prearranged signals. If all three sets of shutters were open it meant "All clear." If the left-hand window was shuttered it meant "Supplies delivered." If the right-hand window was shuttered, like now, it meant "Danger."

Nikulin slowly lowered his binoculars until they were dangling by the thong. He felt momentarily depressed at the thought that he would still be on active service with his regiment if he hadn't let them talk him into taking on this assignment.

He turned away. The best thing would be to maintain his routine unchanged. The success of his mission—in fact, his own survival—depended on it. Besides, routine was his only weapon against the monotony of the endless days and nights. Moura Toumanova had severed all contact with him since the Englishman's death. He'd expected that.

He'd made a habit of never using the same route twice so as not to leave tracks, with the result that it took him nearly an hour to reach the Horses' Graveyard. The old road across the pass had once been a source of dread because the Ural winds could gust so violently that many a horse and wagon had plunged to destruction down the precipices on either side. It was the shattered timbers and bleached bones of mules and horses in their depths that had given the place its name.

The temperature dropped and the drizzle turned to sleet as he toiled uphill. Nikulin treated himself to a brief rest and rolled himself a cigarette with the coarse makhorka tobacco he carried loose in his coat pocket. From where he stood he could just make out Two Brothers Pass and the new road that had superseded the Horses' Graveyard. Beside it ran a single railroad track: the northern arm of the Trans-Siberian Railroad, which traversed the Urals at this point.

He tossed away the remains of his cigarette and raised the binoculars, following the line of the track. The rails and cross-ties were bedded in chips of reddish granite. He could discern no traffic on the road and it was weeks since he last saw a train, but still he continued to peer through the binoculars. Again and again, without really knowing why, he traced the convolutions of the railroad track as it wound its way upward to the tunnel at the head of the pass. And then, as if to reward him for his perseverance, some puffs of black smoke appeared beyond the crest.

They vanished as the train entered the tunnel. Nikulin

waited impatiently. It seemed an age before the train emerged on the near side: a locomotive, a tender, a passenger car, several freight cars, and, bringing up the rear, a flatcar with sandbagged sides and two machine guns mounted on tripods.

With snowflakes whirling around it, the train crawled slowly out of the tunnel and along the level stretch of track near the summit of the pass. Had Govorov known of its arrival in advance? Nikulin had no idea why it should represent a threat to him, but he felt sure it must have some bearing on the danger signal.

He lowered the binoculars with a sigh. Far from being dismayed or alarmed, he experienced a sensation of relief, as if liberated by the thought that his enemies hadn't abandoned the hunt. His short-lived irritation and depression subsided. Every scrap of indecision left him as he headed back to the cabin.

7

T H E train had taken hours to make the switchback ascent to Two Brothers Pass. The journey through the tunnel seemed just as interminable—far longer than Quinn remembered. He tugged impatiently at the strap, but the section filled with smoke when he finally got the window open and he had to shut it again.

Six days and nights it had taken them to reach the eastern foothills of the Urals. They'd trundled for hour after hour through the steppes and forests of Siberia, their progress punctuated by stops of irrational and unpredictable length. Sometimes they barely had time to drink a glass of tea and stretch their legs; sometimes they lingered for hours in remote little stations or open countryside.

It had been a tiring and largely uneventful trip. Although bands of mounted marauders had appeared from time to time, they never dared to take on the machine guns. Quinn had seen few troops apart from the Czech detachments occupying the stations, but signs of the civil war were everywhere: demolished bridges with piers jutting from the water; derailed, gutted, rolling stock; villages reduced to blackened ruins; gibbets erected beside the track.

The compartment was suddenly flooded with light so white and dazzling that his eyelids clamped themselves shut for a moment. He lowered the window again, and clouds of fine snow came billowing in. Having negotiated the short stretch of level ground at the head of the pass, the train began its zigzag descent into the valley. Little of the town could yet be seen through the swirling snow, and Quinn's view of it was further obscured whenever the track ran through patches of forest. Then the trees thinned and the snow turned to drizzle. As far as he could tell, Karmel was unchanged: there were no outward signs of damage. The main impression, as ever, was of a landscape that had retained its pristine charm.

Karmel's career as a mining town had not lasted long—ten years at most. When the gold mine closed down at the end of that phase in its history, it reverted to what it had always been and what Quinn could now see from the window of the train: a mountain resort where the wealthy took refuge from the heat of high summer, where hunting parties gathered in the fall, and skiers disported themselves in the winter. The run-down *dachas* and summer residences had been renovated and joined by new ones: toy castles constructed of timber and set in carefully landscaped gardens. The Karmelites had always loved extravagance.

Quinn left his post at the window. He'd slept very little in the last few days. The only washroom on the train had been permanently besieged by a line of soldiers, so he was unshaven and almost unwashed. He lifted his suitcase off the rack and pulled on his sheepskin coat. The compartment had grown chilly.

54

The train slowed as the track and the river converged. Quinn was temporarily disconcerted and lost his bearings. There had once been a park on the far bank, a gift to the municipality from Prince Diatsaro, with trees, flower beds, graveled paths, and an open-sided pavilion in which the miners' brass band had given Sunday afternoon concerts. The park had disappeared. Enclosing its former site was a ring of earthworks surmounted at fifty-yard intervals by timber watchtowers bristling with machine guns. Motionless sentries under low roofs of split logs watched the train go by without a trace of interest or curiosity.

The train was now traveling at a walking pace. Karmel station came into view, a flat-roofed, single-storied building indistinguishable from the hundreds of similar stations that lined the Trans-Siberian Railroad. Adorning its façade was the red, white, and blue flag of the Czechoslovak Legion.

Quinn waited until the train squealed to a halt. He felt stiff as he climbed out—stiff and a little dizzy from the altitude. He'd sent Davis a telegram from Ekaterinburg, the last stop before Karmel, but he couldn't see anyone on the platform that matched his description.

"Captain Quinn?"

A figure had emerged from the station building. A stocky young man with a plump, rosy face, he was wearing a high-necked, ankle-length fur coat. "Lieutenant Scala," he said, extending his hand. "Scala like the opera house—Dexter Scala. How was your trip?"

"I didn't know anyone was expecting me."

"Visitors cause quite a sensation here. Besides, you've brought the first snow with you. That's supposed to be lucky."

Quinn glanced up at the overcast sky. It was still drizzling. Scala chuckled happily and indicated his fur coat. "Spoils of war," he explained. "I dug it out too soon, I know, but I couldn't wait to show it off."

55

He stood there with his stomach out and his short, sturdy legs splayed. He cut an almost comical figure, but there was something about him that warned Quinn not to take him at face value. If one ignored externals and concentrated on his face, he became another person altogether. His eyes were cold and calculating.

"Forgive me, keeping you standing out here in the rain." Scala turned and beckoned to someone. "Pete!" he called.

There was nothing ambiguous about the man who strode up to them. Around thirty, with fair hair and gaunt cheeks as bloodless as his lips, he was built on a scale that made the pistol in his holster look redundant.

"Sergeant Budyek," Scala said. "He'll be looking after you while you're here. For a start, he'll take you to your billet."

"My billet?"

"The whole town's requisitioned, so I'm putting you up at my place." Scala looked at Quinn. His smile had given way to a look of curiosity. "Or did you have other plans?"

"I hadn't given it a thought."

"I've got plenty of room," Scala said, as if that clinched the matter. "You can even take a bath. Settle in—make yourself at home and I'll join you in an hour or so. I've got a couple of things to do here first."

He turned on his heel and walked off down the platform to the freight cars. Men had already begun to unload them.

"Let's go," said Budyek.

The men were carrying crates from the train to a stone warehouse some distance from the station. Quinn could see another train standing in a siding nearby. It consisted of baggage cars with paintwork of so vivid a blue that they seemed almost luminous in spite of the drizzle. Quinn counted fourteen of them, sandwiched between a pair of locomotives, all identical, all brand-new. Plus a diner and a Pullman car. Sentries were pacing up and down the tracks on either side of this unusual-looking train.

Quinn felt his heart miss a beat. It couldn't be just because the cars looked so smart compared to most of the shabby trains he'd seen, including the one that had brought him here. No, this must be the train Alexander Katov had mentioned— the one visible in the aerial photographs he'd taken. What was it about Karmel station that interested Fitzmaurice so profoundly?

Sergeant Budyek swore in Czech, then lapsed into broken English. "You like stand here in rain?"

Quinn briefly considered ignoring Scala's invitation, but what would be the point? Where would he stay? With Davis? He would have to find him first. Diatsaro? He didn't even know if the prince was still living here. Whatever Scala's status in this town, he seemed to wield some influence.

"All right, let's go," he said. "How far is it?"

"Nothing far in this place." Budyek picked up Quinn's battered suitcase and set off.

They made their way to the end of the train and crossed the tracks. The station forecourt, once frequented by horse-drawn cabs, was deserted. The one unsurfaced street that led into town had been turned into a ribbon of mud by the rain, but boardwalks flanked it on either side. The houses were set back from it, each in its own garden or grounds, so all Quinn could see of them were their carved gables and ornamental turrets.

Snow must have fallen that morning in the valley, too, because the roofs were coated with a thin layer of white, but most of it had melted. The trees were dripping with moisture and the snow had failed to lie even on the higher slopes. The wooded hills above the town looked somber, almost black, in the fading light. Only the ridges and one or two jagged peaks still bore a dusting of snow.

Quinn recalled how he'd gone hunting in the neighborhood. There were deer and chamois to be had—even bears.

He made a mental note to ask Scala if the Czechs had slaughtered all the game.

Scala hadn't exaggerated: he wasn't short of space. Everything in the house was sumptuous, outsize, exaggerated, and its erstwhile owner must have had a thing about birds—parrots, from the look of it. Almost every room was equipped with a cage or cages, now empty.

Quinn's first-floor quarters comprised a sitting room, a bedroom, and an adjoining bathroom. He got the impression that the suite had been specially prepared for his benefit. The parquet floors gleamed, the furniture and gilt-framed pictures had been dusted, the bed was freshly made up.

He had a bath, shaved, changed, and lingered awhile on the landing, listening to the sounds from below. One was a strange, muffled, intermittent clicking. Then he descended the curving marble stairs to the spacious lobby, whose walls were embellished with tapestries and statues in niches. The source of the unidentifiable sound lay beyond some double doors at the far end, which were standing ajar. All was explained when he pushed them open and went in. Scala, brightly illuminated from above, was playing billiards by himself. He straightened up and leaned on his cue.

"Settled in okay?"

Scala had changed too. His U.S. Army uniform identified him as an RTO, or railroad transportation officer. He was wearing the khaki pants, shirt, and tie but had draped his jacket over a chair. "How about a game?" He indicated the billiard table. "We won't be eating for another half-hour."

Quinn selected a cue from the wooden rack against the wall. A log fire was blazing on the open hearth. "A winter palace. You've got this place all to yourself?"

Scala grinned. "I told you I had plenty of room. Shall we play for a dollar or two?"

"My game's not good enough," Quinn said. "Who did this place belong to?"

"A guy named Yurovsky—I guess that's why it's known as Yurovsky House."

"What became of his birds?"

"No idea. The cages were empty when I got here. Maybe Yurovsky wrung their necks because he'd taught them to say 'Long live the Czar.' "

"You turned him out onto the street?"

"Never set eyes on him, more's the pity. I'd like to have made his acquaintance." Scala put the red ball on its spot. "You kick off. Yurovsky was one of Karmel's wealthiest citizens, so they say, but he made a deal with the Bolsheviks. I admire guys like that. He took off with the Red Guards when the Czechs arrived."

Quinn came to with a start. This luxurious house, coupled with Karmel's outward appearance and peaceful surroundings, had temporarily dispelled his awareness that the town had been occupied by the Bolsheviks. "Were you here when the place was liberated?" he asked.

"I've been present at several so-called liberations," Scala said, "and picnics they weren't, but nothing like that happened here. The Czechs just marched in like conquering heroes."

"At Omsk one hears miraculous tales about this Czech general of yours."

"Wajda? Sure, a year ago he was just an officer's orderly." Scala laughed. "I've got nothing against a guy who gets places fast."

"I'm surprised the Reds didn't put up a fight," Quinn said. "All they'd have needed to do was dynamite the tunnel and block the pass."

"Wajda didn't bring his troops over the pass. He skirted the Urals and advanced on Karmel from the plain. Instead of a stronghold, the town became a trap overnight. The station was the only obstacle. Some of the Reds held out there for a while. The rest showed the white flag." Laying his cue aside, Scala went over to a table and poured two drinks. He came back and handed one to Quinn. "What makes you so interested?"

Quinn held the glass in his hand without drinking. "I'm simply curious why battles like this are won or lost. And why fighting continues or settles down. Those earthworks by the station, for instance—does Wajda intend to dig in here for good?"

Scala took a swallow of Scotch, regarding Quinn with the same look of curiosity he'd noticed at the station. "You'd better ask him that yourself."

"If a humble lieutenant lives like this"—Quinn indicated their surroundings—"how does a general fare? I'm expecting him to show me some magnificent hospitality."

"Our young god of war has requisitioned himself a prince's mansion—complete with the prince's daughter." He chuckled. "Even gods have their human side."

"No wonder he's lost his taste for fighting."

Scala nodded. "Can you blame them? These poor damn Czechs have been fighting for a year now, but they're farther from home than ever. They haven't had any pay for over a month. They're going around in rags and eating mule meat— have been for weeks now. I think they'd sooner stay put than go on." Scala refilled his glass and returned to the billiard table. "You aren't drinking," he said, "and you won't play for money. Don't you have any weaknesses—aside from hunting, I mean?"

Quinn waited for Scala to bring up the subject that had brought them all here.

"You really think you'll find gold here?"

"Gold?"

"Come off it. You're here on account of the mine, aren't

60

you? I'm told they closed it down because it wasn't worth exploiting."

Quinn debated for a moment. Had Fitzmaurice spread the rumor as a form of smoke screen? "Okay, so I'm checking it out," he said evasively. "Now I see why you're being so hospitable."

Scala's expression grew serious. "If you ever do find gold in worthwhile quantities, you won't be able to ship an ounce of it out of here without my help. I may be only a humble lieutenant, but nothing moves on the railroad without my say-so."

Quinn recalled his last night in Omsk and Hollis's allusions to Catania and the Mafia. "I did hear something along those lines," he said.

Scala laughed aloud. "You know, whenever the Russkis capture a town—Reds or Whites—the first person they shoot is the guy in charge of the railroad station." He drained his glass. "It's damned difficult to keep this system going. They've let everything go to pot—rolling stock, tracks, everything. I've got over a thousand cars marooned in sidings in my area alone. Either I don't have the locos to shift them, or the track's been destroyed."

"What about that train I saw in the station?" Quinn asked. Scala's hesitation was quite perceptible. "Those blue baggage cars . . ."

"Oh, them? They're my private collection." Scala deposited his glass on the edge of the billiard table. "Come with me and I'll show you something."

Quinn couldn't help thinking of Tom Cutter as he followed Scala out. Pool, billiards, snooker—Cutter had excelled at them all, and he played for money as a matter of course. Had the two men met? Had they spoken together in this very

61

house? Something told Quinn that it would be wiser not to betray an interest in Cutter yet.

The room into which Scala ushered him was a library, though the unread books on the shelves were purely decorative. Lofty French windows overlooked an expanse of garden with a big building at the far end. The library was in darkness when they entered, so its lighted windows caught Quinn's eye.

There was a lamp on a table in the middle of the room. Scala switched it on and went over to a lacquered cabinet, which he unlocked. He returned with an oval object cradled in both hands and set it carefully down on the table. Quinn saw that it was a large enameled Faberge egg. Scala drew the lamp nearer and pointed to some fine silver lines on the green and blue enameling.

"You see what they represent? The Trans-Siberian Railroad system!" His voice was hushed and breathless. "Now, press that button—no, better let me do it."

The upper half of the egg clicked open and Scala folded it back. Inside, reposing on an oval stretch of silver track, was a tiny model of the Trans-Siberian Express: a locomotive, a baggage car, and a parlor car. The locomotive's headlights were two diamonds, the taillights two rubies. Scala inserted a key in the base and wound it several times. The wheels began to turn. He switched the light off. The cars were illuminated from within: trunks could be seen in the baggage car, minuscule men and women were taking their ease in the parlor car, children playing on the floor. It was the work of a master jeweler. . . .

Quinn gazed at the miniature train until the wheels slowed and the lights inside dimmed. A final flicker, and the mechanism whirred to a stop. Scala switched the light on again, his face glowing with pride.

"It must be worth a fortune," Quinn said. The atmosphere of the room, of the entire house, had amused him so far. Now it was charged with tension.

Scala mightn't have heard. He shut the Faberge egg, replaced it in the cabinet, turned the key in the lock, and rejoined Quinn at the table.

"I bought it," he said quietly. "Not for its true value, of course. The man I bought it from was—well, in a bind. He was one of the guards at the Ipatiev place in Ekaterinburg, where the czar and his family were detained."

"And murdered," Quinn said.

"Right. Maybe I bought it from a murderer—does that shock you? The Trans-Siberian was built by convicts. They say a man lies buried under every tie. Eight thousand miles at four hundred ties per mile: work it out for yourself. What's one murder more or less? The world's full of acquisitive types. I'm one of them."

Quinn strove to shake off his persistent and oppressive feeling of tension. Again he sensed that the same scene had already been enacted here. He felt as if he were eavesdropping on a conversation between Scala and Tom Cutter.

"Tell me . . ." Quinn couldn't complete the sentence. The silence was so profound—and what happened next so unexpected—that the shots sounded as if they had been fired inside the library itself. Several volleys rang out in quick succession.

They came from the garden, Quinn realized. Then they ceased, and in their place he heard shouts. One of the library's doors opened onto a terrace. He heard Scala's voice behind him as he headed for it.

"No, it's pointless. Stay here!"

He wrenched the door open and went outside.

Yurovsky's garden lacked the florid ostentation of his house. Everything about it had the austere and uncluttered look of a municipal park: dead-straight graveled paths, rectangular flower beds and stretches of lawn, neatly trimmed shrubs and hedges. Quinn could make out every detail because the scene was illuminated by two powerful spotlights mounted on the roof of the building at the far end. Their harsh white glare lent the garden an even more formal appearance.

Even the men might have been performing some kind of ceremony. Quinn saw a dozen of them converging from all directions. They were still shouting, but in some Slavic language other than Russian—Czech, presumably. They reached their destination and formed a circle around something on the ground.

Quinn hadn't heard any footsteps behind him. He merely felt a hand on his shoulder and heard Scala say, "Come back inside."

Still he didn't move. The glare of the spotlights enabled him to see, through a gap in the circle at the far end of the garden, that the thing on the ground was a motionless human form.

The hand detached itself from his shoulder, gripped his arm, gave it a tug. He saw two men pick up the inert body and carry it away between them. "What was that all about?" he demanded. When Scala didn't reply he shook off the American's restraining hand and rounded on him. "Scala, I want an answer."

Scala pursed his lips. "It means," he said, "that my nice, cozy quarters have one minor drawback: they're too near the pokey, and the inmates make a break for it now and then."

"A prison in the middle of town?" Quinn took another look at the building. He vaguely recalled that it had once been the regional governor's residence. "That place, you mean?"

Scala nodded. "The Cheka used it while the Reds were here."

"And the Czechs took it over. Who do you keep in there?"

"Nobody in Karmel likes questions. You ask too many. You'll find that out soon enough."

Quinn followed Scala back inside. For the moment he felt like the victim of a hallucination. The library was just as it had been: the books stood arrayed on their shelves, the gilt lettering on their leather spines caught the light, the parquet floor was as lustrous as old French polish, while the marble fireplace might have been carved in ice. . . .

But then he was assailed by a vision of the men clustered around the figure on the ground. Quite suddenly, he had the feeling that he himself was encircled.

8

Q U I N N dreamed of nothing on his first night in Karmel. He slept long and soundly, and his host had already gone out by the time he came downstairs. A Russian manservant brought him breakfast in a room overlooking the grounds, where two gardeners were busy raking the trampled flower beds.

He left the house immediately after breakfast. The rain had stopped. Mist still clung to the wooded slopes above the town, but the day promised to be fine once it cleared.

Two sentries were on duty outside the house. They took no notice of him, nor did he see any sign of Budyek as he set off for the station.

The telegraphist was busy tapping out a message while a Czech officer dictated the text. Quinn waited outside. Some men were refurbishing the train that had brought him, scraping rust off the metalwork and repainting the wooden freight cars. The other train, the one made up of blue baggage cars, was still guarded by a double cordon of sentries in the siding near the stone warehouse that had once belonged to the mining company. On the far side of the river, where khaki tents stood in serried rows, two companies of Czech infantry had paraded for inspection.

The Czech officer had finished with the telegraphist. Quinn went into the office and inquired about the telegram he'd addressed to Davis. The operator, a stoop-shouldered old man, mumbled something about having too many telegrams to cope with. Hadn't he passed it on? His shoulders seemed to sag another few inches. "Can't you see I'm busy?" Did he know where the Englishman was staying? He glanced around nervously and said, "Try the railroaders' settlement. Ask for Sonya Kuklin."

The railroaders' settlement, which lay west of the station, turned out to be a double row of timber-framed cottages flanking a narrow dirt road. The tiny gardens at the rear had already been stripped of summer produce. The dirt road evidently became a quagmire in winter, because the stoops at the front were separated from it by short flights of wooden steps.

Quinn saw no one as he made his way along the dismal little street. The last cottage was no different from the rest, except that some withered plants stood in pots on the stoop. He knocked on the plank door, which was weatherworn and split. No response. He seemed to hear some faint sounds from inside the house, but the timbers might simply have been working out in the sun.

He knocked again, harder this time, and this time he heard footsteps. They paused just inside the door. "Who's there?" A woman's voice.

"Captain Quinn," he said. The fact that he'd used his rank told him how tense he was.

The door creaked open. The woman had dark, luxuriant hair done up in a bun on her neck. She was in mourning, but everything about her—the opulent figure and fresh, rosy complexion—was in conflict with the funereal black of her dress.

"May I come in?" he asked.

She stood in the doorway, one hand on the jamb, the other grasping the nape of her neck as if to prevent her bun from coming undone.

"You can't see him now," she said at length in Russian. "He isn't well." Her voice was low and husky, so Quinn was doubly startled when she broke into a sudden, schoolgirlish giggle. "Come back this afternoon."

"It's urgent."

Her sigh conveyed that resisting the opposite sex wasn't her strong point. "All right, you'd better come in then."

The ground floor of the cottage appeared to consist of a single room that served as a kitchen, living room, and bedroom combined. It was furnished with the barest essentials only. The woman pointed to a flight of stairs at the end of a passage. "The door on the right," she said. "He really isn't well, though."

The room was in semidarkness, but one glance told Quinn that it was a woman's room. It was crammed with all the furniture the room downstairs lacked: a display cabinet full of glass ornaments and knickknacks, small tables bearing oil lamps and framed photographs, several upright chairs, an overstuffed armchair. Even the carpets on the floor lay two deep, and the drawn curtains, which admitted only a sliver of light, were of heavy velour.

The ornate bed cried out for an occupant with soft, pink, feminine flesh. Frank Davis, ensconced in a nest of ruched pillows, looked thoroughly out of place in it. His dark eyes stared at Quinn out of a pallid, unhealthy face with sunken cheeks and a stubbly chin. Instead of pajamas he wore an army-issue undershirt buttoned up the front. He was so emaciated that his ribs showed through the coarse gray wool.

"God Almighty," Quinn exclaimed. "What's wrong with you?" He made for the window.

"Please don't," Davis said behind him. "Leave the curtains the way they are."

Quinn turned to face the bed again. "A little light and fresh air wouldn't hurt you."

"They wouldn't do me any good either. You're Quinn, I suppose?"

"Yes, I was expecting you to meet me at the station. Didn't you get my telegram?"

67

"I thought those bastards at Omsk had forgotten all about me."

The capacious armchair, which was upholstered in some kind of plush, stood closest to the bed, but Quinn eschewed this in favor of an upright chair farther away.

"What's really the matter with you?"

Davis gave a wry smile. "I always look this way—it's nothing, honest. Care for a drink?"

Quinn intercepted a glance at the armchair. He leaned forward, lifted the cushion, and found what he expected: a bottle half-full of colorless liquid.

Davis laughed. "A mind reader—just what the doctor ordered." He relieved Quinn of the bottle. "You'll find some glasses over there."

"It's a bit early in the day." There were a couple of dirty glasses on top of the cabinet. Quinn could visualize Sonya Kuklin and Frank Davis boozing together, he lolling back against the frilly pillows while she lounged in the armchair beside him. He opened the cabinet, took out a clean glass, and handed it to Davis. Then he sat down again and gestured at the room. "How long have you been here?"

"Christ, nearly two months now." Davis poured himself a drink—half an inch of vodka only, but he didn't touch it at once, just nursed the glass in his hand. "Are you a Yank?"

"No, English."

"You don't sound like it."

"I've spent half my life in Canada."

"I'm a Londoner—an East Ender. I bet you can tell, can't you?"

"I want to talk about Cutter." Quinn waited, but Davis made no reply. The room was so quiet that the woman could be heard moving around downstairs. Davis listened intently, then looked at Quinn as if he were surprised to have company at all. Quinn decided not to hurry him. "Nice-looking woman, your landlady," he said. "Is she a widow?"

68

"Sonya?" He looked back in surprise. "Well, she's hardly my sister, if that's what you mean."

Quinn couldn't help smiling. "How do you two communicate?"

"In Russian. I've tried to teach her a few words of English, but it's hopeless. Me, I learned this crazy language while I was a mechanic with Rolls-Royce. Russia used to be a big export market—the Russkis bought more of our cars than the rest of the Continentals put together." Davis downed the finger of vodka and poured himself another. "The trouble was, they couldn't repair them, so the firm sent me out here. I became a sort of mobile service station, always on the move from one Rolls to the next. That's how I picked up the lingo."

"And now you're a radio operator."

Davis grunted and settled himself more comfortably. "Somebody in the War Office heard I knew Russian and got the idea. I didn't mind. It was dead cushy to start with. I stayed in London with the monitoring service while everyone else went off to the trenches. Then they sent me here. But I guess all good things come to an end sooner or later—usually sooner." As he said this Davis's face underwent a transformation. Quinn couldn't decide whether his expression was pained, suspicious, or apprehensive, but one thing he knew for certain: it wasn't the effect of a hangover. Frank Davis was a very uneasy man.

Quinn said, "Was it Fitzmaurice who teamed you up with Cutter?"

"Why don't you get yourself a glass? It's no fun drinking alone." Davis held the bottle up to the light. It only contained one more shot, and he'd clearly decided to save it for later. "Fitzmaurice?" he echoed. "Do you work for that bastard?"

"A pilot I spoke with told me you were brought here from Omsk by plane."

"Some plane! A few old sticks and strips of cloth held together with glue and piano wire. We were put down in the bloody backwoods near Yelabuga, east of Kazan. I spent a whole week out there on my lonesome. Cutter pushed off the same night. 'You stay put, Frank,' he said. 'Wait here for me—I've got some business to attend to.' " Davis gave a derisive grunt. " 'Business,' he called it!"

"Where did he go?"

"Kazan. He had a girlfriend in Kazan. Of course. Women went for Cutter like nobody I've ever seen."

"So he spent a week in Kazan. Then he radioed a report to Fitzmaurice in Omsk?"

Davis had decided that it was time for another drink. He splashed the remaining vodka into his glass and knocked it back. Quinn waited. His question had obviously unsettled Davis, but again he resolved not to hurry the man. "And after Kazan?"

"After Kazan we went to Perm."

"And I suppose it was the same story all over again—Cutter going into town, leaving you behind on your own?"

"Look," Davis said, "don't get the wrong idea. What I've told you—it may sound like we didn't get along together, but it wasn't really so bad. We were just different, that's all. I was jumpy, not being used to this kind of . . . well, a job like this. When I insisted, he let me go with him to Perm." He stopped. "In the end I wished I hadn't gone. Perm was a huge, filthy, louse-infected hospital town. I spent the whole time in a bar near the station while Cutter went out gathering his information."

"What kind of information?"

"Anything he could pick up from railroad employees. But don't ask me why he was so interested. I've no idea. Anyway, after that, our next step was Karmel. I liked it much, much better."

"Was the town still occupied by the Red Guard when you got here?"

Davis gave a nervous laugh. "We almost didn't make it at

70

all. There's nothing between Perm and here but bare, open plain. We legged it by night and lay low during the day. At dawn on the second or third day we came to a peasant cottage—one room with a married couple living in it. . . ." Davis laughed again as if recalling something intensely amusing. "It was obvious right from the start that the woman had taken a fancy to Tom—she kept giving him the eye. My God, her husband had hardly gone off to work in the fields when they were rolling around on the bed! I had to keep watch outside, and lucky for them I did. The husband came back with a sawed-off shotgun. . . ." Davis drained his glass and put the bottle on the bedside table. His hand was steady, but he was so thin and in such poor shape that Quinn wondered how his body could withstand so much alcohol. "There's another bottle in the cabinet," Davis said.

"I'll get it for you when I leave," Quinn told him. "I need to know when, exactly, the two of you got here."

"Let's see . . . We blew up the track on the twentieth . . ."

Quinn leaned forward and stared at Davis in surprise. Hollis had mentioned something of the kind, but he'd begun to have his doubts about that story too. "The track between here and Perm?" he said.

"Yes, we dynamited the bridge across the river ten miles outside town. That was in the small hours of August twentieth, the day the Czechs launched their attack on this place. Not that there was very much fighting. The Reds just rounded up a few dozen of the locals, right at the very last minute, and herded them into a cattle car. Then they locked the doors and riddled it with heavy machine guns. Like a sieve, it was. We found it in the station when we got here, with blood still dripping from the holes in the sides. . . . Ask Sonya—her husband was one of the men on board. . . ."

Quinn sat quite still, waiting for him to go on.

"The Czechs didn't behave much better. Once they'd occupied the town they conducted a roundup of their own. You

71

wouldn't believe the stories one hears about that prison of theirs, the interrogations and so on. . . ." It seemed a physiological impossibility, but Davis's face grew paler still. "I'll tell you, Quinn, it shames me as an Englishman to be party to all these atrocities."

Quinn rose and went over to the cabinet. He took out the new bottle and handed it to Davis. The house had fallen silent. Nothing was stirring.

"Do me a favor, will you?" Davis said at length. "Get Fitzmaurice to recall me."

Quinn nodded. "Where's your transmitter?"

Davis indicated a table in the corner of the room. Quinn turned to look. On it stood a sort of suitcase made of battered gray metal. He turned back to Davis. "What was Cutter's real assignment?"

Davis was staring down at the bottle in his hand. "He never told me."

"Come on, man! You were the one that radioed his signals to Omsk."

"They were in code."

"Of course they damn well were, but you must have known what was in them!"

"Cutter enciphered them himself. Only he and Fitzmaurice knew the code."

"You were living in Cutter's pocket for nearly two months. However much he may have tried to keep his mission a secret from you, you must have formed some idea of it."

At this Davis simply shrugged. "Look," he said at last, "if you want to get yourself killed that's your business. Just leave me out of it." Davis had hardly raised his voice at all, as if he couldn't muster the energy for a full-blooded outburst.

"How did you hear of Cutter's death?"

"Someone came here. That Yank, Scala. He said the Reds had executed him."

"Did he offer you any kind of proof?"

"He's dead all right, you can bet on that. His luck was bound to run out sooner or later."

Strange, thought Quinn, that two men as dissimilar as Fitz-maurice and Davis should use the same words. "Have you requested Fitzmaurice to recall you to Omsk?"

Davis nodded. "The weather could close in any day now. Karmel's an icebox in winter, Sonya says, and I've always hated the cold. Will you help to get me out of here?"

"I'll do what I can." Quinn rose. "Cutter's last signal was clear: 'If anything happens to me, take care of Moura Toumanova.' "

Davis seemed to emerge from his torpor. "Really? I thought it was just a joke."

"Why?" Quinn asked.

"Because it was so unlike him. Take care of her? Tom didn't care for women, not that way. Still, maybe she was an exception."

"Did you know her?"

Davis laughed uncomfortably. "He never wanted us to meet. But yes, I know of her. Everyone does. She's the tough-est, most high-strung prostitute this side of Kazan!"

"Where can I find her?"

In the act of raising his glass, Davis noticed that his hands had started shaking and put it down again. He reached for a cigarette case on the bedside table. It cost him a considerable effort to open it and extract a cigarette. "At the old gold miners' village."

Quinn still wasn't sure that Davis had told him everything. But he knew he couldn't stand another minute in this dark, stuffy room. He said, "I hope you'll be feeling better the next time I come."

"There's only one thing that'll make me feel better. Fitz-maurice has got to recall me."

This time there was nothing ambiguous about the look on

Davis's face: it was only too plain. "You're scared of something," Quinn said. "What is it?"

Davis lowered his eyes. "If you want to do me a favor, get me out of here." The words were almost inaudible.

Sonya Kuklin was waiting at the bottom of the stairs. "How is he?" she asked. She patted the bun on her neck in an exact repetition of the gesture she'd made at the door.

"He's lucky to have you," Quinn said.

"You think so?" she replied with an uneasy laugh.

Looking at her, Quinn involuntarily pictured her in a colorful, low-cut gown that showed off her opulent bosom and her bare, rosy shoulders. "I'm sure you're good for his morale," he said.

She blushed. "Nice of you to say so."

"Did you ever meet the other Englishman?" He wasn't sure what name Cutter had used. "His friend, I mean."

"Oh, yes! He was quite different!" She blushed again. "He always made me laugh. . . ." A nod in the direction of the stairs. "Frank's difficult sometimes. I do my best to cheer him up, but I don't always succeed. . . ." Her voice trailed off.

"He's frightened of something," Quinn said.

"If you'll excuse me," she said, her manner cooling suddenly to one of formality. "I must go and see to him."

"Perhaps he'd feel better if he confided in someone—you, for instance."

She shook her head so vigorously that her bun came undone. The long, dark hair cascaded down her back to her hips.

"I don't want anything to do with it," she said.

"With what?"

She opened the door and hustled him outside. At the last moment she whispered, "The house opposite—keep your eyes open. . . ."

Quinn descended the wooden steps. The cottage across the

way was like all the rest. He set off, then swung around as if he'd forgotten something. A shadowy face was glued to the downstairs window. Even as he looked, it vanished abruptly.

So what, he told himself. A Russian woman, and a widow into the bargain, living under the same roof as an *Anglichanin?* Of course her neighbors were curious—nothing could be more natural.

And yet . . . just as in the library the previous evening, he was overcome with the feeling that Karmel was a town in a state of siege.

9

THE search for gold in Karmel had originally been conducted by individual prospectors. A number of local place-names—Yakov's Pit, Two Brothers Gulch, Prospectors' Folly—still survived from that period. The only mine to have been exploited on any real scale was the Xenia, so called after the wife of its owner, the elder Prince Diatsaro.

The gold had been transported by narrow-gauge railroad from the smelting works to the secure warehouse near the station and stored there until it had accumulated in sufficient quantity to be forwarded by rail to the mint at Ekaterinburg. The rusty track was now half-hidden beneath a knee-high tangle of withered grass and weeds.

Quinn paused awhile at the point where the railway diverged from a cart track running parallel to it. The miners' village occupied the last available stretch of level ground. On the hillside above it Quinn could make out the sealed-off entrances to the abandoned mine and, perched on a man-made plateau in front of them, the remains of some timber-framed buildings. A waterfall was gushing down the steep rock face beyond the plateau. Above it, clothed in larch and

75

fir, ridge after mountain ridge ascended to the distant skyline like the tiers of some vast amphitheater.

Nearly five hundred men had worked at the Xenia when it opened in the first flush of the boom. Ten years before, when Quinn had visited the place to compile his report, the population of the miners' village had dwindled to less than a hundred. All he could now see on either side of the dusty street were deserted, tumbledown shacks. The windows of the former commissary were smashed, its roof was falling in, and the makeshift hospital had been gutted by fire. The long, low barn across the way had served as a church, but its wooden belfry was in ruins.

Quinn reached the central square. It was overgrown with withered grass, and the only tree had been split by lightning. On the far side of the square stood a stone building less neglected and dilapidated in appearance than its neighbors. A hotel and bar, it had been patronized by overseers, miners, mule drivers, gamblers, and women of easy virtue.

A succession of high-pitched whistles rent the air—not so much a melody as a discordant scale performed on a primitive flute. Quinn looked over at the hotel. Running along the front was a veranda supported by white wooden posts, and seated on a crate beside the entrance was a man, a thickset, barrel-chested Mongol with a close-cropped head of massive proportions.

Quinn climbed the veranda steps. "I'm looking for Moura Toumanova," he said in Russian.

The Mongol removed the flute from his lips. At his feet lay some freshly whittled shavings of willow and the knife he'd been using to fashion the instrument. He shook his head. "She's not expecting anyone."

Quinn could hear someone moving around inside. He paused for a second, then opened the door and entered the gloomy barroom. A man was sweeping the floor. The room had whitewashed walls, a few chairs, a single table, a stove, and a bar counter. The shelves behind the counter were bare. The only form of decoration was a prospector's pan hanging on the wall.

He abandoned the cheerless barroom and went outside again. There was no chair on the veranda, so he sat down on the top step. The Mongol had started work on another flute. Quinn thought of his former partner. Tom Cutter would have handled the Mongol quite differently. No one had been more adept at making friends or more popular with his fellow prospectors. Even if some of them later regretted having put their trust in him, their liking for him remained unaffected. Cutter spoke their language. Where Quinn himself was concerned they'd always kept their distance as if aware that he could never really be one of them.

He continued to wait in silence. The Mongol had finished carving his flute and was trying it out. All at once he broke off and the brutish look on his face abruptly softened. He jumped up, ran down the veranda steps on his stubby legs, and made for the coach house beside the corral where the mining company had kept its mules and horses. It was only then that Quinn caught sight of the one-horse wagon and the woman on the box. She was wearing a man's hat, but there was no mistaking the color of her hair even at a couple of hundred yards.

The Mongol helped her down. He must have said something to her, because she turned and looked in Quinn's direction. Then, leaving him to unhitch the horse, she headed for the hotel.

Quinn waited for her at the foot of the steps. She took off her hat as she came; her hair was an incandescent red, so vivid that it seemed to absorb the sunlight and reflect it with redoubled intensity. She was a white woman, but her face was tanned—like amber, Quinn thought—and her dark eyes and high cheekbones lent her an almost Asiatic appearance. She was clearly a powerful woman, but she moved with a suppleness, a dignity, a grace. . . . Quinn stood transfixed, as if gazing for the first time at some rare forest creature. Surely this was no common prostitute—she was the finest woman he had ever seen.

He was so obviously transfixed by the sight of her hair that she burst out laughing when she finally reached him. "Everyone looks twice at it," she said.

Moura Toumanova was so unlike the poor, bereaved, harassed woman he'd been expecting that Quinn said the first thing that came into his head.

"It's just startling—the color, I mean."

"It's my greatest asset," she said. Then, as if wanting to get things straight from the start, she added, "It governs my price."

He thought that over. "My name is Oliver Quinn," he said eventually, "at your service."

She smiled at the gallantry but held herself even more stiffly erect than before. The sun was shining full in her face, and her skin, like her hair, seemed to radiate the sunlight it absorbed. She was beautiful, but her face had the rigidity of a statue. Quinn found it impossible to read her thoughts. He hoped she couldn't read his—he had picked the mingled scents she gave off, at close range, of flower-scented hair wash and fine harness leather.

"You are Moura Toumanova, aren't you?"

She walked past him up the veranda steps. She was wearing riding boots under a long black skirt. Her peasant blouse was open at the neck, and a thin gold chain nestled against the tanned skin of her throat. From the way it hung taut between her breasts, he guessed that there must be some kind of pendant or charm suspended from the bottom of the loop.

"I have to speak with you," he said.

"I only see clients by appointment," she replied, mocking his discomfiture by seeming so at ease herself. "They have to book well in advance."

She was putting on an act, Quinn thought—or was that

simply what he wanted to believe? For a moment he tried to imagine how Cutter would have reacted in his place, then just as quickly hated himself for having the thought.

"What did you want to speak to me about?" she asked.

"A mutual friend."

She said nothing, and her expression became even more uncommunicative.

"Maybe you knew him by another name. He was an Englishman like me, Tom Cutter . . ."

She broke into a flood of imprecations. The language was so foul-mouthed, so obscene, that Quinn stared at her as if she were tearing the clothes off her very body. He heard the onrush of footsteps behind him too late: an iron hand chopped him on the side of the neck, his wrists were gripped, and his arms twisted agonizingly behind his back.

The girl had stopped swearing, though Quinn was so preoccupied with the pain in his neck and arms that he scarcely noticed.

"No, Timur!"

"I kick his head in!" The voice in his ear was hoarse with rage.

"Let him go," she said, quite calmly now.

The pressure on Quinn's wrists eased. His arms were numb and his neck and shoulders hurt so much he could barely move his head. The Mongol was standing beside him with his eyes narrowed, a grim smile on his face. Quinn massaged his neck and looked at the girl.

"Follow me." She led the way into the barroom and silently indicated one of the chairs. Quinn remained standing behind it with his hands resting on the back. From outside came the strains of a flute, as unmelodious as before.

"Did he manhandle Cutter like that?" Quinn asked.

"It was never necessary." Her expression was cold and impersonal.

"True," Quinn agreed. "There weren't many women that

79

ever fought him off. But tell me—what did he want from you?"

"A woman in my profession? What a strange question."

"Is it?" Quinn replied. "It seems very strange to me that a man like Cutter should ever want to pay for something he was used to having for free." Quinn gestured at the room. "An odd place to use for professional purposes."

"There's a war on," she said flatly. "War brings all kinds of people together in the oddest places—and doing the oddest things."

"Would you like to get away from here—leave Karmel, I mean?"

Her eyes narrowed.

"You could leave the country if you want," he went on. "I could provide you with the necessary papers and enough money to make a fresh start. Anywhere you like."

She seemed to deliberate. "What would I have to do in return?"

"Nothing. It's a parting gift from Cutter."

For a moment she seemed to forget her self-appointed role. The haughty expression vanished, and all that remained was a look of infinite weariness. The shadows beneath her eyes suggested that she hadn't slept much recently.

"I don't believe in gifts," she said at length. "Especially ones that drop out of the sky."

He reached in his pocket, produced the folded slip of paper on which he'd copied Cutter's signal, and handed it to her.

She glanced at it and handed it back. "I can't read English."

"It's a message from Cutter—the last one he ever sent: 'If anything happens to me, take care of Moura Toumanova.' "

The shadows beneath her eyes seemed to deepen. She took hold of the gold chain around her neck and toyed with it. Then, noticing the direction of his gaze, she quickly lowered her hand. "What *is* all this," she demanded fiercely, "a bad joke?"

It sounded like the prelude to another round of profanities. The flute fell silent. Footsteps clumped across the veranda and paused outside the door.

"You know," Quinn said after a moment, "everyone I talk to in this town is terrifically jumpy."

She indicated the piece of paper in his hand. "May I see it again?"

He handed it to her. She genuinely couldn't read it, by all appearances. She simply held it in her hand, fingering it the way she'd fingered the gold chain. Then she gave it back. "And that's what brought you all the way from Omsk? Charity?"

He hadn't mentioned where he'd come from. He pocketed the slip of paper without pursuing the point. All he said was, "What did Cutter really want from you? What did he hope to find here with your help?"

"I have no idea."

"How did you learn of his death?"

"What the devil does that matter. He's dead. I'm sorry I can't help you."

"Cutter asked you questions too, didn't he?"

She started shouting again. The door burst open and the Mongol came charging in, but this time Quinn was ready for him. He sidestepped and made for the open door.

As he stepped through it he caught one last glimpse of the girl whose anger only seemed to make her more beautiful. He'd never seen a woman so unladylike—or, truly, so exciting. This was different from anything he'd ever felt for Catherine. After her death, there had been other women in his life, but he had never fallen in love with any of them. Sooner or later those relationships had ended in disappointment. And he had never seen the reason why until this moment. Standing here, in this doorway, he realized that every woman in his past had attracted him because she reminded him of Catherine. But this Moura was different. He would find nothing familiar in her, nothing whatsoever to remind him of his old passion or his old grief. She was wild, completely untamed by convention or sentiment: truly a natural woman, of the sort Quinn had previously thought could only exist in fantasy.

The air outside, which had turned colder, seemed to hint that snow was in the offing. Quinn retraced his steps across the square to the coach house. The unhitched wagon was standing in a lean-to, the horse could be heard moving around in its stable. He went over to the wagon. Lying under the driver's seat was a stiff cowhide packsaddle with two side pockets. It was the kind of packsaddle commonly used for transporting gold on muleback. He could tell, when he picked it up and weighed it in his hands, that it was empty.

10

''Y O U ' L L find the whole gang over there," said one of the Czech sentries guarding the main entrance. "They call it their hunting lodge." He hawked and spat with gusto. "The Reds kicked them out of the big house—and personally, friend, I couldn't care less."

Quinn, peering through the wrought-iron gates, could just discern the outlines of the Diatsaros' vast mansion at the end of the drive. It looked as out of place as an opera set. The old prince, an amateur archaeologist, had named it "Amneris" after some pharaoh's daughter whose tomb he had unearthed in Egypt.

Quinn made his way along the stone boundary wall and through a side gate into the grounds. Like the great house itself, they testified to the old Prince Diatsaro's extravagant tastes. Trees native to the region were interspersed with exotic imports such as California red firs and cedars and cypresses from the Eastern Mediterranean. There was even an avenue of palm trees, though these had not long survived transplantation, and all that remained of them was a double row of brown, hairy stumps. Pine trees clothed the rising ground on the far side of the estate, where the hunting lodge stood. It was a large timber building adorned with carved balconies and gable ends, resembling an outsize Swiss chalet.

Quinn could see no one at first, but the monotonous sound of a handsaw drew his attention to an open fronted shed. Bent over the sawhorse inside were two men so dissimilar in height that they found it hard to coordinate their movements. The ground around them was littered with sawn logs.

Sergei Diatsaro, the old prince's son, seemed hardly to have changed in the ten years since Quinn had last seen him, though his hair was a shade grayer and his face a trifle leaner. The sight of Quinn brought him up short. He stopped sawing and looked momentarily embarrassed, as if caught in the act of committing some breach of etiquette. Then he laughed.

"This must be the first time you've ever seen me doing something useful!" He strode up to Quinn with his hand extended, then hesitated. "I'm afraid I've forgotten your name. . . ."

"Quinn. Oliver Quinn."

"Of course! The gold expert—the man my mother pinned all her hopes on!" He massaged his jaw and hollow cheeks, which were frosted with stubble. "Forgive me, but it's days since I saw any reason to shave. What on earth brings you to Karmel?"

"Coincidence. Can we talk somewhere?"

"Of course." Sergei Diatsaro was wearing a fawn linen suit more appropriate to the French Riviera. He reached for the jacket, which he'd removed, but his assistant was too quick for him and helped him into it, standing on tiptoe to do so. Diatsaro thanked him and turned back to Quinn. "As you see, we cling to the old customs here," he said with a smile.

He emerged from the shed. The light was fading fast and the treetops were already veiled in mist. The last rays of the setting sun gilded the windows of the hunting lodge as they approached, lending it an even more picturesque appearance.

Diatsaro paused just outside the door. "The place is packed, but don't worry. I won't bother to introduce you all around. Just stay close."

There must have been at least twenty people in the spacious, lofty hall. They all fell silent and turned to look at Quinn as he followed Diatsaro inside. The room itself was equally daunting. Most of the light came from some upended logs blazing in a big open fireplace, but two manservants in striped vests were going around lighting candles in the enormous gloom. Now that Quinn had a closer view of the apprehensive, inquisitive faces he noticed that the majority of those present were women, and that many of the men wore uniforms encrusted with medals or medal ribbons.

The prince took his arm and led him along a passage to a sort of gun room. The little daylight still filtering through the windows revealed paneled walls and an alcove containing gun racks. The guns themselves were missing. A dog, an elderly red setter, was stretched out on the threadbare carpet. It raised its head when they entered, thumped the floor with its tail, and went back to sleep.

Diatsaro lit the lamp and waved Quinn to one of the two chairs in the room. He himself sat down behind a desk piled high with books, some of which he pushed aside to make room for his elbows.

"You saw that crowd in there?" he said. "They're supposed to be related to our family in some way, every last one of them, but don't ask me who they all are. They've been turning up in groups since October 'seventeen. Did you notice those uniforms? They only put them on in the evenings so as not to wear them out. To hear them talk, you'd think the whole of the late Czar's High Command had taken up residence here."

He laughed, but only with his lips. There was no amusement in his keen, gray-blue eyes.

"I'd have thought you would move back into the big house when Karmel was liberated."

Diatsaro surveyed his surroundings. "We're comfortable enough here. Besides, the new occupant pays us rent. We can't feed ourselves on the entries in my mother's account books. According to them we're still disgustingly rich. Mother still inhabits a world in which we own brimming safe-deposits in Moscow and St. Petersburg and receive a steady income from our foundries and coal mines in Perm. . . ."

"I hope she's well."

"The same as ever. She's probably praying for the czar at this moment. He's as much of a reality to her as our imaginary bank balances."

"It's a wonder you survived the Revolution," Quinn said, sitting back in his chair. "Were you here in Karmel at the time?"

"Yes. The whole family fled here—I told you, they thought it was the safest spot."

"Was it bad here?"

The prince's gaunt face broke into a melancholy smile. "No worse than elsewhere. Besides, we had a guardian angel— Pavel Pavlovich Govorov. Didn't we go hunting with him once?"

"I'm not sure."

"One of our gamekeepers—an ex-poacher."

"I don't recall."

"Then it must have been after your time here. There have always been poachers in this part of the world. Most of them were miners who'd lost their jobs and went poaching to keep the wolf from the door. But Govorov was something else entirely. He always shot the pick of our game—he and our head gamekeeper waged a regular war for years before he was caught and tried. The sentence was ludicrous: ten years' hard labor. My father—he was still alive then—got him out of prison by claiming that he'd taken him on as an assistant gamekeeper."

The prince's laugh sounded more resigned than mirthful.

"None of us had any inkling that Pavel Pavlovich was a revolutionary, a longtime Bolshevik. In October 'seventeen he became Karmel's strongman overnight—head of the Party organization, first secretary of the District Committee. At all events, we owe our survival of the Red October to 'Comrade' Govorov. He took us under his wing."

"I don't suppose his kindness to you cut much ice with the Czechs."

"He didn't wait around to find out. He vanished into his beloved mountains." Diatsaro smiled again. "Things change so fast these days I can hardly keep up with them."

"Is he back in Karmel?"

"He'll reappear soon enough if the Bolsheviks come back."

Quinn thought for a moment, then said, "Tell me—do you believe in the White cause?"

"Do you?"

"I'm not a Russian," Quinn said. "This isn't my country."

"Russia could survive without the Diatsaros, that much I do know."

"And yet you stay."

"What else would I do—sell life insurance? Emigrate to Paris and play the piano in a Russian nightclub on the Champs-Elysées? I ask you, do I look the part?"

The setter stirred in its sleep. It rose, stretched, rotated on the spot, subsided onto the carpet again, and dozed off in exactly the same position as before.

"But you didn't come here to listen to me ramble on," Diatsaro said.

"I came on account of an Englishman. Tom Cutter. Does the name mean anything to you?"

"No."

"He came to Karmel and was shot by the Reds, or so it seems. I'm trying to find out what he was after. From what you say of Govorov, there was a strong Red cell here."

"Yes, thanks to the starvation wages paid to the miners by my mercenary mother. This district was known as the Red Urals years before the Revolution and with good reason."

"The Cheka maintained an outstation here—a whole detachment housed in the former governor's residence. Why? What was so important about Karmel?"

Diatsaro's sudden uneasiness was not lost on Quinn. His brooding eyes had become alert. "What do you really hope to discover?" he countered.

"I'm groping in the dark. I don't know what goes on here, but everyone I question seems scared of something."

"When did you arrive?"

"I got here yesterday."

"Where are you staying?"

"With an American. He's living at the Yurovsky place. Did you know Yurovsky?"

"Only slightly. You must ask my mother—she had business dealings with him. There was a government mint at Ekaterinburg. Vitov Yurovsky was the director."

Quinn raised his eyebrows. "I'm told he made a deal with the Reds. Wasn't that rather surprising?"

"No, quite in character. Yurovsky is a born survivor."

"Does the Xenia Mine still belong to your family?"

"Technically, yes, but it's never really shown a profit. But you should know that better than anyone."

"What about the hotel at the miners' village? Are you familiar with the name Moura Toumanova?"

"She's the one who rents the place. Nobody knows why, exactly. But nobody worries about it. All my mother cares about is that she pays—more punctually, by the way, than that Czech general. He's two months behind."

"So she's been here a while."

"A few months—I don't know exactly." Diatsaro leaned across the desk. He looked like a marksman drawing a bead on a target, Quinn thought: one eye was almost shut. "These rumors," he said, slowly and deliberately, "—there's nothing in them. Rumors always abound when gold's involved, but they don't mean a thing."

The prince rose, walked to the window, and stared out for a moment before resuming his seat. Quinn was reminded of the setter turning on the spot and settling down again.

"My God," Diatsaro said fiercely, "Karmel was a wonderful place before our family had its 'stroke of luck.' I was only nine or ten at the time, but I remember the day vividly. A geologist brought the news: gold had been found—enough of it to justify mining the stuff commercially. Our family had been living beyond its means for generations, so this seemed a heaven-sent chance of restoring our fortunes. My father reacted as if he'd trodden on a snake, but my mother—well, if it hadn't been for her, there would never have been a mine here at all. It was she who raised the bank loans, bought the equipment, built the village, and recruited the labor. The Xenia Mine was named after her as you probably know.

"Still, it was my father who had the last laugh. We'd struck gold all right, but the mine never paid enough to make us rich. It only broke even in the good years, probably because the workers were paid such a pittance, and we wound up deeper in debt than ever." Diatsaro paused. "Did my mother ever pay you for that report you wrote?"

There was a knock on the door, and the scrawny manservant entered bearing a tray. Diatsaro looked at Quinn inquiringly.

"Would you mind?"

"Don't let me stop you."

On the tray were a towel, a shaving brush, a razor, some shaving soap, a bottle of eau de cologne, and a basin of hot water. The manservant set them out on the desk and withdrew. Diatsaro, having removed his jacket, proceeded to lather his face.

"The rumors you mention interest me all the same," Quinn said.

Diatsaro nodded. "You should have seen it. The Czechs embarked on an all-out search as soon as they occupied the town—they didn't even wait to bury the dead. Dozens of detachments headed for the old prospectors' diggings in the mountains."

"All for a burnt-out gold mine," Quinn said, watching. "Imagine."

Sergei Diatsaro turned. The lather on his cheeks intensified the gray-blue of his eyes. "Oh, no," he said. "They were after nothing less than the czar's gold."

Quinn's eyes widened in amazement.

"The *what?*"

Diatsaro laughed. "We're talking about rumors, don't forget. But that's what they thought—that the Xenia Mine might hold our national gold reserves. The Bolsheviks are reputed to have found them intact in the vaults of the Imperial Bank when they captured St. Petersburg in October 'seventeen. The whole of the nation's wealth in bullion—an astronomical sum, so it's said."

"We know it fell into their hands," Quinn said thoughtfully. "But I thought they transferred it to Moscow when the government moved there."

"They did," Diatsaro went on, "but by early August 1918 it wasn't felt to be safe there either. The Bolsheviks didn't know if they'd be able to hold Moscow. The Revolution was on the verge of collapse and their leaders were preparing to go underground, so saving the gold was their prime concern. It would have enabled them to finance a second revolution."

Quinn had a vision of Fitzmaurice in his palatial train at Omsk. Fitzmaurice couldn't have failed to know all this, even

89

with so few active agents at his disposal, and it had been early in September when he'd landed Cutter and Davis behind enemy lines near Kazan.

"It all sounds quite feasible," he said.

Diatsaro, who had finished shaving, tested a patch of skin on his jaw and lathered it again. "They loaded the gold into a special train," he went on. "What they were looking for was a safe place, a natural fortress, a redoubt. Bringing it to Karmel was Vitov Yurovsky's idea, so they say."

"The train in the station? Fourteen brand-new freight cars, one of them with a radio antenna, and so heavy they needed two locomotives to haul them."

Diatsaro shook his head. "Just speculation," he said.

"Someone must have seen them at it," Quinn said. "I was told the Czechs found a locked freight car full of bodies when they got here."

"These things happen in a civil war."

"Except that I've checked the names on the gravestones and asked around. Most of the victims had some connection with the railroad: the stationmaster, a switchman—even the owner of the station barbershop. It looks as if they eliminated every potential witness of the transfer."

Diatsaro laid the razor aside. He shook some eau de cologne into his palm and patted it onto his cheeks, then dabbed them with the towel. He didn't look younger clean-shaven, oddly enough. The smooth skin only accentuated his haggard appearance.

"Rumors, that's all," he said.

"The Czechs did just what the Reds had done before them: they rounded up all the locals who could possibly have known anything and interrogated them at the Cheka's former headquarters. Same cells—same methods too, probably. It seems inconceivable that anyone would do such a thing on account of a mere rumor."

The prince put his jacket on again. He seemed to find it

90

something of an effort without his manservant there to help him. At length he said, "What can I do for you?"

"Put me in touch with Govorov."

"The gold—you really think it's here? Is that why you came? You and the other Englishman you mentioned?"

"He probably came for the same reason. I don't know for sure, but it would explain a couple of things. His death for instance. For now, all I want is a word with Govorov."

"Pavel Pavlovich has gone into hiding. From time to time he turns up unannounced with half a dozen game birds or a haunch of venison for me, but I have no way of contacting him." He mused over the idea for a moment. "I often wonder how all these aristocratic relatives of mine would react if they knew the meat on their plates had been provided by a god-damned Bolshevik."

Approaching footsteps could be heard in the passage. The door opened and a young woman entered without knocking. She had Diatsaro's dark hair and vivid gray-blue eyes. "You're missing dinner," she told him, ignoring Quinn. Then peering at him closely, she raised her eyebrows in amazement. "You *shaved?* What's the occasion?"

"This is my daughter Aina," Diatsaro said, but the girl had already left, not troubling to close the door behind her.

Quinn recalled what Lieutenant Scala had said, but the prince got there first.

"There's a rumor she shares General Wajda's bed. I suspect it's true. Our young hero is the uncrowned king of Karmel, after all, and the Diatsaro womenfolk have always had an eye to the main chance." Diatsaro's eyes twinkled for a moment, then grew serious again.

"Try to fix up a meeting with Govorov," Quinn persisted. They left the gun room and walked back along the passage. The entrance hall was deserted, but a hum of conversation was coming from beyond some double doors on the left.

"Our evening meals are depressing affairs," Diatsaro said.

"Bad for the digestion and worse for the morale; otherwise I'd ask you to stay."

"Do let me know if you hear anything though."

"Of course—though I still fail to see why you want to waste your time," Diatsaro replied. He held out his hand. "If I see Govorov I'll mention you to him."

Quinn made his way back through the grounds. It was dark now, and the fir trees jutted into the sky like tapering black fingers. The palatial house at the end of the drive was ablaze with lights.

He made a mental inventory of the items of information he'd gleaned since his arrival. They resembled the pieces of a jigsaw puzzle, and fitting them together produced a kind of pattern: Fitzmaurice at Omsk, aware that the bullion had been transferred; his instructions to Cutter to find out where it was; Cutter at Kazan, then Perm, and finally Karmel; the probable route taken by the gold; the Czechs' swift advance . . . Only one part of the pattern remained blank: Why hadn't Fitzmaurice told him the truth?

Passing the sentries on the main gate, he headed back to town. The road was unlit and he met no one on the way.

11

HE'D been waiting in the chill of the night for an hour or more, pacing up and down to keep warm. The railroad station was visible in outline against the dim glow of the sentries' log fire. It had snowed during the day. Although the snow in the valley had thawed, the air was dank and the dense ground mist made breathing an effort.

Not the kind of weather for an asthmatic like Fitzmaurice, thought Quinn. He struck a match and squinted at his watch. Govorov had arranged to meet him at one o'clock, here, where the old track led to the derelict gold mine, and it was now nearly two in the morning. He was just wondering if it was worth waiting any longer when he heard the soft scrunch of footsteps on the branch line's gravel roadbed.

A figure loomed up out of the mist—a stoop-shouldered man in dark clothing. Quinn glimpsed an unkempt mustache and a pair of alert, wary eyes.

"Govorov?" he asked.

"Come with me!"

"Govorov was supposed to meet me here at one o'clock— Govorov, no one else."

The man turned on his heel without a word and started back the way he'd come. A few strides, and he was just a vague shadow in the murk.

Diatsaro's message had reached Quinn that afternoon, but his hopes that a meeting with Govorov would prove informative had waned. He'd been waiting for over a week, and it now seemed less and less likely that anything of value would emerge. His feeling that Karmel was a place where everyone was hiding some dark secret had dwindled day by day until he almost shared Diatsaro's belief that the whole story was a rumor.

They'd left the railroad track and were somewhere near the river on the outskirts of the miners' village. The mist was even thicker here. Quinn continued to follow his guide until the dim figure came to a halt. It was only then that he made out the tumbledown shack ahead of them.

The man knocked four times on the clapboard wall, employing a special rhythm, then turned at once and vanished into the gloom. Nothing happened for a moment. Quinn stood there, tense and silent, until the door creaked open and someone inside cleared his throat. A hoarse voice said, "All right, come in."

The shack was in darkness. Quinn felt tamped mud beneath his feet, smelled tobacco smoke as the man came toward him.

93

A pair of hands ran deftly over his body, apparently looking for a weapon.

"Are you Govorov?"

"Let's assume so."

The man stepped back and lit an oil lamp on a table bearing the remains of a meal. Quinn got his first sight of the man's features when he used the dying match to light a cigarette. The deepset eyes were two dark cavities in a gaunt face. Although their color was indiscernible, the resemblance to Sergei Diatsaro was so striking that Quinn gave an involuntary exclamation.

"Don't let it bother you," Govorov said with a hoarse laugh. "Others have noticed the likeness too: Sergei is my ghost."

He spoke with the self-assurance of someone in command of the situation, not like a man on the run. "Did Sergei tell you why I wanted to see you?" he asked.

"He did." Govorov stowed the remains of his meal in a canvas satchel and swept the crumbs off the table. Together with a straight-back chair, it was the only piece of furniture in the shack. "We can leave right away."

"Where to?"

Govorov slung the satchel over his shoulder. "You'll see when we get there." He bent down and blew out the lamp.

There was a second door at the back. Govorov opened it and stepped outside. He whistled three notes. Somewhere in the darkness, someone echoed them in reverse order.

They'd been climbing steadily for over an hour, most of the time through pine forest. There was no mist here, and Quinn could see the sky between the treetops, but the few stars visible were an insufficient guide to the direction they were taking.

Govorov maintained the same brisk pace even when the

terrain became more rugged and precipitous still, never hesitating for an instant when they changed direction. Having twice crossed the branch line to the Xenia Mine, they encountered it a third time at the foot of a steep escarpment. Govorov waited in the shadows for Quinn to catch him up.

"Need a breather?"

"Only if you do." Quinn was sweating hard, but he felt rather proud of himself for having kept up. Govorov was a true outdoorsman.

"Wait here."

The Russian stole off without a sound in his light, rubber-soled boots. Quinn waited. The clouds seemed low enough to touch at this altitude, but there was just enough light for him to detect that the track had recently been cleared of brushwood and undergrowth at the point where it rounded the foot of the escarpment. From above came a muffled, continuous roar.

Govorov reappeared so silently that he might have sprung from the ground. He'd divested himself of the satchel and was carrying a miner's safety lamp. "Let's go," he said.

"Are we near the Xenia?" Quinn asked.

Govorov's sole response was to set off up the escarpment. It was steep, stony, and overgrown with brambles in many places. The roaring sound grew louder the higher they climbed, but it wasn't until they reached the plateau at the top that Quinn discovered its source: clearly defined against the dark trees at the far end of the plateau, pale threads of water were cascading down the mountainside.

The derelict mine was a scene of devastation. The whole plateau was strewn with rubble and debris, charred timbers from the conduit that had supplied the turbines with water, rusty components from the hammer mill that had pulverized the ore. Overgrown with weeds and brambles, the place made a doubly desolate impression in the nocturnal gloom.

Govorov had paused to light a cigarette. He offered the pack to Quinn, who shook his head.

"You did well." Govorov pulled at his cigarette, and Quinn was struck once more by his startling resemblance to Diatsaro.

"Right," Govorov said. "Let's get this over."

As Govorov led the way across the rubble-strewn plateau, Quinn reviewed what he knew of its structure. The mine had originally been opencut, but the gold content of the surface ore soon diminished and tunnels had been driven into the mountain, together with a system of lateral galleries and vertical shafts. The main tunnel had long since been walled up. Govorov made his way past it to one of the side entrances.

"Stay close behind me," he said, lighting the safety lamp. This entrance, too, had been walled up, but the lamplight revealed a narrow aperture in the masonry, apparently of recent date.

The air inside the gallery was absolutely still but even colder. The first stretch was wide enough for them to walk abreast. Govorov moved with the same unerring self-assurance as before, never pausing or faltering. Sometimes, when turning off into a side passage, he would raise the lamp aloft. Pitprops and walls of rock swam into view, but there were no directional aids that Quinn could see. They turned left down one crumbling gallery, then right along another so low that they had to negotiate it in a crouch. Water trickling down the walls had formed a rivulet in the middle of the passage.

Govorov came to a halt and waited for Quinn to catch up to him. The gallery had widened out into a semicircular chamber with no other exits or entrances.

The Russian's mood had changed, Quinn could tell. His face was pale and tense, almost as if he were less at ease in this subterranean world than Quinn himself.

The floor of the chamber was strewn with sharp, fist-size chunks of rock. The white beam of the carbide lamp groped its way over the walls, wavered uncertainly, and came to rest on a hagged hole with blackened edges. It had been blasted out of the living rock by an expert who knew precisely how much dynamite would make a hole just big enough for a man to squeeze through. Govorov pointed to it. "Go on," he said, "see for yourself."

There was a mound of rubble beneath the hole. Quinn made his way over to the foot of the mound, then scrambled over the loose rock and squeezed through the aperture. It was pitch-black inside and the air had a different smell. He might have been standing in a pharaoh's tomb. When Govorov followed him in, the lamp revealed a spacious, vaulted chamber hewn out of dry limestone. The walls were lined with stout shelves, and arrayed on these were serried rows of wooden boxes. Quinn recognized them instantly: they were the rectangular blue chests in which the Imperial Bank of Russia had customarily transported its bullion.

He heard Govorov laugh. The echo bounced from wall to wall as it died away.

"Well, what are you waiting for? Take a look, see for yourself." Govorov's voice was little more than a whisper now. "Here's your gold. . . ."

Gold . . . gold . . . gold . . .

The last word circled the chamber, sounding less like human speech than the low growl of some wild beast.

Govorov shone his lamp on one of the chests. The emblem of the Imperial Mint had been branded into the wood, Quinn noted. Each chest was designed to hold forty one-kilogram bars, and there must have been hundreds of them. He felt a pounding in his chest—less a result of the gold itself than of the knowledge that, having seen it, Govorov would never let him out of here alive.

So that was what had happened to Cutter. . . .

He moved away from the wall and the chests. Govorov was

visible only as a shadowy figure beyond the glare of the safety lamp. Quinn stared at the light until his eyes hurt.

Govorov went to the nearest shelf, took hold of a metal carrying-handle, and tugged. The chest slid off the shelf and fell to the ground with a crash. The lid, which was loose, flew off. Govorov shone the lamp: the chest was empty. While Quinn was still staring at it, Govorov proceeded to haul other chests off the shelves at random and send them crashing to the ground with ever-increasing speed and abandon. At last he stopped and came over. His tone was less hostile than contemptuous.

"You're too late, *Anglichanin.*"

Quinn surveyed the empty chests littering the floor of the chamber. "I might have guessed. You'd never have brought me here if the gold were still *in situ.*"

He followed Govorov out through the hole in the wall. At the last moment he turned and looked back, but not to assess the value of the gold that had been stored in this subterranean vault. He was wondering if Cutter had been here too—if Cutter had seen what he himself had seen. Or more . . .

The wind had dropped, but the overcast had broken up and it was much colder. They were back on the open plateau. A string of rusty dump cars, some of them overturned, marked the end of the branch line. Quinn could trace its downward route, not by the rails themselves but by the swaths of trees that had been felled to accommodate the track. Karmel lay somewhere at the foot of those dark, wooded slopes, but all he could see was a faint glow of reflected light.

They hadn't exchanged a word on the way out of the mine. Now Govorov looked up at the sky. "It'll be daybreak soon. Can you find your own way back?"

Quinn nodded, doing some mental arithmetic. If all those chests had held bullion, their contents would have weighed a hundred tons or more. London banking circles had naturally formed estimates of Czarist Russia's gold reserves, though their accuracy was in doubt because the Russians had never numbered their bars consecutively, preferring to use a confidential system of their own. If a hundred tons corresponded to three years' output, however, as the estimates known to Quinn suggested, the bullion in question must have represented the entire gold reserves of the Imperial Bank.

"So now you know," Govorov said. "The gold was here. It came in by special train. The one in the station. They unloaded the stuff and transferred it to the mine using a special squad of hand-picked men. A dozen of them, no more. All the witnesses were eliminated all right, but I had nothing to do with that. I didn't even know that gold was involved, not at first. Officially, the chests contained Party records and membership lists."

"And where is it now?" Quinn asked, wondering how much the Russian would be willing to divulge—and why.

"Somewhere safe," Govorov said flatly. "Nothing else matters."

"But it can't have left by rail," Quinn pursued. "The train's still there, and besides, the line to Perm has been cut—somebody demolished the bridge. Moving a hundred tons of gold isn't that easy."

"There are ways," Govorov told him. "Mules, for instance."

Mules, Quinn reflected. Yes, that was feasible, if the bars had been transferred to packsaddles.

"Tell me," Quinn said, gesturing at the mine. "Did Cutter even see where the gold was stored?"

Govorov pulled at his cigarette. His taut, tense expression betrayed that he was nowhere near as calm as he pretended. "Who the hell's Cutter?"

"An Englishman—an agent. He was on the track of the gold."

"And he's dead, no doubt?" Govorov tossed away the remains of his cigarette. "Dead like all who've taken too close an interest in it."

Quinn felt a sudden upsurge of anger. "Your friends killed him, damn it!"

"I wouldn't be sure of that." Govorov removed the crumpled pack from his pocket and extracted another cigarette. "Ask *your* friends in Karmel," he said. "Ask that Czech general. Ask him what would have happened to the stuff if he'd managed to get his hands on it."

"What does that have to do with Cutter?"

"Gold seems to have a special smell," Govorov said. "It attracts human sharks. They hunt their prey in packs, but once they find it they all compete for the biggest bite and they don't care if they eat one another up in their frenzy. They needed each other at first, the Czech and the *Anglichanin*. But maybe they fell out—maybe the *Anglichanin* got in General Wajda's way . . ."

Quinn stared at him. "You think Cutter was killed by his own side?"

"I don't have any more proof than you do. I don't say you've got to trust me. All I'm saying is, how far can you afford to trust your friends? Think it over."

Neither of them spoke for a while. They both looked up as a bird took wing nearby. A shadow whirred overhead and disappeared into the darkness. Quinn indicated their surroundings. "Is this where you're hiding out?"

"I'm a woodsman. I'm at home anywhere in the mountains."

"Sergei Diatsaro told me you used to hunt here together as boys."

"Times change." The words were almost inaudible.

"I tried to talk him into leaving the country."

"Don't bother. I managed to save his skin the last time, but I'm not convinced I did him much of a favor."

100

"Why did you do it at all?"

"I owed him."

"I'd have thought Prince Sergei Diatsaro symbolized everything you despise."

"Perhaps he does," Govorov said. "And yet, unlike so many in these parts, he is an honorable man. Good night."

With this, Govorov turned on his heel and strode off. Quinn stared after the Russian until he was swallowed up by the gloom, then set off down the mountainside himself.

12

LIEUTENANT Scala drove through the gates and up the avenue to the Diatsaro mansion. Tires bit into gravel as he braked hard and pulled up outside the main entrance, a frieze-adorned portico reposing on four massive columns painted blue and gold. Standing motionless between the columns were sentries in long, picturesque Cossack coats bristling with cartridge cases. Cossacks they weren't, however. Their European cast of feature made it seem more likely that they were Czechs.

Quinn said, "Your General Wajda likes to keep up appearances."

Scala turned his head and glanced at Quinn with the nervous speculative expression that had monopolized his face ever since Wajda's summons reached him. He got out and hurried up the steps. "He hates to be kept waiting," he said, opening the door.

The entrance hall had been stripped of its statues and furniture. Rifles stood in racks and field telephone cables straggled across the checkerboard marble floor. A blue, white, and red flag hung from the gallery at the top of the stairs. Soldiers were bustling to and fro.

Scala headed for a door flanked by two more sentries, but it opened before he could get there. A man in a snug-fitting gray uniform emerged. He had black hair as sleek as his uniform and parted in the middle, and his pallid face was dominated by a pair of fanatical eyes.

Quinn wondered briefly if this could be Wajda, but the man stepped aside to let them pass and followed them in. Stained glass windows in the background reduced the morning sunlight to a subdued glow. Maps lined the walls and another Czech flag hung in one corner. The man seated behind the desk at the far end of the room looked startlingly young—far too young for his general's blue uniform and the order suspended from his neck. His face, Quinn thought, was that of a pampered prince who'd inherited the throne before his time.

A carafe of water and several glasses stood on the desk in front of him. "Sit down," he said.

Scala hovered behind the chairs facing the desk. "Will you be needing me, General?" he inquired. "I have an appointment with the guys from the repair shop."

Rudolf Wajda ignored him and focused his gaze on Quinn. His lustrous brown eyes and long lashes would have graced a beautiful girl.

"Sit down," he told Quinn. "Or do you also have a prior engagement of greater importance?"

Quinn complied. Scala reluctantly followed suit, still holding the car keys. For a moment or two, all that broke the silence was the faint clink of metal on metal as he fidgeted with them.

Wajda's hand, a slim hand with slender fingers, reached for the carafe. He picked it up, poured himself a glass of water, and drank it down. Then he said, "I expect you're wondering why I sent for you, Mr. Quinn. To be brief, I feel it would be better for us all if you returned to Omsk."

The man who had opened the door was standing in front of one of the stained glass windows with his arms folded. There

102

was something about his stiff, silent figure that made it hard for Quinn to concentrate on Wajda.

"I intend to," he said. "At the right time."

"At once would suit me better. Scala will attend to your travel arrangements."

"And what shall I tell my superiors when they ask why you object to my presence here?"

"I've got a war to fight with an army which is short of everything. Empty promises are all I ever get from Omsk. I owe them no explanations."

"So you think I'm a spy," Quinn replied. "Well, I assure you I'm not."

Wadja leaned forward and stared at him. "You don't expect me to believe your story? An expert on mineral resources! With all the questions you've been asking? Tell me, Quinn, if you're not a spy, why didn't you come straight to me?"

"You were busy, apparently."

Wadja sighed. "I'm a very patient man, Quinn, but Viktor Ryazanov here"—he gestured at the figure in the background—"has a much shorter fuse. So I'm only going to ask you once, and I expect a thorough reply. Have your inquiries borne fruit?"

"All I've discovered is that you got here too late to lay hands on the gold," Quinn said, surprised to note the three men's reactions and the glances they exchanged. All of them, even Scala, looked relieved. Why? Somehow, he had expected Wajda to contradict Govorov's version of the gold's removal.

"Then I assume," Wadja replied slowly, "that Fitzmaurice doubted my account to him?"

"Fitzmaurice doubts everything on principle. It's in his nature." Quinn was groping in the dark, trying to gain time.

"And you, do you have your doubts too? Cutter was a friend of yours, I gather. He put on a splendid act, your friend. Oh no, he wasn't interested in the gold itself, only in finding

103

it!" Wajda's voice had taken on a shrill, hysterical note. "Except that he changed his mind as soon as he picked up its trail. It wasn't just a rumor anymore, it was there for the taking: a whole trainload of bullion. The temptation proved too much for him. . . ."

Quinn's bewilderment was too complete to leave room for any other emotion, so he said nothing.

"He wanted to make a deal with me," Wajda went on. "What do we care about Fitzmaurice, the White generals, England, the war? Forget them, we'll split the gold between us! That was his proposition." Wajda's agitation had subsided. He chuckled to himself. "He wasn't so wide of the mark, your friend Cutter."

The man at the window unfolded his arms and came over to the desk. His movements were supple, almost feline. "We're wasting time on him," he said.

"You may be right, Viktor, but perhaps Mr. Quinn has enough common sense not to meddle in our business." Wajda turned back to Quinn. "Your friend Cutter changed his mind when he saw he couldn't do business with me. He hit on the dangerous idea of coming to terms with the Bolsheviks. He warned them of our advance and helped them to remove the gold from Karmel at the last minute—in return for a share of it."

"And then they killed him?" asked Quinn.

"They saved us the trouble, yes. Once the gold was in a safe place his only share of it was a bullet—or so one assumes."

Quinn shook his head. "Your story doesn't add up. Tom Cutter was capable of a lot of things, but not that." It was a strange sensation, defending Cutter's integrity.

Ryazanov walked around the desk, and again Quinn was reminded of a lithe beast of prey. He sat there without moving a muscle. It was a great effort to do more than just hold the man's gaze.

A long silence ensued. Wajda studied his fingernails as if

they needed attention and polished them on the sleeves of his uniform jacket, first one hand and then the other. Scala cleared his throat. He leaned forward, reached for the carafe, and poured himself a glass of water.

Wajda seemed satisfied with his nails at last. He looked up. "I don't really know why I'm being so tolerant. One last try: stay away from that gold."

Quinn was feeling tired more than anything else. Lack of sleep had taken its toll. "Go to hell," he said.

"You can tell Fitzmaurice to do the same when you get back to Omsk. He can forget about the gold. Unless, of course, you can tell me why you British lay claim to it—or the Whites for that matter? What entitled them to regard it as theirs? Plenty of Czechs have fought and died for that gold. You think Fitzmaurice loses any sleep over them? We've been trading our lives for empty promises ever since the war started. Well, we've made enough sacrifices for everybody else. If we fight again it'll be for our own country."

"I'm beginning to understand," Quinn said. "A country needs gold reserves. And naturally you have no personal interest in the bullion."

Wajda's breathing could be heard in the silence that followed. It was fast and irregular. "Yes," he said, "I want it. And I'll get it. All of it."

"But you don't know where it is," Quinn said.

"Don't fret, we'll find it. Without your help. I told Fitzmaurice it wasn't necessary to replace Cutter and he agreed. That's why I'm surprised he sent you here. Was it really his idea?"

"It was his idea. And I'll most certainly be leaving. As soon as I know what really happened to Cutter."

Wajda glared at him in disbelief, but it was Ryazanov who really alarmed him. The man's pale face darkened and a menacing glint appeared in his eyes. Quinn knew that look from his prospecting days: it was the look of a man who would kill for nothing.

"Cutter's dead," Ryazanov said. "Careful you don't wind up the same way."

Quinn got up. He looked Wajda full in the face. "Can't you speak for yourself? What is he, your watchdog?"

"Viktor's a very persuasive man, I've found. An irresistible negotiating technique. But I hope he won't be needed, Mr. Quinn." Wajda sat motionless in his chair. His eyes narrowed, and the crow's-feet that appeared at their corners made his boyish face look older. "It's an odd thing about that gold. It brings bad luck to everyone who comes into contact with it. First Cutter and now poor Mr. Davis . . ."

No one spoke for quite a while. Glancing at Scala, Quinn saw that he had turned pale and looked as if he might be sick at any moment. He reached for the carafe again.

"Cutter's friend was overly fond of the bottle, as I expect you noticed," Wajda pursued. "He went for a stroll last night. He'd been drinking, and the result was a regrettable accident. Near the station. One of our sentries challenged him in the regulation manner. Receiving no reply, he opened fire. It's still too early to say if the man exceeded his orders, but we've placed him under arrest pending inquiries. Once the other members of his picket have been questioned we'll forward a full report to Fitzmaurice."

"An accident?" Quinn said.

"Davis seems to have been unaware of the risk he was taking by walking so close to a restricted area. But then, things of this sort happen frequently during wartime."

Again no one spoke. Scala finally summoned up the energy to pour himself a glass of water and put it to his lips. Quinn, hearing him gulp it down fast, yearned for a glass of water too. His head was aching. Someone was breathing heavily, audibly: himself.

Wajda had risen to his feet. Like Fitzmaurice he was a

106

surprisingly short man, but like Fitzmaurice he seemed to have no complexes about his size.

"So," he said, "I see you have made up your mind. You'll be leaving . . . when?"

"Give me twenty-four hours." Quinn was surprised to note how natural his voice sounded.

Wajda nodded. "I sympathize, Quinn. It's only natural for a man to want to finish what he's started, but sometimes it's wiser to cut your losses."

"Where is Davis?"

"In the morgue at our field hospital. Scala will drive you there if you wish." Wajda put out his hand.

Looking at the slender, well-manicured hand, Quinn felt a strong disinclination to touch it. But he'd always been a man who considered the odds carefully and never hesitated to back down when they were too high. He grasped the proffered hand.

Wajda's face relaxed. He was transformed once more into the pampered youth who knew that no one could ever refuse him: General Wajda, the uncrowned king of Karmel. Perhaps he already saw himself back in his native land, thought Quinn: King Rudolf I, returning home in triumph with the Russian gold reserves . . .

Ryazanov was standing there with a face like marble. Wajda turned to him. "Go and get it," he said.

Ryazanov left the room. He returned a moment or two later carrying a double-barreled shotgun of Belgian manufacture: a Lebeau-Courally, a magnificent collector's piece inlaid with silver.

"Accept it as a memento of your stay here," Wajda said. "You're an enthusiastic hunter, I hear." He produced two boxes of shells from a desk drawer and held them out. "A pity Fitzmaurice didn't send you here in the first place," he added. "We might have hit it off together."

Quinn took the gun and the boxes of shells. "Thanks," he said. The word was little more than a hoarse grunt. He turned calmly and walked to the door. Scala hurried on ahead and opened it for him.

13

H E knocked loudly at the door of Davis's house, but there was no response, no sound of approaching footsteps. He depressed the latch—the door wasn't locked—and went in. The room was in chaos. Whoever had searched it hadn't bothered to hide his tracks.

"Sonya Kuklin?" he called.

Still no response. A chill pervaded the room. He picked his way across the ransacked room and climbed the stairs.

She was sitting in the big armchair facing the bed in which Davis had received him. The bed was empty, no Frank Davis propped up against the pillows, but nothing in Sonya Kuklin's pose conveyed that she was aware of his absence. She continued to sit there, staring at the bed.

"Sonya?"

She hadn't turned to look when he entered the room. Nor did she do so now. She was wearing a woolen robe over her nightgown, perhaps because she'd put it on when the men came to search the house and hadn't bothered to get dressed when they left.

"Remember me?" he said. "I'm Quinn, the Englishman."

He was still holding the bundle of Davis's clothes they'd handed him at the field hospital. He'd been so disconcerted by the sight of the dead man—the bare feet protruding from under the sheet, the emaciated body, the hollow cheeks and bony chin with their sprinkling of stubble—that at first he hadn't bothered to unroll them. Later he'd forced himself to go through the contents. Davis's clothes were caked with

108

blood. All he'd kept was a cigarette case that had fallen out of one of the pockets, an enameled case bearing the Rolls-Royce monogram. He'd noticed it on the bedside table during his earlier visit to the house.

He deposited the bundle on the end of the bed. Sonya Kuklin came to life at last. "Take it off!" she snapped.

He removed it and put it on the floor instead. A glance at the room told him that someone had searched it too. Everything was in disarray apart from the bed, which suggested that the woman had remade it afterward. The radio transmitter had gone from the table in the corner. He went over to the display cabinet, took out a glass, and returned to the bed. He sat down and held out the empty tumbler. She just stared at him, her eyes red-rimmed, her cheeks ashen.

"I need a drink," he said.

She'd hidden the bottle behind her when he came in. He took it from her, poured a drink, and handed it back.

"When did they tell you?" he asked.

The robe had fallen open, revealing her breasts. She did up a button or two and brushed the hair out of her eyes with a smile that almost turned Quinn's stomach. Its intention was seductive, its effect merely pathetic. He raised the glass to his lips and emptied it in one swallow.

"I've been wondering why Davis went out last night," he said at length. "Did he make a habit of it?" Even as he spoke he reflected how little he knew about the man.

Sonya Kuklin was staring at the bed and the plumped-up pillows with the bottle in her hand. Quinn saw her mouth pucker as she tilted the bottle and took a swig. Then she lowered it and tried to say something, but all that escaped her lips was a muffled groan.

"Did you hear him go out?"

She nodded. "The house isn't that big," she replied with an effort. "I begged him not to go!"

"And of course he had been drinking."

"If you mean was he drunk, no!"

"Still, even a drunk would know better than to hang around the station at two in the morning."

"At the station? But—I thought he was meeting you! Oh, I wish he'd never set eyes on you. I told him that message was a trap!"

"What message?"

"I'd never seen the man before, but I didn't trust him."

"A Russian?"

She shook her head. "He might have been Czech, from his accent. But I don't really know."

"Can you describe him?" Quinn had a sudden idea. "Fair-haired, around thirty, built like a boxer? A Sergeant Budyek?"

"My God, I begged Frank not to go but he wouldn't listen. He said it was important—he had to see you. And to leave home with nothing but a notebook—"

"What notebook?"

She glanced at the corner where the transmitter had been. "I never looked at it—I can't read English—but he used it to keep a record of the messages he sent."

"He copied them out?"

"Yes, as soon as he was alone—as soon as the other Englishman had gone."

Quinn was sure it hadn't been among Davis's personal effects.

Untidy strands of hair straggled over her eyes, and she brushed them aside with an impatient gesture. "*Gavno! Gavno! Gavno!*" she said angrily. "He's gone and left me all alone, the bastard!"

If Quinn had expected tears to follow this emotional outburst, he was mistaken. She eyed him coolly now. He wondered why Davis hadn't listened to her. He felt sure the man's death was no accident, but why kill him? For the sake of the notebook in which he'd recorded his radio messages, apparently without Cutter's knowledge? To throw a scare into him,

110

Quinn, and ensure that he really left Karmel? He'd seen men fight to the death over some trivial argument in the goldfields, but this coldblooded murder was different. He held out his empty glass.

"May I have another?"

"That's all the bastard left me, one lousy bottle!" Although she spat out the words as furiously as before, she surrendered the vodka without protest.

She struggled to her feet while he was refilling his glass. Much drunker than he'd thought, she swayed and almost fell before regaining her balance. She drew the robe around her and knotted the belt more tightly. Then, with her arms outstretched like a sleepwalker's, she tottered across the room and blundered down the stairs.

He sat there sipping his vodka and listening to the noises from below. It sounded as if she was looking for something. When she returned she was holding a small bundle of envelopes tied up with ribbon. She laughed and tossed her head. "Letters from my husband," she said, "when he was a conductor on the Trans-Siberian. He used to pass the time by writing to me whenever there was a delay on the line."

She sat down in the armchair with the letters on her lap. She seemed to have forgotten them already.

"I was fond of him, you know," she said. "Frank, I mean. I'd never spent so much time with any man—during the day, that is. I felt at home with him. He got depressed sometimes, but still, we had some laughs together." She eyed the clothes at the foot of the bed. "Did you see his body?"

Quinn nodded. He felt increasingly uncomfortable in her presence. "What about the letters?" he asked, feeling somehow guilty for pressing her on the subject.

She started to undo the faded red ribbon that held them together. The envelopes were old and dog-eared. She leafed through them until she found what she was looking for: a blank, unstamped envelope. She handed it to Quinn without a word.

He took it. It was so thin he thought at first it must be empty.

"Frank asked me to hide it for him." Her tone was calm, almost businesslike. "I suppose they didn't think there could be anything of interest in a bunch of old love letters."

Quinn weighed the envelope in his hand. It was sealed, and he was reluctant to tear it open for fear of destroying something, so he simply sat there holding it.

"Did Davis say what it was?"

"No, only that I was to give it to you if . . . Oh, leave me alone, damn you!"

"The men who searched the house—when did they come?"

"Sometime early this morning."

Quinn said, "Is there anything I can do for you? Do you need money?"

She looked at him as if he'd thrown a glass of water in her face.

"What do you think I am, some kind of whore? Get out!" she screamed. He pocketed the envelope and stood up. "Get out!" she screamed again. "Go away and don't come back, not ever!"

The last word turned into a sob. She struggled to her feet and threw herself on the bed. The letters slid off her lap and fell to the floor. Quinn stood there irresolutely for a moment. The room had grown dimmer, as if someone had drawn the curtains. Glancing at the windows, he saw that it had begun to snow.

He walked to the door and turned to look. She was still lying on the bed with her face buried in the pillows. He heard her burst into tears as he closed the door behind him, but he couldn't bring himself to go back in. He knew there was no way to console her about anything; she was too proud to allow him that luxury.

He made his way downstairs and left the house. Big fat snowflakes were drifting down out of a heavily overcast sky, and before long everything was mantled in white.

He was reminded of what Frank Davis had said about the snow, and how much he'd hoped to get clear of Karmel before the first real snowfall of the winter.

14

T H E sleigh emerged from the woods and turned out onto the track. Quinn ran to meet it through the snow, which was already knee-deep, and barred its path with his arms spread wide. Moura Toumanova reined in and pulled up beside him. Her hair was almost completely hidden under a big fur hat, her face wind-whipped and rosy-cheeked with the cold. He looked up at her, and although the sight of her didn't dispel his sense of foreboding he somehow felt as if he were waking from a fitful sleep.

She didn't speak. Her expression, betraying neither surprise nor annoyance, was just as he remembered it. Her features were almost too regular to be true, like those of a beautiful statue. He would never see *her* hair straggle over her forehead, *her* mouth wrinkle at the corners, *her* eyes fill with tears. Even now, as she laughed at him, her laughter bore no resemblance to the agonized sound that had issued from Sonya Kuklin's throat.

"How long have you been waiting out here for me?" she asked.

The question reminded him how cold he was. He shivered in his sheepskin coat. "I came because they killed Cutter's friend," he said. "I need to talk with someone about it." He made his way around the sleigh. The horse's coat was lathered with sweat. From the way the beast was panting, it had been toiling uphill for quite some distance.

113

Her face remained impassive. She shifted sideways on the seat and said, "Get in," as if it were the most natural thing in the world for her to be the only one he could trust. He wondered whether there was any sincerity in her response, or, whether it was simply the skilled manner of a woman whose profession consisted of anticipating the desires of men. Though he found her sexually exciting, Quinn sensed that Moura could only be handled warily, if at all.

He brushed himself down and stamped his feet to rid them of clods of accumulated snow before climbing in beside her. She shook the reins and drove on, and for a while the world consisted of nothing but falling snow, the creak and jingle of harness, and the hiss of metal runners.

He'd waited for her for several hours. The light was fading by the time they reached the tumbledown shacks on the out-skirts of the miners' village. When the sleigh turned into the square and headed for the coach house Quinn saw the sturdy, thickset figure of Timur the Mongol emerge from the shelter of the hotel veranda and run toward them.

The girl got out and handed Timur the reins, then pro-ceeded to the house. Once beneath the overhanging roof of the veranda she stood and waited for Quinn to catch up. The barroom was deserted and unheated. She opened an inner door and pointed along a passage. "I'll get us something hot to drink. Get out of those wet things," she said firmly. "I'll only be a couple of minutes."

He was grateful that she asked no questions and received him like a friend. The paint was peeling off the door at the end of the passage. The room beyond it was unlit, but the last of the daylight filtering through the window showed that it con-tained little but a low table, some stools upholstered in leather, and a few cheap, colorful rugs. The end of the room was partitioned off by a curtain, and standing in one corner was a cylindrical cast-iron stove. The Mongol must have stoked it, because the metal sides were glowing in the semi-darkness.

The girl came in with a samovar and some tea things on a brass tray. She'd removed her coat and fur hat. Beneath it she wore the same long black skirt and floral blouse in which Quinn had first seen her. Where melted snow had moistened her hair it had gone curly and looked even more luxuriant than usual.

She kneeled and put a match to the kerosene lamp on the low table, then sat down beside it cross-legged.

Impassive as ever, she filled two glasses, stirred in some sugar and brandy, and handed one to Quinn. The lamplight lent her skin a radiant quality, and he thought again how inconceivable it seemed that she would ever look into a mirror someday and detect the first signs of age. He couldn't have said why the thought disturbed him.

"I have a few questions," he said, "and you're the only one I can ask. Listen to me for a moment—"

"There's no need to explain."

"Did you ever meet Frank Davis—the man who came with Cutter? You must have heard of him."

She rose and went over to the curtain, and drew it aside. The alcove behind it contained a big couch covered with a kilim. Gaudy cushions lined the walls.

"This is better than any explanation."

She said it quietly and unemotionally, almost soberly. He had never heard a woman speak so directly, and although her meaning was unmistakable, there was nothing crudely seductive about the invitation.

That, perhaps, was just what he found so titillating. He went over and gazed into her face with its dark eyes, high cheekbones, and flaming red hair, overwhelmed by the intensity of his desire for her. He fought against showing it.

"Don't you . . . agree a price first?" he asked, hoping that his voice gave no hint of his true feelings.

115

She laughed deep in her throat. "Not when I'm the one that wants it," she said. "And believe me, *Anglichanin,* I do."

They were so close that their bodies and faces were almost touching. His heart was pounding wildly . . . the present, this moment . . . The only shadow across this feeling was the man who had died. . . . He wanted her, but not here, not this way. Not on Cutter's terms. He took hold of the curtain and wrenched it shut.

She stiffened as if he had mortally insulted her. He had a momentary fear that she would start cursing and swearing like the first time. But finally she went back to the table and reinstalled herself beside it, crossing her legs. "More tea?"

He nodded and took his coat off. She refilled their glasses with tea, sugar, and brandy. He sat down on a stool opposite and watched her, sipping his tea in silence.

"I hear you're leaving Karmel."

"Then you will also have heard what happened at the station last night?"

"You're right to leave here," she said.

"How about you? Have you thought it over? If I do go, will you come with me?"

"I didn't take your offer seriously."

"But I meant it. What is there to keep you here?"

She looked back at him. "What's so much better about anywhere else?"

Why couldn't he banish the shadow? Why didn't he just tell her what he'd felt earlier? Was it *her* reaction he feared? Or did he mistrust his own feelings? He groped in his pocket for a cigarette. It was only when his fingers closed on Frank Davis's cigarette case that he found he'd forgotten to leave it behind. He opened it and took out a Russian cigarette with a cardboard mouthpiece. Just as he was lighting it she said, "May I have one?"

He offered her the case and gave her a light. Still holding the case in his hand, he said, "It belonged to Frank Davis." She looked blank. "Cutter's friend," he amplified. "I suppose you heard that he had an unfortunate accident. Well, it was no accident."

The envelope given him by Sonya Kuklin had contained a single sheet of paper. It bore the key to a numerical code, but it was useless without the notebook in which Davis had copied out Cutter's signals. On the back, in clear, was the heading "Perm" followed by a list of names inscribed in Davis's handwriting, which was microscopically small and looked like printing. The names meant nothing to Quinn.

She puffed at her cigarette. He could see that she wasn't a habitual smoker. "I still don't understand why anyone should want to kill him."

He was about to take the envelope from his pocket, but some caution told him not to. "I don't understand it either. Yet. Davis knew nothing. Cutter never took him into his confidence, not completely."

She put the cigarette down, leaned forward, and picked up her glass in both hands before putting it to her lips.

"What did you know about the gold?" he asked.

"I heard rumors like everyone else in Karmel."

"Oh, come on!" he said angrily. "You knew it was here and you knew the sort of quantity involved! People have been threatening me ever since I got here and started asking questions. Now stop holding out on me!" He had a mental picture of a pallid face and a pair of dark, fanatical eyes.

She regarded him with frank surprise. "What is it you want to know?"

"Start with Viktor Ryazanov," he said. "What's his role here?"

"Ryazanov?" She gazed at him steadily over her cup. "Stay away from him. He used to command the Cheka outstation in Karmel."

Of course, Quinn thought. He could see the man vividly now, standing motionless in front of a stained glass window with his arms folded and a look of menace in his eyes. "How on earth did you manage to survive?"

"It was Ryazanov who surrendered the town to the Czechs. He betrayed his former comrades without a second thought."

"I'm amazed the Czechs didn't execute him on the spot. They hate the Cheka."

"They took him prisoner, lashed him to a tank, and paraded him around the town in triumph. They were just about to execute him when General Wajda stepped in. He and Wajda had a private chat. No one knows what they talked about."

Quinn digested this in silence. Then he said, "Ryazanov must have known about the gold—was that what he offered Wajda?"

"I don't know what the deal was. I only know they've been inseparable ever since."

"Were you already in Karmel at the time?"

Her voice became entreating. "You're nothing but trouble."

"I'm not convinced you've told me all you know."

She laughed bitterly. "You're catching on at last. You can't trust anyone in this place. Get out of Karmel while you can. We have enough heroes here—and every one of them is dead."

She had to put the cup down, her hands were shaking so badly.

Quinn said, "I had already made up my mind to leave here when they killed Davis. That changes things."

"He's only one among hundreds, thousands, dying every day in this area. . . ."

"Frank Davis was a harmless soul who wound up here by chance and against his will. He didn't know what he was letting himself in for. He shut himself up in his room and drowned his fears in drink, and they lured him out by faking a message from me. I don't like to feel responsible for his death. . . ."

Neither of them spoke for a while. The embers in the stove subsided with a whisper. The building was hushed and seemingly deserted. When she finally broke the silence, she sounded unsure.

"I've tried to help you—in my own way." She smiled, but even her smile had lost its cool self-assurance. "For some reason, I have a good feeling about you."

He looked at her again. He'd given up hope of meeting another woman he could live with, and now he sensed that Moura Toumanova could be that woman. Here, in the middle of a war, everything between them seemed so immediate, so obvious. Then he saw her fingers toying with the chain around her neck, and the sight turned his emotions to ice.

"Was it the same with Cutter?" he asked brusquely. "Do you always take men to bed before they die?"

Her eyes went wide in astonishment. "Get out!" she yelled. Quinn reacted swiftly for fear of provoking another confrontation with the Mongol. He kneeled down beside her and put his arm around her shoulders. She was trembling in every limb, but then she calmed down.

She slowly turned her head and stared at him in surprise. She said nothing, just stared at him with that strange and incongruous look.

"You can congratulate yourself," she said eventually.

"On what?"

The smile had returned to her eyes. "Shutting me up," she said. "Only one other man has ever managed to do that. He used to put his arm around me when I blew up."

Quinn held her. At length he started to remove his arm, but she said, "No, stay like that."

He swallowed hard. "You were making me jealous," he said. The words were almost unintelligible, his throat felt so dry.

"You've no reason. It was . . ." She broke off. "I'm all right now, it's over. You can take your arm away. Give me a cigarette, would you?"

He produced Davis's case again and held it out. Her hands trembled as she took a cigarette and bent over the chimney of the lamp to light it. She handed it to Quinn, took another, and lit that too.

"Why can't you talk openly to me?" he asked.

She blew smoke in his face and laughed. "I've seldom been so talkative in my life."

"So who was it who used to put his arm around you?"

"Oh, that? My father." She eyed him gravely. "You can't help me, *Anglichanin*, and I can't help you, not in the ways you want. I'm sorry, for you, for us both. But I can't. Please try to understand."

"I know Tom Cutter came here on account of the gold. And now I'm here."

"I've never flattered myself that he was interested in anything else. Just as I never flatter myself about you."

"I've heard a remarkable story," he said. "Cutter found the gold and made a deal with the Bolsheviks. That was how they managed to spirit it away before the Czechs got here."

She remained silent, toying with the chain around her neck. He wanted to ask her to show him whatever was suspended from it, but he would have felt as if he were asking her to strip off in front of him.

"General Wajda seems to think they took the gold to Perm," he added.

He took the envelope from his pocket and removed the sheet of paper. "This is a list of names," he said. "They're probably Cutter's contacts in Perm."

She glanced at the list and shook her head. "You're asking too much of me."

He waited a long time. Then he replaced the piece of paper in the envelope and got up. She rose too, and for a moment they stood facing each other in silence.

"Thanks for the tea."

"Please try to understand," she said. "I can't do anything more for you."

"It all began with a message from Cutter," he said. " 'If anything happens to me, take care of Moura Toumanova.' The wording surprised me from the start—it just didn't sound like him. I now think he meant something else: 'If anything happens to me, get in touch with Moura Toumanova. She knows all the answers. . . .' "

She said blankly, "If you really want to do something for me, get out of Karmel."

"Scala has fixed me up with a train tomorrow morning. You've still got time to change your mind and come too."

"You think if I'm somewhere else, then I'll talk?"

"That's right. Because someplace else, things might look different for us."

"I think you meant what you said just now. That you were really jealous."

"Yes."

She leaned forward and kissed him so lightly that he barely felt her lips brush his cheek. Then she drew back. "Don't miss your train."

Silently, she accompanied him as far as the veranda.

"*Do Zvidanye,* Moura."

"Good-bye, *Anglichanin.*"

He stepped out into the freezing night. It was still snowing heavily. He heard the horse stir restlessly as he passed the coach house and recalled his first sight of Moura in the wagon with the packsaddle at her feet—a mule's packsaddle. What did she use it for? Where did she go on her excursions? He hadn't put those questions to her, and they weren't the only ones that puzzled him. She wasn't talking—but he wasn't finished with her yet.

He trudged on, making plans. The snow was so deep that he had difficulty in finding his way back to Karmel.

121

15

THE morning was cold, with a biting wind, but it had stopped snowing. The sentries guarding the station had made themselves a log fire and were clustering around it for warmth. Sergei Diatsaro, by contrast, had come to see Quinn off in a pearl-gray duster with a worn fur collar.

"You forget," he said when Quinn raised his eyebrows, "I'm inured to the Russian winter. Besides, I've got a weakness for this coat, and vanity always comes first with a Diatsaro."

Quinn, waiting with him under the station's overhanging roof, shivered in spite of his sheepskin coat. The train, a locomotive and three cars, was still in a siding. Two uniformed men emerged from the mining company's former warehouse carrying a plain wooden coffin and loaded it into a section under Scala's watchful eye. Scala shut the door and affixed a lead seal to the handle.

The wood-fired locomotive's smokestack emitted a series of hoarse puffs, the smoke thickened, the wheels began to turn. Quinn picked up the shotgun, which was leaning against his suitcase in a canvas sheath, and held it out.

Diatsaro cleared his throat and shook his head. "I don't go hunting anymore."

"Why not give it to Govorov?"

"You saw him, then? Was he any help? No, he wasn't. I can tell."

Quinn continued to hold out the gun. "You're so alike you could be brothers."

Diatsaro gave a wry smile. His cheeks were stippled with several days' growth of beard. "There's a rumor we share the same father." He took the gun. "I'll give it to him."

"Sorry, I didn't mean to be indiscreet." Quinn handed over

the cartridges as well. "You've got my address in Omsk. Don't hesitate to call on me if you need any help in getting away from here."

"With the entire Diatsaro clan? Don't worry about me, I've nothing more to lose." He snorted. "You may find it hard to understand, but that's an immensely reassuring thought."

Quinn was glad when the train pulled out of the siding and into the station. The leading car was the one in which he'd come, and the same section had been reserved for him. Scala came hurrying along the platform with a broad smile on his face. He nodded to Diatsaro. "Our friend didn't stay long after all, did he?" The hostile silence that greeted his words didn't seem to surprise or annoy him in the least.

Quinn turned away, opened the door, and climbed aboard. The compartment was overheated. He lowered the window and leaned out. "That telegram to Omsk," he said to Scala, "—did you send it?"

"Sure, though I couldn't give them your exact time of arrival." Scala handed a sealed envelope through the window. "Details of the accident, complete with the autopsy report and witnesses' sworn statements."

"The *accident?*" Quinn couldn't restrain himself.

"I wouldn't advise you to call it anything else."

"So Sergeant Budyek never paid Davis a visit or lured him here with a message purporting to come from me?"

Scala looked grave for a moment. "You're all in one piece, Quinn," he said. "You're traveling first-class while Davis is making the trip in a box. Be grateful for the difference."

Quinn's pent-up fury got the better of him. "It's because of lies like that, and people like you, that I know I'll be back."

Scala stared at him, more hurt than angry. Then his face cleared. He gave Diatsaro another nod. "Our friend is far too smart to mean what he says—I hope." He stepped back and signaled to the engineer before turning to Quinn again.

123

"Maybe I got the old Russian proverb wrong. Maybe it's luckier to leave with the first snow than arrive with it."

The train got under way. The two men standing side by side on the platform couldn't have been more ill-matched: Sergei Diatsaro the prince's son, tall and erect in his threadbare coat, his gaunt face frosted with stubble and set in an expression conveying long acceptance of the fact that his world was at an end; and Dexter Scala, son of an immigrant laborer on the Pacific Railroad, a short, stocky figure with sturdy legs and a prominent gut whose outlines were perceptible beneath a heavy fur coat, his rosy moonface betraying that these were vintage years for him and his kind—years when everything they touched turned to gold.

The sun had been almost invisible down in the valley—just a pallid disk inching above the mountains—but the light grew stronger as the train toiled up the switchbacks, and by the time it reached the pass the sky was clear and sunny. Cold air streamed in through the window, reminding Quinn only now that he'd forgotten to close it.

His anger slowly waned as he gazed out at the snow-clad mountains. It was as if every additional mile that separated him from Karmel restored his energy and his capacity for rational thought.

What a fool he'd been to let Fitzmaurice deceive him. Why had he been sent to Karmel blindfolded? Had Fitzmaurice been afraid that he would have refused a potentially lethal assignment? Had he calculated that, once he was deeply enough committed, he wouldn't back out? If that was what the bastard had banked on, well, the bastard was right.

He shut the window. Scala's envelope caught his eye as he sat down again. From outside came the shriek of the locomotive's whistle, and everything went black as the train entered the tunnel.

OMSK

November 11, 1918

C L O U D E S L E Y Hollis opened the door rather tentatively. Although the evening was gray and frosty, Fitzmaurice hadn't turned on the lights in his Pullman car. Even the curtains were drawn. Hollis peered uncertainly at the figure behind the desk.

"Sorry I'm late, sir," he said, "but the town's in chaos. Everyone seems to be celebrating. . . ."

As though to underline his words a wave of noise flooded in through the open door: tin trays clashed like cymbals, shots were fired in the air, men's voices mingled with the strains of a brass band. Hollis shut the door behind him, wondering why Fitzmaurice was sitting there in the gloom. "Has the generator packed up again?"

"Turn on some lights if you like."

The wall lights flickered for a while and then steadied. Fitzmaurice opened a desk drawer and produced a bottle and two glasses. "The war's lasted long enough. Celebrations are in order, I suppose. Help yourself."

Hollis poured himself a Scotch and sat down. Fitzmaurice's uncharacteristic mildness continued to puzzle him, but he was too relieved to worry about it. This morning's rumor had

125

finally been confirmed: the Germans had just signed an armistice at Compiègne.

"They're planning a big fireworks display in Omsk," Hollis said.

"So they're all bright and cheerful, eh?" Fitzmaurice sipped his Scotch. "We've got grounds for celebration too. I was right about Oliver Quinn."

"Right in what way, sir?"

"My assessment of him was correct."

Hollis, feeling that it would be wiser to remain sober, put his glass down. "I wish you hadn't made me party to your scheme. I don't like it. Anyway, I'm glad he's coming back."

Fitzmaurice looked up from his glass. "Only Davis is coming back."

"Scala's telegram from Karmel was quite explicit."

"Quinn's a remarkably persevering type," Fitzmaurice broke in. "That's what I like about him."

"Sir?"

"Have another drink." Fitzmaurice shoved the bottle across the desk. "Quinn *is* on board that train, officially, and it's your job to convince everyone of the fact. He's resigned his post here—he'll take the next express to Vladivostock and sail for home from there. That's the official version."

"Then where the devil is he really?"

"At this moment? On the airfield at Tyumen." Fitzmaurice dismissed any further questions with an airy wave of the hand. He rose and went to a window, drew the curtain aside, and wiped away the condensation. It had been snowing almost incessantly for two weeks, and the snow lay three or four feet deep.

"Our friend Katov can't have done much flying lately," mused Fitzmaurice.

"No," Hollis said, "there's too much snow."

Fitzmaurice turned back from the window. "All the same," he said with a complacent smile. "I can't imagine that a man like Alexander Katov will be deterred by a little cold weather."

"What are you planning?"

"What am *I* planning? It was Quinn's idea, not mine. He insists that Katov is the man to fly him out of Tyumen."

"Where to?"

"Some lonely little spot within reach of Perm . . ."

A long silence followed, broken only by riotous sounds of rejoicing outside. Hollis eyed his empty glass. "Behind the enemy lines, you mean?"

"Surprising, eh?" Fitzmaurice said. "However, I can assure you the idea was his. He sent me a message from Tyumen. Of course, I won't pretend I'm not delighted that I summed him up correctly."

Hollis reached for the bottle and poured himself another drink, not caring if Fitzmaurice noticed how badly he needed it.

The pandemonium outside grew louder still, punctuated by the sound of fireworks being set off prematurely. To Hollis they sounded like the opening shots in a new campaign.

PART THREE

PART THREE

THE SENTINEL

F Y O D O R Nikulin had waited until nightfall before fetching the saddlebag of fresh provisions from its hiding place. He was returning to his cabin when the fireworks started. Unsure at first what they signified, he paused and stared at the colorful starbursts in the sky above Karmel.

The snow was deep enough to carpet every surface and muffle every sound, so the distant detonations were almost inaudible. This lent the exploding stars and multicolored cascades an appearance of even greater unreality. Nikulin was so used to seeing Karmel shrouded in darkness at night that the blaze of light made him doubly uneasy.

He wondered what they were celebrating down there. The saddlebag had contained only the single message for him: that the visitor from Omsk had left on time. He had no immediate cause for concern.

Another salvo of rockets soared into the sky and exploded into downward-drifting showers of colored sparks. It was a magical sight, but his uneasiness persisted.

He switched the saddlebag from one shoulder to the other and forced himself to walk on without looking back. He'd changed into winter clothes when the snow set in and was now wearing a long fur coat, a fur hat, and fur-lined boots. The steeper the gradient, the warmer he became—uncomfortably so. Because of the deep snow he was sticking to the tracks he'd made on the way down. This now struck him as an unforgivable piece of carelessness.

He branched off the old route. He was in no hurry to get back to the cabin. Nothing awaited him there but solitude, and solitude was his one real source of anxiety. He was afraid that the long, lonely days and nights might sap his determination.

He started to curse aloud, then laughed angrily at himself.

Of course more snow would fall, and of course the temperature would drop still further. It would aggravate the hardships of his life in the mountains, but who cared? Conditions that were adverse to him personally would only make his job as a lookout easier.

He'd done well, by and large. Things were going his way. The enemy had lost track of him, and the harder the winter the safer the gold and himself.

For all that, Fyodor Nikulin would almost have welcomed it if the surrounding silence had harbored some hint of danger, some promise of contact—even hostile contact—with another human being.

For the first time in weeks he thought of the *Anglichanin*. The recollection didn't anger him. He hoped the man's grave had been left undisturbed by marauding beasts. Tomorrow he would go and look. A dead man was better than no company at all.

And Moura Toumanova? Should he send her a message? He missed their conversations. If Nikulin felt any hunger, it was a hunger for words, for her voice, for their history together.

16

THE DH-9A banked in preparation for landing. Beneath them was a white void, an infinity of whiteness. The rising sun, a pale yellow sphere, dipped below the horizon as they descended. The slipstream buffeted Quinn's streaming eyes. He shut them and hoped Katov knew what he was doing.

The plane was a single-engined two-seater reputed to be one of the most modern machines in service, but Quinn's first sight of it on the airfield at Tyumen had made him recall Davis and wonder how on earth the rickety contraption would ever hold together. It had taken over an hour to start the engine and divest the struts and stays of accumulated ice. Quinn had been as little reassured by these preliminaries as he was by Katov's final act before takeoff: the Russian ace had leaned forward and kissed the St. Nicholas icon screwed to his instrument panel.

Quinn didn't open his eyes again until he felt the ski-plane touch down. Snow whirled up into his face, blinding him. Dazed and dizzy from the flight, he sat motionless for some seconds after the machine had slid to a stop.

His relief that they were finally on the ground began to wane. He had some difficulty in releasing his safety belt. Katov swiveled around in his seat with a look that demanded to know what was keeping him.

He hoisted the bundle onto his lap, heaved it over the side, and climbed down after it. The idling propeller sucked up more clouds of blinding snow and flung them into his face. "See you in ten days!" he yelled. Katov responded with a thumbs-up. "Ten days!" he yelled back, but the eyes behind the goggles looked less sanguine than the words implied.

Quinn picked up the bundle and trudged off through the

snow. When he paused and looked back he saw that Katov had already turned the plane into the wind.

The drone of the engine dwindled to a distant hum. Then the hum, too, died away, to be replaced by another sound: the whistle of the wind driving fresh snow over the frozen crust of old snow beneath. Nothing else disturbed the early morning hush.

Having made his way across the field to a bank that offered some protection from the wind, Quinn proceeded to undo the bundle. Katov had brought the outfit he was wearing from Omsk: a new set of clothes, underclothes included, all of which accorded with his new identity. Fitzmaurice's arrangements could not have been more thorough, he was relieved to note. Only two items of equipment had given him pauses for thought: the seven-shot Browning automatic, 1910 model, and the cyanide capsule.

He'd meant to ask Fitzmaurice about the latter when they were speaking on the telephone last night, but the connection was poor and their conversation had been limited to essentials. Quinn thought Fitzmaurice had already hung up when he heard the major's voice once more: "I'm counting on you, Quinn, but it's not too late. You can still back out." Then, if at all, would have been the moment to broach the subject of the cyanide capsule. . . .

The bundle was wrapped in a shelter half. The money belt he was already wearing, the other things he stowed about his person: the gun, the two sets of forged papers, the map and compass. The food went into a shoulder bag. Everything else—notably the torches he would need to illuminate the landing place if Katov returned in bad visibility—he repacked in the shelter half and concealed in a shallow hole scooped out of the bank with an entrenching tool. Then he covered the spot with snow and snapped a branch to mark its position. He couldn't do anything about the airplane's tracks, but with luck more snow would protect them from chance discovery.

He took out his map and compass and climbed the bank. The sun had crept above the skyline again, and its feeble light was sufficient for him to take a bearing on a dead tree half a mile away, which stood conveniently on his line of advance.

The plane had followed the Trans-Siberian in the direction of Kazan before turning north and landing him some forty miles southeast of Perm. The nearest town with a railroad station was Kungur.

He pocketed the map and compass and set off. He walked into the wind. Not an animal stirred, not a bird took wing at his approach. The cold air, the desolate landscape, the physical exercise—all these combined to relax him. At Karmel he'd been unable to distinguish friend from foe; from now on he would be surrounded by enemies at all times, and the sooner he got used to that feeling the better.

It took him four hours to reach Kungur station, which lay outside the town itself. There seemed to be no approach road, not even a path, just the single-line track and the inevitable line of telegraph poles. He waited at a safe distance and lunched on some sandwiches and cold tea. Another hour passed before he sighted the smoke of a westbound train on the skyline.

He entered the station shortly before the train pulled in. Peasants were waiting on the platform with sacks and baskets full of agricultural produce. Katov had handed Quinn some rubles on Fitzmaurice's behalf. The woman clerk who sold him his ticket accepted them without hesitation.

Hitched to the rusty old locomotive were two reeking cattle cars and a decrepit passenger car. Every section was jam-packed, and he only just managed to squeeze aboard at the last minute.

* * *

135

Perm's central station was a brick building with glass-roofed platforms, but melted snow was dripping through gaps in the panes overhead. It was already dark, and only a scattering of lights had been switched on. Quinn was the first to emerge from the crowded section, but he stood aside and let the other passengers overtake him.

They streamed toward the exit, then slowed to a standstill. Uniformed sentries were checking travel documents and baggage. Quinn looked around for an unguarded exit, but there almost certainly wasn't one, and a fruitless search for it would only arouse suspicion. Taking the Red Cross arm band from the outer pocket of his coat, he slipped it on and wormed his way through the crowd rather than be the last in line.

He reached the barrier and held out his papers. The two soldiers on duty gave his photograph a perfunctory glance. Then he caught sight of another man, a civilian in a long overcoat so tightly belted that it seemed to cut his body in half. He had close-cropped hair, deepset eyes, and a face the color of parchment.

"Just a minute! Your papers." He stopped Quinn with a gesture. Taking the papers, he stepped aside to examine them under an overhead light, then turned back. "You're with the Swedish Red Cross?"

"Yes."

"Where have you come from, Achim Lundeberg?"

"Motovilchinskoyo." It was a Perm suburb where the Red Cross maintained a camp for refugees from neutral countries awaiting repatriation.

"You've been boosting your compatriots' morale?"

"That's all your authorities permit us to do."

The Cheka officer—there could now be no doubt about his identity—was still holding the Swedish passport in his hand. His eyes traveled from Quinn's photograph to his face and back again. "Let's see your ticket."

Quinn turned cold, but only after the event. The prospect

136

of getting off at Motovilchinskoyo and fighting his way aboard another overcrowded train, just to arm himself with a local ticket and shake off anyone tailing him, had almost deterred him from breaking his journey there. He searched his pockets one by one, taking his time. When he eventually produced the ticket he even managed to look the man in the eye.

"Why so suspicious?" he demanded.

The man returned his passport. "You can go."

Quinn was so relieved he couldn't restrain himself. "Is that all?" he said. "Aren't you going to search me?"

The man put his hands on his hips. "Another time, perhaps. State Security is no laughing matter, comrade. Now get going—the exit's over there."

Quinn turned away, forcing himself to walk slowly. His brief sense of triumph ebbed away. The big square was hushed and almost deserted by the time he emerged from the station. A few figures hurried across it and disappeared into the adjoining streets. Banners adorned with slogans were suspended from the station's overhanging roof and the buildings nearby.

The sky was gloomy enough overhead, but gloomier still on the other side of the river, where ascending spirals of smoke could be seen. Perm's munitions factories were doubtless working around the clock. A smell of coal dust hung in the air. Sentries were manning a barbed-wire barrier at the mouth of the street that led to the main bridge over the Kama.

Two droshkies were waiting beside the station steps. Quinn felt tempted to hire one and drive to the Swedish Mission. He needed a secure base from which to pursue his inquiries, and Fitzmaurice had provided him with a contact there. He would be given a clean bed and a heated room—even a bath, perhaps—but he dismissed the idea. For the moment at least, he would feel happier relying on no one but himself.

He walked across the deserted square toward the roadblock, feigning nonchalance.

This time he encountered no secret policeman. The Red

Guards manning the barrier had weary faces. But for their ragged uniforms, they might have been replicas of the British sentries guarding the bridge at Omsk the night Sergeant Rice drove him back from Boloto and his abortive hunting trip. It seemed an age ago.

They merely glanced at his papers and waved him on.

17

H E ' D been watching the cul-de-sac for quite a while. Perm's Chinatown was situated on the north side near the river. There were no street lights, and the few lanterns bracketed to the houses shone dimly through the river mist.

He was reminded yet again of Omsk. The narrow alley with its cramped little houses resembled the street from which he'd collected Hollis after his binge at the "Divan," except that this one was lined with shops. The Chinese characters on the hanging signs indicated that some of them sold antiquities while others housed astrologers, letter-writers, and dealers in herbal medicines.

He paused for a moment when he reached the house at the far end of the blind alley. The windows were shuttered, but patches of melted snow on the roof indicated that the house was occupied. He knocked on the shiny red door, heard shuffling footsteps, sensed that someone was observing him through a peephole.

"Who is it?"

He said the first thing that occurred to him. "A customer."

The door opened to reveal an entrance hall bathed in a warm glow by shaded wall lights. He stepped inside and found himself confronted by a Chinese woman in a long silk gown slit up the side.

"What can I do for you?" she asked in Russian.

"I'd like a word with Chen Teh."

"You're sure you have the right address?" She had the sharp, watchful eyes of a nighthawk. "What did you wish to discuss?"

"Business," he replied.

"Wait here, please."

He waited. The house was as silent as the grave, but a minute later he heard voices in the distance. The Chinese woman reappeared, nodded mutely, and padded off again. He followed her along a maze of passages until they came to a door, which she opened. She showed him in and then withdrew.

The walls of the small, low-ceilinged room were adorned with ink drawings and a Tibetan banderole. Chen Teh was seated on a divan with an opium table beside him. The night light on the table, a simple oil lamp with an exposed wick, provided the only illumination.

"Good evening, Chen Teh, and good health." It was Chen Teh's dignified bearing that prompted Quinn to greet him with such formality. His broad Mongol features and slit eyes clearly stamped him as a native of northern China. A man of sixty or thereabouts, he had a shaven head and a sparse beard, white around the mouth but still dark at the edges. His left hand was a prosthesis in a leather glove, but the capacious sleeve of his blue silk jacket concealed this fact from Quinn until he moved it. He laid aside the opium pipe he'd been lighting and looked up.

"Do you have a name?"

"I'm sorry to disturb you at this late hour," said Quinn.

"I'm always ready to talk business."

"That was a white lie, I regret to say. All I want is a few minutes of your time."

Chen Teh nodded. "Sit down."

Quinn lowered himself onto a floor cushion. For the first time since he'd left the train at Perm he felt a slight lessening of tension.

"May I offer you some refreshment?" Chen Teh inquired. "You look tired—worried, too. That was what my wife said: 'There's a man outside who wishes to talk business with you, Chen. He looked worried. He's a foreigner—probably an Englishman. . . .' " He indicated the little table and its neat array of opium smoker's utensils. "Will you take a pipe with me?"

Quinn shook his head. "I've never tried it."

"You should. Opium helps one to see things in a better light. One even entertains strangers who neglect to introduce themselves."

"You can call me Lundeberg," Quinn said. "Not that it's my real name."

"I quite understand. Aliases are a sensible precaution these days." He leaned forward and adopted a conspiratorial tone. "How is our mutual friend?"

Quinn reached in his pocket and produced Davis's cigarette case, which he'd kept. He opened it and removed one of the cardboard-tipped papiroshi. "What makes you think we have a mutual friend?" he said warily.

"What else would an Englishman be doing in Perm but looking for another Englishman?" The man's voice seemed to invite trust. "You're a friend of Tom Cutter's, aren't you?"

Quinn made no move to light the cigarette between his fingers. Chen Teh's name had headed Davis's list. He had to trust him—he had no choice.

"Would you tell me why Cutter got in touch with you?"

"We're old acquaintances. Hasn't he ever told you about Nerchinsk?"

Quinn, wondering what the name signified, made no reply.

"It was a gold mine I owned in Siberia. Our friend worked for me there for a time."

"You still haven't told me what he wanted from you."

The Chinese seemed engrossed in his own thoughts. "I was a youngster of fifteen when I first came to Nerchinsk, a coolie like a thousand others working in the gold mine there. When

140

the owner ran short of labor the governor put soldiers at his disposal. They raided the villages across the Chinese border and rounded up as many men and boys as were needed." The heavy silk sleeve rustled as Chen Teh made an angry gesture with his leather glove. "Workers were so easy to replace at Nerchinsk that they hanged anyone caught hoarding even a few grains of gold. I suppose I should be thankful they only chopped off my hand."

"You said Cutter worked for you."

"Why should a coolie try to change the world? When I had the chance to become rich, I seized it. I ended by owning the mine, yes, and Cutter worked for me."

"Are you still in the gold business?"

"No, it's a fool's game. Dreams are my business now—or, if you prefer, prostitution and gambling."

"In a Red-occupied city? Is that a good business to be in?"

"The best in any city of whatever color."

"Cutter came to see you early in September?"

Chen Teh nodded. "Look, no one would risk coming here without a very good reason. Why not make up your mind to trust me?"

"Cutter may be dead," Quinn said. "The Reds may have killed him. According to another version, he's still alive."

The Mongol face remained impassive. "Which version do you favor?"

Quinn didn't answer at once. He wasn't sure how far he could afford to go, but he felt relaxed in Chen Teh's company, soothed by his calm voice and serene manner.

"Tom Cutter was on the track of something," he said eventually. "Something of interest to many people. He was after gold, more gold than you and I have ever seen: a hundred tons of bullion loaded into fourteen freight cars—and there's only one place where so much gold would have been kept: the Imperial Bank at St. Petersburg. But once on the train it disappeared. It was Cutter's job to track it down."

Chen Teh inclined his head. "Then I reluctantly favor your first version. He's dead. With so much gold at stake his chances of survival must have been slim. And you—you must be mad to have come here. How can you be sure the Cheka won't turn up here at any moment, alerted by my wife? A man in my line of business needs protection."

Quinn found it a supreme effort not to turn his head and look at the door. "It was a risk I decided to take," he said at length.

The Chinese sighed. "If that's why you came, I should tell you that Cutter never even mentioned the gold. Perhaps he thought I wouldn't help him—under the circumstances. But of course I guessed what he was after from the questions he asked and the people he wanted to meet with. I had some idea of his objective, but not of its magnitude."

Quinn was still holding the cigarette he'd taken from Davis's case. He snapped off the shorter end containing the tobacco. There was a knife with a jade handle on the brass-topped opium table. He slit the cardboard mouthpiece length-wise and unrolled it. Inside was a slip of paper bearing a copy of Davis's list of names.

The Chinese took the paper and glanced at it. He frowned but said nothing.

"Are those the people Cutter visited here?" Quinn demanded. "Your name heads the list as you can see."

Chen Teh held the paper over the night light until it caught fire. Quinn made no attempt to stop him; he had memorized all the names.

"Merely to have survived for as long as I have is quite an achievement on the part of a former coolie," Chen Teh said at last. "What's more, I'm only just beginning to enjoy life. It took me sixty years to discover what I was made for: not gold or riches, but a tranquil existence. My ambition is to grow old in peace." The slip of paper had burned away to almost noth-ing. He dropped the remains, which resembled a scrap of black silk, onto the opium table. "You'd be wise to forget the whole affair." He pointed to the neat row of opium pipes. "Are you sure you won't smoke a pipe with me?"

Quinn shook his head.

"How would a girl suit you?"

"For a moment," Quinn said, "I thought you'd help me."

"Did Cutter find what he was looking for?" asked Chen Teh.

"He found out where they took the gold—Karmel in the Urals. What happened then isn't clear. It may even be here in this city."

Chen Teh ran two fingers over the sparse beard and mustache that framed his lips, first on one side, then on the other. The effect was peculiar: a smile appeared at each corner of his mouth in turn. "Well, if you're intent on staying here," he said, "our first step must be to find you somewhere safe to lie low. These things cost money, of course, but I'm happy to help you out."

Quinn nodded and followed his host across the garden behind the house. A pale moon visible through rents in the clouds showed that the snow covering the beds was fresh and untrodden. Chen Teh paused before a door in the garden wall, unlocked it, and stepped outside. Long swaths of river mist were drifting over a stretch of open ground.

Quinn followed close at Chen Teh's heels so as not to lose sight of him. They'd gone only fifty yards or so when he sighted the boats moored along the bank. Chen Teh turned and raised his hand. "Wait here," he said.

Quinn saw him walk the last few yards to the water's edge and hail a junk whose clumsy lines, three stumpy masts, and rolled sails were just discernible in the murk as it stirred and swayed with the current. A figure appeared in the feeble light of the single deckhouse lantern.

The two men conferred. "It's only a matter of courtesy," Chen Teh had explained. "Hu Long is a member of the family—he's my wife's brother. You can trust him. Besides, if you have to leave Perm in a hurry, the river's the safest route."

He turned and beckoned to Quinn. The man on board the junk, who was waiting to greet him at the end of the gangplank, wore a long black robe and a small black skullcap. Quinn paused at the foot of the gently seesawing gangplank. "Thank you, Chen," he said.

"Stay on board—don't go off on your own. Get some rest, and if you can't sleep, consult my brother-in-law."

"I'm tired enough to sleep."

"Any man who can say that of himself is fortunate indeed."

With a nod to Quinn, Chen Teh turned and walked off. The mist swallowed him up only a few feet from the riverbank.

Quinn's sleeping quarters were in the steeply raked stern. The cabin was surprisingly snug, with mats on the floor and a comfortable couch in one corner. He undressed, extinguished the lantern, and lay there in the dark, conscious of little but the boat's gentle movements and his own exhaustion.

An hour later he was still wide-awake and had given up all hope of sleep. If he'd been able at that moment to put the clock back, he would probably have abandoned the whole venture. He felt entrapped and unequal to his present predicament.

He could hear someone quietly pacing the deck overhead. The sound only heightened his sense of isolation and triggered a new thought in his mind: he would never get to sleep unless he had a woman first.

It came after him with almost unprecedented intensity, this straightforward lust, this yearning to feel a naked body in his arms, to touch bare flesh and revel in its warmth. . . .

He got up, bathed in sweat, and lit the lantern again. And

144

then he realized that the object of his persistent desire was one particular woman, and that her name was Moura Toumanova. He pictured her drawing back the curtain on the alcove where the bed was, recalled the way her dark skin seemed to absorb the light, heard her deep, husky laugh, heard her say, "This is better than any explanation."

Although his desire was unabated when he lay down again, it had lost its gnawing, agonizing intensity. It was as if the thorn had been extracted from the wound, and the memory of the woman in Karmel left him wrapped in a serene sense of well-being.

Never in all the years since Catherine's death had he felt such a sensation. He tried to stay awake and savor it. He knew now that he was going to see her again. Then the long, gentle billows of sleep engulfed him.

18

QUINN'S vantage point at the end of the street afforded a view of the square in front of the freight depot. This was the city's east side, where all the slaughterhouses were situated. Every Monday and Thursday freight trains arrived from the flatlands laden with horses for sale in the square. The inhabitants of Perm had been reduced to eating horsemeat for months.

He'd seen the first train arrive and the first consignment auctioned at dawn. Women and children were now busy collecting the dung the horses had left behind in the trampled snow. A gray sky brooded over the bleak and dismal scene, and the east wind chilled Quinn to the marrow as soon as he stopped moving.

Another train pulled in. Armed with sticks, drovers in long, grimy smocks manhandled ramps up to the freight cars. The first of the horses, pitifully emaciated beasts with prominent ribs, tottered out onto the platform under a hail of blows.

Quinn heard a plaintive exclamation behind him. Young Pei was one of Hu Long's sons, a comical-looking youth of sixteen with a round, spotty face and a pair of steel-rimmed glasses perched on his snub nose.

"Take it easy," Quinn said.

"I hate the way they treat those animals, that's all."

Quinn was surprised Pei could see anything at all, the lenses of his glasses were so dirty.

"The bank opens in another half-hour," he told the boy. "It's time we went."

He turned and set off along the street, forcing himself to walk slowly and keep watch for any sign that someone might be tailing them. A hundred yards down they passed the side street that led to the abattoirs, squat buildings whose smoke-stacks jutted into the gloomy sky and spewed forth plumes of noisome smoke that darkened it still further. The butchers' shops lining the street were still closed. There were a few stand-up bars, but they too were deserted at this hour and would not fill up until the drovers had finished work. The only distinctive building was a branch of the former Imperial Bank, a pretentious three-storied edifice built of brick and situated at the mouth of a cul-de-sac.

Quinn paused on the other side of the street. Lights were burning and shadows moving around beyond the barred windows. The clock above the main entrance indicated that there were twenty minutes to go before the bank opened.

Everything seemed unusually quiet—too quiet for Quinn's liking, though he told himself that the silence was quite natural at this hour and put his uneasiness down to impatience. He gave an involuntary start when Pei touched his arm.

"That car's still there!"

The unmarked Ford was parked at the far end of the cul-de-sac with its windows up. It had been there when they checked the environs of the bank an hour ago.

"Shall I go and take a look?" Pei said.

"No!" Quinn scrutinized the car more closely. He couldn't tell if there was anyone inside. It was an effort to breathe calmly, control his nerves, brace himself for a decision. . . .

He'd spent six days in Perm without making any progress. "Be patient," was Chen Teh's recurrent advice. "Give me time. I'll find the man you need, but it can't be done overnight." There was nothing for it but to spend those days and nights below deck in the junk, and inactivity was the thing he hated most. Then, forty-eight hours ago, he'd set out on his first reconnaissance trip with Pei. That, too, had borne no fruit—or not, at least, until he came across a familiar name.

Vitov Yurovsky, ex-director of the mint at Ekaterinburg, was now the manager of the branch in Perm. Quinn had sent him a message yesterday, and Yurovsky, in return for a substantial sum in foreign currency, had agreed to a meeting.

Again Quinn felt Pei grip his arm. "You really mean to go?"

He shook off the boy's hand with an impatient gesture. "You stay here and watch that car. If anyone gets out, signal me."

"I'll take off my glasses."

"Good, and if anything unexpected happens don't dream of coming to my assistance. We'll split up and rendezvous at the landing stage."

Before Pei could say a word he was out in the roadway and heading for the bar across the street from the bank.

The air inside was thick with tobacco smoke. The men at the counter stared at him for a moment and then, apparently losing interest, turned away. It surprised him that a stranger should attract so little attention. He paused in the doorway, watching the men but listening for the sound of hurried footsteps or a car starting up. Nothing happened, so he went up to the counter. The barroom was unheated, and the customers

147

were drinking some kind of hot toddy. The man behind the counter, who had a broad face and a broken nose, leaned forward and said, "You're up early, Comrade. What's it to be?"

"Nothing, thanks. I'm waiting for someone."

The man looked puzzled. He rubbed his ruin of a nose. "The Comrade Manager, you mean?"

"Yes."

"Comrade Yurovsky," the man continued to rub his nose, "is expecting you over at the bank."

The others stared at their glasses and didn't budge. Again Quinn sensed that there was something false and unnatural about the prevailing silence. "How do you know?" he asked as calmly as he could.

"Because he called in half an hour ago and told me to send you across."

Quinn left the counter and walked to the window. He could see the bank's main entrance over the top of the grimy half-curtains. The hour hand of the clock above the door was already pointing to nine. As he watched, the minute hand jerked into place: it was nine o'clock precisely. Yesterday at this time a good dozen horse dealers had been waiting for the bank to open; today there was no one to be seen.

He waited. Pei, still wearing his glasses, was standing on the other side of the street. At five past nine the double doors opened and a man emerged, a dark-suited figure with sparse hair carefully distributed over a balding scalp. He descended the steps, glanced up at the clock.

"There's the Comrade Manager," said a nasal voice behind Quinn's back. It was the barman, sounding edgy. "I thought you wanted to see him."

The banknotes for Vitov Yurovsky were in an envelope in the breast pocket of Quinn's coat, but the first thing he reached for was the Browning. Releasing the safety catch, he stuffed it in his waistband and continued to wait.

148

Yurovsky took another look at the clock, squinted this way and that, smoothed his hair down, hovered at the foot of the steps as if about to go back inside. Then, changing his mind at the last moment, he slowly headed for the parked car.

Quinn followed him with his eyes. Yurovsky made his way around the car and seemed to be talking to someone inside. His body was hidden from view, but Quinn could see his head. He spoke with mounting vehemence. Then the rear doors of the Ford burst open and two men jumped out and grabbed him. Yurovsky tried to fight them off, broke away, and ran for it, but they easily caught up with him. He yelled and lashed out, only to be clubbed to the ground and hauled back to the car. The men bundled him inside, dived in after him, and slammed the doors shut. The car moved off, jolting over the cobblestones as it picked up speed.

It was only now that Quinn became aware of the barflies clustered around him, watching the scene, and only now that he noticed Pei—without his glasses—dashing across the street. The Ford had reached the mouth of the dead-end street and was just turning left when the driver trod on the brakes. The car slewed and skidded to a stop. The two men in the back abandoned their inert prisoner and jumped out, guns in hand.

Overcoming the fear that had temporarily paralyzed him, Quinn drew his own gun and made a dash for the barroom door. Pei raced past just as he emerged. His pursuers reached the spot an instant later, their whole attention focused on the fleeing youngster. They were muscular fellows, and Quinn would have stood little chance against them on his own, but surprise was on his side.

He charged straight at them. The first man went sprawling under the impact, the second tripped over him and let go of his gun. Before they could scramble to their feet, Quinn was away and running.

149

Escape was his one and only thought. He could see Pei ahead of him, a hundred yards in the lead.

"Stoy! Stoy!"

The cries came echoing along the street. He ran on with his head down, waiting for the blow in the back, the bullet that would stop him, but it never came. The cries faded and died away, to be replaced by a sound he couldn't at first identify, a thunderous crescendo that swelled until the very air rang with it.

He didn't see the horses until sheer surprise caused him to slow and look up. They filled the entire width of the street ahead of him, hundreds of them being driven to the slaughter-houses, and it was the drumming of their hooves that had impinged on his consciousness.

Pei came to a halt, looking helpless, and started to run in the opposite direction. Quinn caught him by the arm and urged him forward. The oncoming beasts were less than a hundred yards away, the thunder of their hoofbeats drowning every other sound.

Quinn dragged Pei into a doorway and forced him back against the woodwork. And then the herd was upon them, a sea of tossing heads, foaming mouths, rolling eyes, heaving flanks with protruding ribs. They heard terrified whinnies, were buffeted by blundering bodies coated with lather. Pei threw up his arms to shield his face and fell to the ground.

Suddenly there was space around them again. Drovers ran past, lashing out at stragglers with their long sticks. The surf-like roar of hooves receded and grew fainter. Quinn hauled Pei to his feet. They sprinted to the end of the street, dodged into an alleyway, and stopped to listen. All was quiet again.

Quinn turned to look at Pei. The boy was panting hard, like himself. He had a cut over his right eyebrow.

"How did that happen?" Quinn asked.

"I collided with the doorpost—one of those poor old nags

tossed its head at the wrong moment." Pei gingerly probed the cut with his fingers. It started to bleed again.

"You should have stayed where you were."

The boy hung his head and said nothing.

"Where are your glasses?"

"Oh, them. They came off while I was running."

"Do you really need them?"

Pei's face relaxed. "They were only window glass," he replied with a smile. "Everyone makes fun of me in night school. I thought I'd look older in glasses." He turned and set off down the street.

"Follow me," he said, youthfully self-assured once more. "We'll go back a different way."

They returned to the Chinese quarter by a roundabout route. A rowboat was waiting for them at the landing stage downstream, and the last part of the way there took them across a stretch of open ground on which thousands of refugees were bivouacking between the city's outskirts and the river.

Quinn kept close behind Pei as they traversed the camp. The nearer they came to the river, the denser the close-packed humanity around them. They might have been making their way through a vast open-air hospital. Scores of inmates died daily now that the cold weather had set in, to be collected every morning by a working party and carted off for burial in mass graves outside the city.

Pitiful figures dressed in rags sat huddled on the sodden, trampled ground. The more fortunate owned handcarts piled high with their belongings and were reclining on mattresses. Those who were really wealthy by local standards had erected makeshift huts and were seated around meager camp fires.

The nauseating stench that hung in the air gave way near the river to a smell of decaying fish and stagnant water. On the other side of the Kama, the smokestacks of the munitions

151

factories loomed against a dark gray sky. Quinn noticed that no smoke was rising from them today.

The junk's dinghy lay moored at the end of a narrow, rotting jetty. Souen, one of Hu Long's sturdy Chinese crewmen, had been guarding it in their absence. He cast off as soon as they were aboard and headed upstream.

They made slow progress against the current, and it seemed an eternity before they cleared the narrow channel between the other boats anchored there. When the dinghy at last drew level with the junk's squat hull, which had an eye painted on the bow, Quinn was relieved to see familiar faces looking down at them.

A rope ladder came tumbling over the side. Pei grabbed it and hung on. The cut above his eye had stopped bleeding. He tried to smile, but he still looked tense. Quinn climbed aboard. Hu Long was his usual laconic, imperturbable self. The midday meal was ready, but Quinn excused himself. He went below and lay down to reconsider his position.

"I have news for you," said Chen Teh. "Some good, some bad."

He normally visited Quinn aboard the junk, but not tonight. They were closeted in his house ashore.

"Let's hear the bad news first," Quinn said.

"Very well. The Cheka turned up at the Swedish Mission this afternoon. They wanted to interview a man named Achim Lundeberg."

"And the good news?"

Chen Teh raised his eyes from the pipe he'd been smoking when Quinn entered. "A man has agreed to speak with you."

"Who? When?"

Chen Teh ignored the first question. "Tomorrow night." He indicated the little table and its array of opium smoker's implements. "Be patient. Would you care for a pipe tonight?"

"I'd sooner accept your original offer."

Chen Teh pointed to the Tibetan banderole on the wall. "Take that down. Behind it you'll find a mirror. No one will be able to see you, but you can make your choice at leisure. There are more ways than one of soothing the soul. . . ."

Back aboard the junk two hours later, Quinn found that nothing had changed. He lay sleepless on his couch below deck, elsewhere in mind and body, thinking of Karmel and of Moura.

19

T H E rickshaw came to a halt. Quinn could see nothing through the curtains, but their trip in the enclosed two-seater had taken so short a time that they must still be in the Chinese quarter.

Chen Teh, sitting beside him, made no immediate move to get out. Whispers were heard. Then the curtain was drawn aside. "This is indeed an honor, Chen," a man's voice murmured. Through the mist, Quinn saw that they had pulled up outside a garden with a phoenix carved on the gateway.

The man who greeted them was a Chinese like Chen Teh, but there the similarity ended. Tall and heavily built but surprisingly light on his feet, he led the way through the ornamental garden to a door, which he opened. Ushering them inside, he preceded them along a corridor to a second door. Beyond it was an unlighted walkway with open arches on one side.

At the far end, beyond yet another door, lay a room in which some thirty people stood clustered around two roulette tables. The croupiers were Chinese. One of them had just spun his wheel, and his high-pitched *"Rien ne va plus!"* was followed by the click of the ball as it caromed off the rim of the bowl.

153

The gamblers, most of whom were also Chinese, included a sprinkling of Russians. Chen Teh and the proprietor of the "Phoenix" paused inside the door. "The omens are good, Chen," the big man whispered. "It's always easier to do business with a loser."

The croupier sang out the winning number. "*Trois, rouge, impair, manque.* Nothing *en plein!*"

"Yes, he's losing again," whispered the proprietor. "He must be down at least ten thousand."

Chen Teh raised his eyebrows. "You allow him to play on credit?"

"Only as a favor to you, Chen."

The proprietor showed them into his inner sanctum. Apart from a desk and several armchairs, the richly carpeted room contained a number of lacquered display cabinets. Illuminated from within, they were filled with collector's pieces, some of bronze, others of porcelain.

"This is an honor," the proprietor repeated. "No one will disturb you in here."

Chen Teh produced a velvet case from his robe and opened it. Inside was a small blue object in the shape of a bird's head.

"A Chao phoenix!" The proprietor took the case and examined the contents reverently. "I've never yet succeeded in acquiring one from the Chao period."

"The dealer sold it to me as such," Chen Teh said. "I was far from sure."

"Many thanks, Chen, you're far too generous. Shall I let Borodin know you're expecting him?"

Quinn might have been invisible for all the notice they took of him. The proprietor secreted the velvet case beneath his robe. "Don't be so generous with Borodin, Chen," he said. "He may soon lose the power he has now. . . ."

Chen waved Quinn into an armchair as soon as they were alone. "Sit down, Mr. Quinn. I have two things to say." He strolled over to one of the cabinets and eyed the pieces on display. "First, leave me to negotiate a price . . ."

Quinn took out the envelope of banknotes and deposited it on the desk without a word.

"Second," Chen went on, "whatever Borodin tells you, pretend to believe it."

The man who entered was wearing a well-tailored tuxedo, which looked like a uniform on him. He walked erect and stiff, and his ascetic face conveyed aloof detachment. Quinn found this surprising. Gamblers fresh from a losing streak at the roulette table usually made quite a different impression.

"Good evening, Yegor," Chen Teh said. "It's a pleasure to see you out of uniform for once, and not on a matter that concerns us personally."

Yegor Borodin was standing with his hands in his jacket pockets. He removed one, and Quinn saw that it was holding two oval chips—chips of gold-lacquered sandalwood that glittered as he toyed with them. "How much do you propose to pay?" he asked.

"I know how important you are to me in your capacity as chief of police," Chen Teh said patiently, "and *you* know how quickly times can change. I hear the workers in the munitions factories have gone on strike. I hear the army is falling behind with its executions of mutineers and deserters. I hear of plans to strengthen the city's defenses. Perhaps these are merely rumors—I'm sure you know more about such things than I. You're a farsighted man, Yegor, so please sit down and speak with my friend. Then we'll agree on a price."

Borodin sat down facing Quinn on the extreme edge of his chair. The chips in his hand made a faint clicking sound. "I'm a gambler," he said, "but not suicidal. You've touched on a dangerous subject. I'll give you some advice you needn't pay for: drop it."

155

Quinn wished he had some chips to fiddle with—anything that would help to steady his hands. "Chen gave you a list of names," he said. "If you'd start with Vitov Yurovsky—"

"Have you no common sense?" Borodin snapped. "Didn't you see what happened at the bank yesterday?"

"So they were from the Cheka," Quinn said. "I *knew* it." Borodin merely stared at him.

"What did Yurovsky hope to gain by giving our rendezvous away?"

"Haven't you noticed? Frightened people do the silliest things." Borodin leaned forward, and the chips stopped clicking for a moment. "Fear is our greatest ally."

"If you'd been quicker off the mark I'd never have called on him in person," Quinn said.

"A list containing a few innocuous names? You must have known what it would lead me to."

Quinn glanced across at Chen Teh, who had retired to a chair in the corner of the room and was sitting there with his chin on his chest and his eyes shut.

"Why didn't you tell me it was really a death list? With the exception of this Chinaman, everyone on the list was taken to Cheka headquarters and haven't been heard of since. Even my friends there couldn't—or wouldn't—tell me what happened to them. The cases were handled by a special commissar from Moscow, Comrade Chaikin. Well, I said to myself, I'll be damned if I'll meddle in an affair like that. Not even Chen Teh, for all his generosity, could make it worth my while." He chuckled. "Maybe I really am a gambler by nature."

Quinn studied the man not knowing what to make of him. "But Vitov Yurovsky is still alive."

"I admire jugglers—what a knack, keeping half a dozen balls in the air at once! But even the most skillful juggler can panic. That's what happened when I called on Yurovsky. I can tell when someone's frightened, and Yurovsky was paralyzed with fear."

156

The sound of the chips was beginning to annoy Quinn. Suppressing an urge to ask Borodin to put them away, he silently counted to ten.

"He confided in me," Borodin went on, "I don't know why. Perhaps he'd simply had to keep his mouth shut too long and couldn't restrain himself. Vitov Yurovsky was a custodian of the nation's wealth. As vice-president of the Imperial Bank at St. Petersburg, he was responsible for the country's gold reserves. When Petrograd went 'Red' he performed his first juggling act: he ensured that the contents of the Imperial Bank's vaults fell into Bolshevik hands intact. That, I presume, is what saved his neck until now, giving him all of it, including the reserves of the Romanian government which were transferred there when war broke out."

"Did Yurovsky say what they were worth?"

"Five hundred million rubles—gold rubles. The ingots were stamped 'I.B.' They also bore the double eagle, the weight, and the titer."

"And they were all transferred by special train to Karmel in the Urals?"

Borodin put his chips on the desk, slid the envelope toward him, and removed the wad of high-denomination British banknotes. He counted them with the dexterity of a bank cashier, Quinn noticed, then replaced them in the envelope.

"So *that's* what interests you," he said, "the gold."

"Not only that," Quinn said. "I sometimes think it's all pure fabrication—that nothing of the kind really happened, there's no gold train, no cache of bullion. That somebody concocted the whole fantastic story to tie up a Czech division needed at the front. But no. What interests me—*really* interests me—is the truth."

"What about the dead?" Borodin demanded. "Besides, Yurovsky obtained a receipt for the gold when it was transferred. I saw it with my own eyes."

"He organized the transfer himself?"

157

"His responsibility for the consignment ceased when he handed it over—but not, of course, his fear of future repercussions."

"Do you know the name of the person who signed for it?"

Borodin looked amused. "We never trust one man alone. It's the same with our Red Guards. They have commanding officers, but every C.O. has a political commissar breathing down his neck. The train commander responsible for the transfer to Siberia was naturally accompanied by a political commissar."

"Yurovsky must have mentioned names," Quinn insisted.

"The train commander was a man named Fyodor Nikulin, the political commissar was Viktor Ryazanov."

Quinn leaned forward. "Ryazanov?"

"Yes, an interesting character—he made a name for himself during the Moscow purges. I could tell you a couple of things that might bring you to your senses. . . ."

"Our paths have already crossed."

"Then you puzzle me more and more."

"What can you tell me about this man Nikulin?"

"A combat soldier. He served in the Czarist army and became one of the few enlisted men to win the highest award for gallantry. He was active in 'seventeen—persuaded an entire sector of the front to mutiny, joined the Red Guard and fought at Petrograd, commanded an armored train that played an important part at every focal point in the war: the Kuban campaign, the advance on Tula, Kazan—wherever there were Whites to be fought. Nikulin had been selected at the highest level, so Yurovsky told me, and the transfer was delayed because he at first refused to give up his frontline command."

"How old is he?"

"I could only guess."

"No details of his background or place of origin?"

"No. Look, I've told you all I know."

Quinn eyed the chips on the desk. It was all he could do not

158

to pick them up. At last he said, "When did the gold come back to Perm?"

Borodin's look of surprise was genuine. "You thought . . ." He shook his head. "It never did. The story was a hoax. They never managed to get it out of Karmel!"

"But that's impossible. It can't be there anymore."

"I have it from an unimpeachable source. The Czechs' advance on Karmel was too swift and unexpected. The situation during August was chaotic. The battlefronts were collapsing everywhere—the Moscow authorities were paralyzed. The order to remove the gold arrived too late. All they could do was fabricate this myth that they managed to get it out in the nick of time. It was just a false trail designed to throw people off the scent—people like you."

Quinn had a mental picture of himself and Pavel Govorov surrounded by empty chests in the subterranean chamber at the Xenia Mine. So they must have had sufficient time to hide the gold elsewhere, either in or near Karmel. But how, in such quantities, and who had engineered its removal? This man Nikulin? And where did Ryazanov fit into the scheme?

He tore his eyes away from the chips. "I suppose I was a fool to fall for the story."

Borodin smiled and shrugged. "Better dumb than dead."

"What about the Englishman whose name Chen Teh mentioned to you: Tom Cutter? Any trace of him in Perm?"

Borodin rose.

"Because it's important to me to know how he died," Quinn concluded.

"Of course it is," Borodin said angrily. "Important to you and sundry other people. No. I'm sorry. None of my contacts knows where or how he died, but they'd all like to find out." He picked up the chips and put them back in his pocket. "One last piece of advice," he said. "Get out of Perm, and be quick about it!"

Borodin turned and walked to the door. He'd reached it by the time Quinn could bring himself to say, "Your money."

Borodin paused. "I sell protection, not information," Borodin said coldly, "as Chen Teh can confirm. I'm corrupt—I take bribes and wink at certain things in return. That's the system, but I didn't invent it. The world is made that way, and not even the Revolution seems to have made any difference. If you know of a better world, tell me where it is."

Quinn glanced toward the corner. Chen Teh had opened his eyes and was blinking as if the light hurt them. He rose and walked quickly across the room to the desk. Picking up the envelope, he went to Borodin and held it out. "Take the money," he insisted. "Information or no information, that was the agreement." When Borodin still didn't react, he added, "How else will you pay off your gambling debts?"

"Very well," he said. "If it'll make you feel easier in your mind, Chen, settle my debts."

He went out and closed the door behind him. Chen Teh stared at the door for several seconds, then turned and handed Quinn the envelope with a look of profound uneasiness.

"When a man like Borodin refuses payment it's best to be prepared for the worst," he said. "You must leave here as soon as possible—preferably before the night's out."

"It's only thirty-six hours to my rendezvous with that airplane I told you about."

"But they have your description," Chen said. "They'll be watching all the railroad stations, checking every train, patrolling the streets. The river's not without danger, but it's your best bet. Upstream in a boat, as far north as possible. At Gajny I may be able to find someone to take you overland to Syktyvkar, which is said to be in British hands."

"You've already done more for me than I could ever have asked of you."

"Come," Chen said abruptly, "let's go pay off his debts."

160

*   *   *

The mist had dispersed, and the ornamental shrubs in the garden looked thoroughly unreal beneath a powdering of snow. Quinn found it a relief to be out in the crisp fresh air.

The two-seater rickshaw was waiting outside in the deserted alleyway. Its black foldback roof was dusted with white, but the cobblestones were wet and glistening. The snow had melted as soon as it touched the ground.

They got in. Quinn, sinking back in his seat as the coolie picked up the shafts, heard Chen Teh's voice in his ear.

"Do you know any prayers?"

"Not many. Why?"

"Start saying them now. Pray there's a boat going north. Pray that the Kama isn't frozen upstream. Pray that I manage to contact someone at Gajny, and pray that Syktyvkar really is in British hands. . . ."

20

QUINN climbed down into the dinghy and seated himself on the thwart in the bow. Souen pushed off and the dinghy drifted clear of the junk. Through the mist, which was still veiling the river, Quinn could make out the figures of Chen Teh, Hu Long, and Pei standing amidships. Chen raised his hand and called something. Quinn didn't catch the words, but they and the gesture were clearly meant to be encouraging.

The outlines of the junk dissolved into the darkness. They were heading downstream, so Souen had little to do but steer with the oars. For a while Quinn heard nothing but the rhythmical plash of the blades dipping into the water.

The three iron spans of the railroad bridge across the Kama came into view less than ten minutes later. Souen shipped his oars and let the dinghy drift. A few feeble gaslights provided just enough illumination for Quinn to make out several sentries armed with rifles and fixed bayonets. They had clearly been reinforced and were checking all pedestrians using the walkway that ran along one side of the bridge.

The dinghy glided silently beneath the central span. Souen resumed rowing. They passed the wooden landing stage near the refugee camp and continued on their way. Then the rhythm of the oarstrokes quickened as Souen headed inshore. The unlovely outlines of a river freighter loomed up out of the mist, black smoke rising from a single smokestack.

The *Ussolye* was bigger than Quinn had expected. She regularly carried coal from a mine near Perm to Gajny, where her cargo was exchanged for flour. "That's why all the bread in Perm looks as if it's made of coal dust," Chen Teh had said, trying hard to sound jocular.

The dinghy swung around and headed upstream. Although Souen rowed with all his might, it seemed that they would be swept away downriver. He fought the current yard by yard until the red riding lights on the *Ussolye* port side reemerged from the mist and Quinn could smell smoke once more. Then the dinghy scraped the freighter's hull.

Quinn had risen and was standing in the bow, waiting for a rope to be thrown, but nothing happened. They were already drifting astern again when he saw something snake down from above. The rope splashed into the water beside him. He grabbed it and made it fast with the help of Souen, who hauled them alongside hand over hand. "Now we must wait," the Chinese boatman whispered, panting from his recent exertions.

Chen Teh had advised Quinn accordingly, so it was a needless injunction, but perhaps Souen needed to speak to calm his nerves.

"A member of the family will be expecting you—a second or third cousin." Souen's chuckle only betrayed how tense he was. "It pays to have plenty of relations."

He fell silent. The dinghy bobbed and swayed. They could not have been far from the freighter's engine, which must have been turning over declutched, because its steady pounding penetrated the hull.

After a long time there was a whistle from above. The dinghy rocked violently as Souen sprang to his feet. A rope ladder hurtled through the air and came to rest against the curving iron plates with a dull clang.

Souen whispered another needless injunction. Quinn had already gripped the rungs and was climbing up the side.

It was more of a climb than he'd thought, and he was grateful for the hand that reached down to help him aboard—the calloused hand of a stoker.

Quinn could see little of the man even when he reached the darkened deck. The shadowy figure turned at once and led the way to a narrow iron door in the stern superstructure.

The steel ladder was slippery, and Quinn had to descend it with care. Then they were in a passage faintly illuminated by a shaft of light from an open bulkhead door at the far end. Just as they reached it the freighter's engine began to cough and shudder underfoot.

The man ducked through the door first. The light came from a naked bulb on the deckhead, and its dim glow gave Quinn his first real sight of his companion. He was a Chinese with an outsize head and a bull neck. The oil and coal dust coating his face made his eyes look bigger than they were, and his chest was bursting out of a ragged, sleeveless undershirt. He looked deformed, because from the waist down his body was as slender as that of an adolescent boy.

"I go my work," he said in broken Russian. "You stay here. No move."

"Thank you."

The Chinese paused in the doorway. "No move," he repeated. "I come when possible."

"Why should I move?" Quinn said, studiously nonchalant. "I'm feeling quite at home already."

The hinges of the bulkhead door squealed as the Chinese closed it behind him. Quinn surveyed his surroundings. The compartment was little more than a locker used for storing unwanted items: cans of paint, drums of lubricating oil, odd lengths of rope. The iron walls were rusty, and lying on the floor were a dirty old mattress and a tattered blanket.

The noises from the engine room increased in volume. Quinn felt the deck beneath him begin to vibrate, then gently sway as the *Ussolye* left her moorings. His tension subsided. The compartment was warm and stuffy. He unbuckled the belt around his sheepskin coat, took the heavy garment off, and laid it on top of the blanket. The clothing and false papers supplied by Chen Teh identified him as a Russian river pilot.

He probably wouldn't be able to sleep, but the best thing he could do was rest and build up his strength. The *Ussolye*'s first port of call would be Berezniki, sixteen hours upstream.

He looked around for a light switch but failed to find one, so he reached for the bulb and unscrewed it, burning his fingers in the process. Somehow the reality of the pain was almost consoling. Now that it was dark he noticed a porthole just above the waterline on the freighter's starboard side. Wavelets were slopping against the glass, but he could make out the faint glow of Perm receding astern.

He stretched out on the mattress with his coat beneath him. The rhythmical pounding of the ship's engine drowned all other sounds. It had a soporific quality, like a steady heartbeat.

He shut his eyes, and a series of faces paraded before him in quick succession: Sednev the old hunter, Rice and Fitzmaurice, Hollis and Katov at Omsk; Scala and Davis, Diatsaro and Govorov, Wajda and Ryazanov at Karmel; Katov again, Chen

Teh, Pei, Yurovsky, Borodin . . . All these and other nameless faces flashed past at lightning speed. Not even Moura Toumanova's image lingered long enough for him to bring it into focus.

And then it was over. The mental picture show ended, and he got the feeling that none of its subjects really existed—that they were all figments of his imagination, products of an overtaxed nervous system.

Something in his immediate surroundings had changed: his closed eyelids were suffused with light. He opened them. A beam of light was playing on the storeroom wall. Then it vanished. He couldn't tell at first what it meant.

The light returned. It slanted down through the porthole and glided along the wall. He lay there with bated breath until it disappeared again. The next moment he was startled by something else: the rhythm of the freighter's engine had also changed. It faltered and slowed until the *Ussolye* seemed to be proceeding at a snail's pace.

He got up and groped his way to the porthole. Nothing but darkness and mist—nothing that would have accounted for the light. He was just about to turn away when he glimpsed the outlines of a river gunboat. It lost way until it was steaming parallel to the freighter. Two spotlights mounted on the deck-house were probing the gloom. When one of them traversed the porthole again, its beam stabbed his eyes like a knife.

The *Ussolye* was almost motionless now, and he wondered if it had dropped anchor. The gunboat was so close he could make out the pom-poms on the foredeck. They were trained on the freighter. A man in uniform was standing at the rail with a megaphone in his hand, addressing someone on the freighter's bridge.

He moved away from the porthole. Moments later he felt a jolt as the gunboat came alongside.

The longer he waited and listened, the more unbearable the darkness around him became. Even the stench of paint and oil seemed more intense. It was all he could do to breathe, as if he'd exhausted all the oxygen in the cramped little compartment. Footsteps and muffled voices were audible overhead.

He made his way to the door and cautiously opened it. The passage was in darkness. He tiptoed along it, feeling better now that he was at least doing something.

At the foot of the companionway he paused to listen. The sound of footsteps and voices had ceased. He waited for the freighter to get under way again, but nothing happened. Then, step by step, he climbed the ladder.

He reached the top and went on deck, sucking in deep breaths of cold, damp air. River mist and falling snow blurred the outlines of everything around him. Only the wheelhouse, which was caught in the beams of the gunboat's spotlights, stood out clearly. Two men, one of them Chinese, were standing beside the rail, but their voices were almost drowned by the gurgle of water lapping along the freighter's sides and the subdued murmur of the engine as it maintained just enough to keep her heading upstream.

Securely lashed to the deck in Quinn's immediate vicinity were a number of crates. Using them as cover, Quinn made his way forward to the foot of the wheelhouse steps. The men's voices became more audible. They were speaking Russian, and he began to pick out individual words.

"Coal, that's all I'm carrying," said one of the voices, evidently the captain's.

"Someone in Perm doesn't like you, it seems," said the other voice.

"Guns? You'll find nothing but coal on board! Who's been spreading such a rumor?"

So that was it! The outbound freighter had been stopped because someone had tipped off the river police that she was gunrunning.

Quinn abruptly lost interest in the two men's conversation. From behind him came sounds of movement, shouts, footsteps. Drawing his Browning, he flipped the safety catch and held it close at his side.

Then he saw a panic-stricken figure racing toward him. It was the Chinese stoker who had helped him aboard and taken him below. He hissed something Quinn didn't catch, seized his arm, dragged him along by main force.

They hadn't gone more than a few yards when a voice hailed them. Almost simultaneously, a single shot rang out. The stoker's viselike grip relaxed. His fingers went limp and he toppled forward. Quinn caught a momentary glimpse of the man's broad back and the frightful dumdum wound between his shoulder blades, a mess of bloody flesh and shredded undershirt.

Figures suddenly materialized from everywhere. Quinn saw flashlights bobbing, heard raucous shouts behind and on either side of him. Although instinct told him to surrender and rely on his false papers, he was given no chance to do so.

They charged him. He went reeling with the impact of the first man, but managed to regain his balance and raise the gun. Another man caromed into him as he pulled the trigger, and the shot was followed by a cry. Breaking away for a moment, he made for the rail.

They caught up with him before he could reach it. Something hit him on the head. He dropped the gun and fell to his knees, arms raised to protect himself, but his reactions were too slow. The next blow was even harder. Blood ran down his forehead and into his eyes.

He no longer had the strength to defend himself. He knew he was not far from the rail. He had to get to it somehow. . . . He started to crawl on hands and knees, only to be flattened by another blow. A boot thudded into his side, hands turned him over on his back, a flashlight blinded him. He heard a babble of triumphant voices, but the only word that penetrated his brain was *"Anglichanin!"* He was unconscious by the time they picked him up.

21

EVERYTHING was rocking and swaying. Quinn drew a deep breath and struggled to open his eyes. The pain was excruciating. He felt sick, and he'd never been seasick in his life, never had such an agonizing headache. He instinctively tried to clasp his brow but found he couldn't move his hands.

It dawned on him that his wrists were handcuffed behind his back, and that he wasn't alone. He could feel two bodies hemming him in, one on either side. He also realized that he wasn't aboard the *Ussolye* anymore: he was lying on a stretcher in the back of an ambulance.

Again he struggled to open his eyes. It was an almost superhuman effort, and not only because of the pain; his eyelids were stuck together as if someone had gummed them shut.

He gave an involuntary groan. One of the men beside him drove a fist into his ribs. The other laughed and said, "Leave some for Comrade Yanson."

He didn't invite another blow by trying to move again, just lay there wondering what had happened to his eyes. For the moment, that worried him more than anything else.

They seemed to have reached their destination at last, because the ambulance pulled up with a jerk. The two men lifted him bodily off the stretcher and bundled him outside. His eyes opened a crack, and he found to his relief that he could still see, though his vision was temporarily blurred. He was in a paved courtyard enclosed by a building with tall windows, all of them brightly illuminated. A dozen or more uniformed men came crowding around as if they'd been expecting him.

168

His guards seized him by the arms and hustled him up the steps. Someone flung the door open, someone else prodded him in the back. He was in a spacious corridor with doors on both sides and rows of coat hooks between them. A school? They thrust him through one of the doors at the far end.

It was a classroom with gray walls. There were no desks or benches, just a single chair in the middle, and seated on it was a man. The guards shoved Quinn forward until he was standing in front of him.

He had difficulty keeping his balance, and his vision was still blurred. The man rose, a uniformed figure with a holster on his hip, the belt so tight that it made him look wasp-waisted. Something about him rang a bell.

He gave an order. Quinn heard hurried footsteps and the slam of a door. Nothing more happened until the footsteps returned and he felt someone swab his face with a wet cloth. He now had a clearer view of the man confronting him: close-cropped hair, deepset eyes. It was the Cheka officer who had examined his papers at the station.

"Remember me, Mr. Red Cross?" The man raised his hand and slapped Quinn's face—lightly, more to humiliate than hurt him. "You thought you could give us the slip, eh, you little bastard?" He sat down again. "Let's start with your name. Your *real* name."

Quinn tried to look at him squarely. He had strange eyes. The irises resembled amber beads with trapped insects deputizing for pupils.

"Don't make things difficult," he said softly. "I guarantee you won't last two minutes."

Quinn was determined not to be provoked.

The man rolled his eyes wearily. "Another tough one. Why do I always get the heroes?" He sighed, obviously experienced in such matters, so experienced that he had no doubts who would get his way in the end. "Your name," he repeated.

"Achim Lundeberg."

169

Quinn looked past him. The far wall still bore a blackboard, and above it was a crucifix that the new occupants had omitted to remove.

The man sat back and nodded to the guards who had marched Quinn in. "Get busy," he said casually. "Don't mark his face though."

His wrists being handcuffed behind his back, Quinn was powerless to take evasive action. When he fell to the floor under this hail of blows, one of the men hauled him to his feet and held him while the other went on punching him. He sank to the floor again, and this time they used their boots. He closed his eyes.

When they stopped he maneuvered himself into a kneeling position, tried to get up, and finally succeeded. His whole body ached.

"Now, what's your name?"

"Lundeberg." He could hardly get the word out.

"Stop lying, you British scum! We know who you are."

"Why ask me, then?"

The man's tone changed. "This isn't a girls' school anymore, so be sensible. You're dealing with the Cheka. More importantly, you're dealing with me, Vassily Yanson. If you think that's the worst we can do to you, you're wrong."

Quinn wasn't sure how much more pain he could take. To gain time he said, "You won't get another word out of me till you remove these handcuffs."

Yanson jumped up and punched him full in the face. Quinn staggered back. He tasted blood in his mouth.

"Your name is Quinn, Oliver Quinn, you son of a bitch. Now talk! How did you get to Perm?"

For a moment Quinn almost welcomed the shock of surprise because it took his mind off the pain. How could they have discovered his name? He hadn't mentioned it to anyone, not even Chen Teh.

170

"My name is Achim Lundeberg. I'm a member of the Swedish Mission."

"Of course, that's why you went into hiding as soon as you got here. Where, exactly?"

"Various places," he said.

Yanson's tone changed once more. "All I want are some names. Who helped you? Who harbored you the whole time? Who got you a berth on the *Ussolye*? Give me their names and I'll leave you in peace."

"I don't remember any names. I stayed in brothels—they don't ask for your papers there."

Yanson lit a cigarette. "Look, are you going to answer my questions or not?"

"Take off these handcuffs."

Yanson jammed the cigarette in the corner of his mouth. "All right," he said, "give the swine a bath."

The full significance of these words eluded Quinn at first, but his body must have grasped it. Even before the guards could seize him and drag him out of the room, fear coursed through his veins like an electric shock.

They hustled him out of the classroom and along the corridor, then down some stairs to the basement and along another corridor. Opening a door, they thrust him into a gloomy cellar. He fell headlong on the flagstones. The stench almost made him vomit. As his eyes became accustomed to the subdued light he made out a circular wooden tub with three men beside it, one holding an oxhide whip.

Two of them pinned him down while the third removed his shoes, socks, and trousers. They had to unlock his handcuffs to divest him of his coat and shirt. Although he knew it was futile, he hurled himself at them. The whip whistled through the air. He heard a scream go echoing around the walls without realizing that the voice was his. They handcuffed him again as before. The oxhide had bitten deep into his wrist, and the searing pain was so intense that he didn't even feel the cold as he stood there naked in front of the brimming tub. Then a hand shoved him in the back. He staggered forward, collided with the tub, and jackknifed, involuntarily kicking up his heels like a frisky horse. The hand gripped his neck and forced his head under water.

He shut his mouth and held his breath. His head swelled to bursting point. There was a roaring sound in his ears. He panicked: he opened his mouth and gasped, but all he inhaled was water. The hand relaxed its grip. He surfaced, coughing and spluttering. The hand thrust him under again and held him there. . . .

He wasn't even aware that they'd hauled him out and stood him on his feet. He retched and vomited a stream of water, but he wasn't aware of that either. Someone was panting hoarsely like an animal. Then he realized that the sound was coming from his own lips—that he hadn't drowned after all. Just as he was beginning to hope that his tormentors had finished with him, they forced his head under again. This time he hadn't the strength to resist. He sucked in water at once, conscious that he was near to drowning.

He was lying stretched out on a stone floor, simultaneously shivering and burning up with fever. His mouth was parched, and the very intensity of his thirst jogged his memory. He started to retch and gasp as if drowning once more. His aches and pains returned too, charting the point of impact of every punch and kick, and his wrist seemed to be enclosed by a bracelet of red-hot iron.

Alone in the darkness, he realized that he was fully dressed again and not wearing handcuffs. He crawled across the floor until he encountered a wall. He couldn't have said how long it took him to haul himself erect, but he finally made it and stood there leaning against the wall before forcing himself to totter along it. Then, mustering all his strength, he crossed the cell unaided. His head was swimming by the time he reached the other side, but he felt a glow of satisfaction.

He forbade himself to think of what had happened and, more particularly, of what might happen next. He knew he wouldn't be able to withstand further torture, and he knew there was only one way of escaping it: the cyanide capsule.

He felt for his money belt, and realized it was missing. The realization jolted him badly.

Sometime later, when the door was unlocked and they came to fetch him, he knew it beyond doubt: his fear was such that he would answer each and every question they asked.

22

THE guards marched him to a chair and sat him down. For Quinn, nothing existed but the desk in front of him. On it, in the cone of light cast by the lamp, lay the things that had been taken from him: the Browning, the forged papers given him by Fitzmaurice, and the money belt.

"Here's your prisoner, Comrade Chaikin."

It was Yanson, the amber-eyed, crew-cut Cheka officer who had ordered his "bath." Quinn froze, sickened by the very sound of his voice.

"Will you be needing me anymore, Comrade?"

Yanson's question was addressed to a man standing at the only window, staring out with his hands clasped behind his back. It was still dark, though a few gray streaks in the sky suggested that dawn was not far off.

The man slowly turned. He was slim, with flaxen hair and an oval, clean-shaven face so effeminately handsome that a woman might have envied it. He glanced at Quinn.

"I thought I told you not to work him over."

173

"That was just a modest beginning, Comrade."

Chaikin strode briskly up to Yanson and prodded him in the chest with his forefinger. "You disgust me!" he said.

Yanson bowed his head. His gray face turned still grayer but remained expressionless.

Quinn was entirely unreassured. He was still feeling sick enough to vomit at any moment, and every painful breath suggested that he had cracked several ribs. He sat bolt upright on his chair for fear of falling.

"Are all your things there?" Chaikin indicated the desk.

"As far as I can tell."

"What about the money?" Chaikin opened the flaps of the cloth belt, emptied the various pockets, and made three piles of banknotes: pounds sterling, U.S. dollars, rubles. "Any idea how much you had on you?"

Although there was nothing to be gained by such a futile gesture, Quinn's desire for revenge was so overwhelming that he couldn't resist it. He told the truth where the pounds and dollars were concerned but multiplied the number of rubles by ten.

Chaikin had already started counting the banknotes. At length he turned to Yanson and thrust the wad of rubles under his nose. "Where are the rest?" he demanded.

"The bastard's lying! He's lying, Comrade, I give you my—" Yanson broke off as Chaikin slapped his face with the money, twice in quick succession.

"Now get out," Chaikin said.

"The filthy swine—"

Chaikin hit him again. Yanson's jaw dropped. He raised his hand, and for one moment Quinn thought he was going to return the blow, but he only clasped his cheek with trembling fingers. He was still clasping it as he turned and strode from the room.

Chaikin leaned back against the desk. "I apologize for his

174

conduct," he said. "I wasn't here, and they informed me too late. How are you feeling? Shall I call a doctor?"

Quinn couldn't raise a reply. It wasn't just the pain. He was still too dazed to think straight, so he merely shook his head.

"What's the matter with your hand?"

The skin was hanging in strips where the plaited leather had curled around Quinn's wrist. The blood had clotted, but the wound looked ugly and he'd tried to conceal it.

"Yanson had orders not to touch you." There was a wash-bowl on the other side of the room. Chaikin produced a clean handkerchief from his pocket, moistened it under the faucet, and wrung it out.

Quinn took the handkerchief and wound it around his lacerated wrist. It hurt even more for a moment, but he was glad of the makeshift dressing. Chaikin had gone over to a small table with a samovar and some tea things on it. He filled a glass and came back.

Quinn felt thirsty and feverish. A big stove burning in the corner of the room made the atmosphere hot and stuffy. It was a former classroom from which the blackboard and cruci-fix had been removed, and the wall behind the desk was adorned with a map. He took the cup and drank. He had to gain time.

"You needn't get your hopes up," Quinn said, taking the cup. He found it hard to swallow, and there was a stabbing pain in his chest.

Chaikin waited in silence. Then he took the empty glass, replaced it on the table, and sat down at his desk. The desk light was shining in Quinn's eyes. Chaikin moved it aside.

"How are you feeling now? Ready to talk?"

"I refuse to give you any names!"

Chaikin ran a hand through his flaxen hair. "Yanson is a birdbrained idiot!" he said. "If it'll set your mind at rest, I'm not interested in any names."

Quinn couldn't help feeling relieved, but he simultaneously

175

resisted the sensation. "Is this your usual technique?" he demanded. "First the iron fist, then the velvet glove?"

"All I want is a quiet chat." Chaikin studied him intently from across the desk. "Just now you implied that Comrade Yanson had helped himself to your money. It was a lie, wasn't it?"

"He didn't touch the money," Quinn said, estimating that it didn't really matter whether he admitted it or not.

"I thought as much, and it told me a lot about you. I said to myself: Here's a man who's prepared to take a risk." Chaikin paused. "You risked a landing behind our lines and sneaked into Perm, a Bolshevik stronghold. Why? Why did you take such a risk?"

Quinn would gladly have replied, given that nothing would happen to him while they were still talking, but he didn't have an answer ready. He said nothing.

Chaikin pointed to the things on the desk. "This is enough to convict you," he said in a calm, matter-of-fact tone. He removed the cyanide capsule from the money belt. "Even your employers must have known that you risked being shot as a spy."

"All it proves is that no one cherishes any illusions about the Cheka's methods."

Chaikin weighed the capsule in his hand. "Would you really use this thing?"

"I might. Are you offering to give it back to me?"

"You still haven't answered my question, Mr. Quinn. Why did you run such a risk? You're a geologist, not an agent."

"Why ask if you know so much?"

"How much did Major Fitzmaurice offer you?"

"Who's he?"

"I'm trying to fathom your motives. Did Fitzmaurice offer you a share—say twenty percent of all the gold recovered?"

"I don't know what you're talking about."

Chaikin laid the capsule aside. Opening a desk drawer, he

produced several sheaves of typescript and held one out. "Run your eye over that."

Quinn took the sheets and leafed through them—awkwardly, because of his injured wrist. They bore nothing but column after column of figures. More precisely, each figure consisted of two Cyrillic characters followed by four digits. "What's this?" he asked, trying to look blank.

"The serial numbers of the bars—the gold reserves of the former Imperial Bank." Chaikin took the sheets back. "The list came from Vitov Yurovsky. You may assume that it's correct and complete." As though simply stating a fact, he added, "Your job was to steal that bullion."

"Why should I steal the late czar's property?" Quinn suddenly found it pointless to prevaricate any longer.

"You considered it your patriotic duty to . . . salvage it, shall we say, on Britain's behalf?"

"Why not?"

"Would you credit me with a similar motive? We're both simply trying to do our job. You want the gold for Britain, I for Soviet Russia. That's our problem."

Quinn detected a certain hesitation in Chaikin's manner. "That's *your* problem, you mean. If your approach doesn't work you'll have to turn me back over to men like Yanson."

Chaikin rose, went again to the window and looked out.

The gray light of dawn was stronger now. Quinn ached all over and could scarcely hold his head up, he was so weary. He glanced at the desk. The cyanide capsule was nowhere to be seen, but his pistol, the snub-nosed Browning, was almost within reach. He leaned forward. Chaikin, possibly alerted by the creak of his chair, turned and walked back to the desk.

"Oh, yes," he said in a cool, businesslike tone, "you could always shoot me and then shoot yourself, but what would that solve?" He indicated the wall map. "How near were you to finding the gold?"

"Near enough," Quinn said.

"And then you fell for their story—that they'd managed to get it out at the last minute?"

"Yes, damn it, though I ought to have known it was just a ruse." The knowledge that the gold was still in Karmel had restored some of Quinn's self-confidence.

"Did you come across Viktor Ryazanov?"

"Avarice isn't a capitalist monopoly," Quinn said. "It's quite possible that neither of us will ever see that gold. It'll wind up neither in the vaults of the Bank of England nor in those of the Bank of Moscow. Ryazanov has acquired two partners worthy of him, a Czech general and an American RTO. They've suddenly all decided that Russia is the land of opportunity."

"They'll have to find the gold before I do, of course."

Quinn was too surprised to grasp the full significance of this remark at once. Had he heard aright? Was Chaikin really ignorant of the bullion's present whereabouts? He remained silent in the certainty that Chaikin would say more. The Russian adjusted the desk light so that it illuminated the map on the wall.

"Come over here and take a look."

Quinn struggled to his feet. It was all he could do to keep his balance, and every step was agony. Once at Chaikin's side he saw that the map was a general staff map of the Karmel area.

"The gold was stored in the Xenia Mine." Chaikin pointed to the spot. "Was it gone by the time you got there?"

"Empty chests were all I saw." The words slipped out before Quinn could stop himself.

"Does the name Nikulin mean anything to you—Fyodor Nikulin?"

"Yes."

"You know he commanded the train in which the bullion was transferred to the Urals?"

"I was told so, yes."

"But you never tracked him down?"

"No." Quinn sensed that his position had improved—that the cards in his hand were worth more than he'd thought.

"Viktor Ryazanov was Nikulin's political commissar," Chaikin went on. "They could only make decisions jointly. When it became clear that the Czechs' rapid and unexpected advance would give them no time to ship the gold out of Karmel by train, they concocted a plan together: they would pretend they'd managed to do just that. In reality, the gold was transferred to another spot in the mountains. Nikulin had less than thirty-six hours in which to shift it. It was Ryazanov's job to remain in Karmel and gain the new masters' trust by surrendering the place without a fight."

"Except that he developed capitalist inclinations," Quinn said.

Chaikin looked at him. "The problem isn't Ryazanov, it's Nikulin." He tapped the map again. "This is where the new cache was supposed to be sited, on the far side of Two Brothers Pass, but when Ryazanov tried to reestablish contact with Nikulin later on, there was no sign of him or the gold. Nikulin had evidently decided not to trust anyone, Ryazanov included, so he chose another spot altogether."

"I can understand the impulse," Quinn said dryly.

Chaikin gestured at the map. "You're familiar with the area—you worked there as a geologist—and you also know how much bullion was involved. Where could Nikulin have hidden it?"

"If I'd had the least idea do you think I'd ever have come to Perm?"

"He didn't have many helpers," Chaikin went on imperviously. "So that limits his radius of action. He must have used mules to transport the gold, which also rules out certain sites, and he didn't have time to bury it. The probability is, he concealed it in another derelict mine."

Quinn stared at the map with sudden fascination. The more he studied Karmel's complex topography, the more con-

179

vinced he became that Chaikin was right. Nikulin would have had only a limited number of places in which to conceal such a quantity of gold. Quinn wondered if a map existed showing the location of all the old abandoned mines in the district.

Chaikin was looking at him intently. "It's possible, isn't it?" he said. "Knowing that it hasn't left the Karmel area, you'd find it sooner or later, wouldn't you?

"But you had a predecessor, a compatriot of yours named Cutter. Wasn't he convinced that she held the key? I'm sure your friend succeeded in gaining her confidence."

Quinn suddenly felt the same old jealousy he'd felt when Cutter—the living Cutter—had made passes at Catherine. How could he be jealous of a dead man? It was absurd, but that was what he felt: jealousy and savage hatred. Once again that man was like a shadow between him and a woman.

"If she trusted Cutter," he said, "why did he die?"

"Not knowing what happened, I can't say. I only know that months have gone by since then. Moura Toumanova may think differently now—she may regret what happened. What have you got to lose by accepting my offer?"

Quinn wondered what choice he had but to go along with the proposal, if only outwardly.

Chaikin leaned across his desk. "Listen! I can protect you from the attentions of Yanson and his like, at least temporarily, but I myself am subject to certain pressures. The gold was already lost when I was given this assignment, so I do have some freedom to maneuver, but don't forget that Moscow expects results!" For the first time, a vehement note had crept into the Russian's voice. "Our armies can abandon whole provinces, lose a dozen battles, absorb a hundred thousand casualties, but we can't dispense with that gold—not that gold, Quinn! We will stop at nothing, absolutely nothing, to get it back. I'm convinced Yanson's methods will get us nowhere in this instance—luckily for you. But if I'm to maintain control of my command—and your life—I need your cooperation."

"Who informed you I was on board the *Ussolye?*"

"I could claim that the Cheka is omniscient and leave it at that. The truth is, somebody tipped us off that the *Ussolye* was gunrunning. It was a routine search. If you hadn't been so careless . . ."

"What exactly would you expect me to do?"

"We'll sneak you through the lines. You'll then make your way back to Karmel and get in touch with the Toumanova woman. You'll try to persuade her to reveal where the gold is hidden. You'll be provided with facilities for transmitting that information to me. Thereafter you'll be free to do as you please. It'll mean betraying your trust, I know. Perhaps you'd like time to think it over. . . ."

"This is all too simple," Quinn said. "What makes you think I won't renege?"

Chaikin fixed him with a steady gaze. "I wouldn't rely on your word alone, of course. You might forget all about our agreement as soon as we released you, and that's a risk I can't afford to take. If you do back out, someone else will have to die in your place."

Quinn looked on impassively as Chaikin picked up the phone. The prevailing tension was perceptible in the Russian's voice. "Has he arrived? Good, bring him in. . . ."

They sat there in silence, listening for the sound of approaching footsteps. The footsteps came, followed by a knock at the door. Chaikin seemed engrossed in his own thoughts. The knock was repeated. At last, in an expressionless voice, he said, "Come in."

23

I T was him and it wasn't. Quinn stared at the pitiful figure in the baggy prison uniform, wondering if it could really be Alexander Katov.

"Your prisoner, Comrade."

The guards thrust him forward. Wrists manacled, head sagging on his chest, Katov stumbled and nearly fell. He seemed unaware of Quinn's presence.

Nothing happened for a moment. Quinn couldn't bring himself to speak. Chaikin, looking pale and somehow puzzled, as if he'd envisaged the scene quite differently, stared straight through the prisoner.

"Alexander . . ." Quinn found it an effort to utter the name at all.

Katov slowly raised his head. The dull, apprehensive eyes swiveled in Quinn's direction. Quinn repeated the name, unsure if Katov had recognized him. The eyes in the haggard face came to life, but they were devoid of hope.

Quinn sprang to his feet, ignoring all pain, mindful only of the gun on the desk. He hoped to hell it was still loaded.

He made a dive for it. His fingers closed around the grip, but that was the most he could manage. He heard shouts and running feet behind him. A hand grasped his wrist and a sharp pain shot up his arm. The gun slipped from his grasp. He was stooping to retrieve it when something hit him on the back of the head.

He cried out. The reverberations of the cry seemed to shatter his skull, the walls around him abruptly heeled over sideways. He felt himself falling, falling, and was unconscious by the time he hit the floor.

* * *

He seemed to be in a moving vehicle. Was it just a continuation of the same nightmare? What with the ring of fire around his wrist and the agonizing pains in his head and maltreated body, he found it hard to concentrate. He had to do something, but what?

He wanted to rub his eyes but found that he was handcuffed again. Slowly, he began to remember. Turning his head, he made out a figure beside him.

"Katov?"

A voice answered him, but why from so far away? "What happened?" he asked.

They were thrown together as the vehicle rounded a bend. Quinn became aware of the stench emanating from his companion's body.

"Where are they taking us?"

Katov was sitting huddled up beside him, silent and apathetic. Quinn nudged him. "Say something! What happened?"

The Russian raised his head at last. His face looked gray in the half-light. "I . . . I gave you away," he said in a faltering voice.

"Just tell me what happened."

"They made me talk, don't you understand?"

"It doesn't matter."

"It was all I had to cling to—the hope that they hadn't found you, and now . . ."

"How did they take you prisoner?"

Katov looked down at his manacled hands. He was fighting back the tears, and Quinn had to look away. He could see through a barred window in the van's rear door that they were driving along a deserted street in the first light of dawn. It occurred to him that he and Katov might be separated when they reached their destination, so he said, "What happened to your machine?"

"I had to make a forced landing not long after I dropped

you. The struts and stays iced up—they were giving way . . ."
Katov gave him a sidelong glance. "I should have dived into
the ground, but I thought I'd make it. . . ." He laughed
insanely. "I landed right in the middle of them. It's my fault
they caught you."

"Stop tormenting yourself."

"I gave away the landing place. Is that where they picked
you up?"

Quinn struggled to collect his thoughts. "No, our rendezvous wasn't till tomorrow."

"Tomorrow? I've lost track of days. . . ."

"Who interrogated you? Chaikin?"

"I thought they were going to shoot me."

"Look," Quinn entreated, trying to keep the man talking,
"whatever you told them, my capture had nothing to do with
it."

"I don't believe you."

"Give it a rest, for Christ's sake! What's more to the point
is, where are they taking us?"

Katov didn't reply.

"A prison?"

"That's what they call it. It's in the city, near the waterfront.
It's where they take you for questioning. You'd better be
prepared for the worst. . . ."

Quinn sensed the effort it had cost Katov to speak at all. His
own head was still aching violently. Worse than the pain it
caused him, however, was Katov's apathy. It was an effluvium
more repellent than anything given off by the Russian's prison
uniform. He told himself that his chances of survival would be
nil if he allowed himself to become infected with Katov's
abject resignation. So far, of course, he himself had withstood
only one interrogation. . . .

He tore his mind away from the thought and began to take
note of their surroundings. Getting up off the wooden bench,
he pressed his face against the barred rear window. The sky

184

resembled a sheet of crumpled gray paper, and their route was now flanked by warehouses. Once, as they passed a sidestreet, he thought he caught a glimpse of leaden water and the misty outlines of some sails. The river's proximity made his pulse race.

They drove on. The van slowed to a stop. Voices could be heard, followed by the sound of a gate opening. The van moved off again, and he saw that they had entered a courtyard enclosed by high walls with watchtowers at each corner. Tripod-mounted machine guns were visible beneath their flat roofs.

Guards surrounded the vehicle as it pulled up with a jerk. The rear door was flung open. Orders rent the air. Katov, who had scrambled to his feet, got out at once. Quinn, slower to move, was seized and dragged to the ground.

"Get up, *Anglichanin!* On your feet!"

A building like a stone cube loomed up in front of him, gray and windowless. When he turned to see what had happened to Katov a guard prodded him in the back with his rifle butt.

"Keep moving!" The man laughed. "It's your last chance for some exercise. Better make the most of it."

Four of them hemmed him in as they made their way along echoing passages and down stone stairways. Even in his present bemused state Quinn noticed a difference in attitude between these men and Yanson's. Theirs was not the naked brutality with which Yanson's minions had treated him. It was a contrast whose significance dawned on him all too soon. Brutality was superfluous in "the Box," as the converted grain silo was popularly known. Kept in solitary confinement and cut off from the outside world, the inmates came to regard death as something more to be desired than feared.

24

H E stood beside the cell door and listened, shivering with cold, before continuing on his way. From the door to the opposite wall, then to the corner, then diagonally across the cell. He was grateful for any variation. Darkness was no handicap. He knew precisely when to skirt his bed and avoid the corner reserved for the stinking bucket in which he relieved himself.

The earth floor of the underground cell had been softened by his endless perambulations, but a film of ice was beginning to form in places. He trudged on regardless until, becoming dizzy, he sat down to rest on the palliasse covering the planks that served as a bed. Then he compelled himself to perform his next exercise: he stood up and flapped his arms until he felt a trifle warmer.

The dim light above the cell door came on. He went over and scratched another mark on the wall with a sliver of bone saved from one of his meals. His calendar told him that this was the forty-second day. He didn't know what day of the week it was, only that it must be late December.

He returned to the door and strained his ears for the footsteps that would soon be heard when the guards brought his daily ration. He'd become inured to the lack of daylight but not to the silence. Many were the times he'd knelt with his ear to the wall, hoping to establish contact with a fellow prisoner, but the cells on either side were unoccupied. All that marked the passage of another day was the sound of approaching footsteps and the opening of the door.

More than once during the first week he'd been roused in the middle of the night and taken by car to Cheka headquarters. Chaikin hadn't threatened him in any way, just offered him a glass of tea and repeated his proposition. He seemed to take it for granted that time was on his side. Hard as it was to have to return to his cell afterward, Quinn had welcomed those interruptions because they helped to convince him that the world outside "the Box" still existed. And then his visits to Chaikin had ceased. . . .

He heard the guards' footsteps in the passage, heard the rattle of the food wagon, and fetched the tin bowl he kept at the foot of his bed. Bolts were drawn and a key grated in the lock. One of the men dipped his ladle in an iron caldron, filled Quinn's bowl with hot soup, and handed him a hunk of gray bread bristling with chopped straw. A second guard stood to one side with his rifle at the ready, looking on impassively.

Quinn had tried at first to engage them in conversation, but they never replied. He'd yelled at them in an attempt to provoke them, but without success. They simply slammed the door in his face.

He resumed his place on the bed with the tattered blanket draped around his shoulders. He broke off bits of bread and dropped them into the unidentifiable liquid, from which foul-smelling steam was rising. It was still an effort to get the mush down, even now, but he forced himself to linger over every mouthful. His determination not to give up was all he had left.

Eat! he commanded himself. Don't get lethargic! Keep up those walks around the cell! Do your exercises! Keep your calendar up to date! If he wanted to leave this filthy hole alive and see Moura Toumanova again, he couldn't afford to become inactive.

Most of the time he succeeded. He resisted the temptation to let things slide even though he sometimes felt he was deceiving himself: he would never leave this dungeon alive— even the guards would forget about him, fail to reappear, leave him to die like a dog at the bottom of a well—

That thought was like a recurrent alarm signal. He rose to his feet and set off, counting his steps aloud. One complete circuit amounted to sixteen paces: four plus two plus two (around the bucket), plus five plus three (to allow for the bed). And around again: four plus two plus two plus five plus three.

25

H E had no idea if it was day or night. The sound that had roused him from his torpor reminded him of a winter thunderstorm, but winter and the cold were his constant preoccupation. Although he was shivering all over, he couldn't raise the energy to sit up. The cell was like a refrigerator, and his clothes and the thin blanket offered scant protection.

The frost that coated the walls had begun at ground level and crept higher every day. In the end the white film reached the scratch marks on the wall and obliterated them. He'd abandoned his calendar days ago.

Again he heard the rumbling sound, and this time he forced himself to sit up. Straining his ears, he thought he heard the clang of cell doors, words of command, distant footsteps.

Panic overcame him. He jumped up, grabbed his tin bowl, dashed to the iron door and hammered on it. He yelled until his voice failed. He'd already given up hope but was still hammering away when the door swung open. They weren't the usual guards; these were soldiers armed with rifles and fixed bayonets. One of them smirked at him.

"You're in a hell of a hurry to die," he sneered.

The warehouse resembled an immense, overcrowded cage. It was thronged with hundreds of prisoners, ragged figures with faces so gaunt that their eyes looked grotesquely large. Ripples

188

of alarm and apprehension traveled the length of the building, filling the air with successive waves of sound.

A row of high windows ran along one side of the warehouse. The lower halves were encrusted with snow, and more snow was drifting down out of a gunmetal sky. Again Quinn heard the distant thunder, which had now become more or less continuous. It sounded to him like an artillery barrage, but he banished the thought for fear of kindling his hopes in vain. He wanted to think calmly.

He'd set off at once in search of Alexander Katov, but progress was slow and his inquiries went unanswered. He was still struggling through the throng, step by step, when he heard someone call his name and caught sight of Katov standing under a window. Quinn scarcely recognized him, he was such a bag of skin and bones. Wondering what he himself must look like, he fought his way over to the window. The rumble of gunfire was growing steadily louder. He gripped Katov's arm. "Alexander, thank God you're still alive! Any idea what's going on?"

Katov seemed barely able to formulate a reply, but to Quinn, starved of conversation for so many weeks, it seemed immensely important that someone should answer him. "What's the date today?" he asked.

A weary smile flickered across Katov's face. "It must be nearly Christmas. Somebody's thought up a present for us."

The windowpanes overhead rattled in response to a muffled detonation. Almost simultaneously, voices started bellowing orders.

"Everyone outside, quick!"

The mass of ragged figures began to move. After a few steps Quinn and Katov were caught up in their midst and swept along. The prisoners ahead of them slowed to a crawl as they crowded toward the exit. The bellowed orders increased in volume and stridency. Guards stationed on either side of the door were hitting out with their rifle butts.

189

And then they were outside on an expanse of open ground illuminated by searchlights. Snowflakes were still drifting down and the air was bitterly cold, but Quinn drew it deep into his lungs with a sense of liberation.

"Halt! You, *Anglichanin*, halt!"

A guard barred his path and thrust him to one side. Quinn tried to push past him, anxious not to lose sight of Katov and become separated from the rest. A second guard came to the aid of the first. They both leveled their rifles.

"It's all right, let him alone!"

The voice came from beside him. Swinging around, he saw Chaikin in a fur-lined greatcoat with the collar turned up. His oval face looked more than usually pale in the glare of the searchlights. "Here," he said, "you'd better have this." He put out his hand. "Take it," he repeated.

Quinn looked down at the outstretched hand. The fingers were closed around something. "What's happening?" he asked.

"We're on the retreat—we're pulling out." Chaikin wiped the sweat from his brow with his free hand. "Hurry up, take it! It's the most I can do for you." His fingers opened.

The cyanide capsule was nestling in his palm. Quinn's momentary sense of triumph and elation vanished. He recoiled a step as if he might be tempted to accept the Cheka officer's parting gift.

"What's going to happen to the prisoners?"

"Take the thing or you'll regret it!"

Chaikin sounded almost like a jilted woman, Quinn thought. He shook his head. "Better save it for yourself," he said hoarsely, and hurried after the others.

The snow-laden wind stung his face, pricking the skin like a shower of ice crystals. The ground was frozen solid and his shoes were falling to pieces.

He stumbled on until he came to a train. Dozens of cattle cars had been shunted into the warehouse siding, and the prisoners were lined up outside in serried ranks. Katov, who was in the last batch, looked at Quinn inquiringly, but Quinn said nothing. The sound of gunfire was almost drowned by the guards' raucous yells.

"Hurry it up! Get aboard there! Faster!"

The prisoners scrambled into the cars like a panic-stricken, stampeding herd. Quinn felt someone catch him by the arm. It was already so dark that all he could see of his fellow prisoner's face was a pair of black eyes surmounted by strange, bushy eyebrows that met in an unbroken line.

"Take your time," said the stranger.

The others were crowding into the car ahead of them. Though half-infected by their fear that there would be no room left, Quinn hung back and waited. He, Katov, and the stranger were the last to squeeze aboard. Eyes glared at them with hatred. Those already on board formed a solid mass and were reluctant to yield an inch. Crushed against the wooden wall and almost unable to breathe, Quinn forgot they were fellow prisoners and used his elbows on them to make room for himself.

The guards had begun to close the doors. They slid them shut, leaving a narrow crack between them, and secured them with planks nailed crosswise. Before long Quinn felt the car lurch beneath him and get under way, worn axles squealing as it jolted along the track.

He applied his face to the crack. There was little to be seen, nor was he sure of their direction, but he could once more hear the muffled crump of shells exploding in the distance.

Half an hour went by. The train came to a halt, waited awhile, and then set off again, rattling and swaying. It seemed to be traveling in a circle. The rhythm of the wheels changed once more as the car slowed. Peering through the crack, Quinn saw that they were crossing the bridge over the Kama.

The pedestrian walkway was alive with movement. Refugees of both sexes and all ages were trudging along through the driving snow, some pushing bicycles, others hauling hand-carts or sleds piled high with their belongings. Every now and then the human tide clogged the walkway and came to a stop. There must have been thousands of them fleeing westward.

The detonations were even louder and closer now. Quinn couldn't decide whether the city was already under fire or the Red Guards were destroying their supplies and ammunition dumps before they withdrew.

When the train speeded up again he saw buildings ablaze along the waterfront and black smoke billowing into the snow-laden air.

26

H E was dozing in a kind of trance. The temperature was far below zero now that it had stopped snowing, and the lower half of his body felt like a block of marble. He was ravenously hungry, too, and his legs, swollen after so many hours of standing, repeatedly threatened to give way under him.

It was still pitch-dark, and silence reigned apart from the rattle and clank of the train. Most of the prisoners had sunk to the floor and were lying in a jumbled heap for lack of space. Their grunts and curses had grown steadily fainter and died away altogether, to be replaced by a deathly hush.

Quinn, too, had half-subsided, and his head was swimming with the effort of hauling himself erect. Little by little, the sky outside paled and the landscape took on shape in the leaden gray light of dawn.

Beside him, the prisoner with the bushy eyebrows cleared his throat. Whenever Quinn had emerged from his torpor, he'd seen the man standing there foursquare as if he were immune to fatigue. Despite its prison pallor his face lacked the

192

starved, emaciated look of the others and made an almost hearty impression.

"Cold enough for you?"

Quinn looked back mutely.

"Better uncomfortable and alive than cozy and dead." The man gave a hoarse laugh. He reached into a cloth bag suspended from his neck. A moment later Quinn felt something thrust into his hand. It was a hunk of bread.

Hurriedly, he broke off a piece and put it in his mouth. Katov was crouching beside him. He bent down and touched him on the shoulder. "Here," he said, handing him the rest of the bread, "breakfast." His morale, he was surprised to note, had markedly improved.

He chewed the bread slowly and perseveringly. The coarse, pulpy mass in his mouth acquired various flavors as he plowed through a long, imaginary menu. He spun it out until the urge to swallow became too much for him. Then his attention was drawn to something else: the clank of the wheels was changing, slowing. He peered through the crack between the doors but could see no sign of a station or village, just an expanse of snowy countryside. The train eventually came to rest at the foot of a gentle slope culminating in a range of wooded hills.

Quinn shot an inquiring glance at the man beside him.

"You'll soon find out, friend."

"What's your name?"

"My name? Why do you ask?"

"I'd like to know whom to thank for the bread."

"They'll give us no time to get used to swapping names. For what it's worth, everyone calls me Tompo. That's the name of the town where I come from."

"You're a Sibiryak?"

"Yes." The man chuckled. "Right now, the temperature at Tompo must be fifty below. By my standards, this is a mild spring day."

The silence outside was broken by voices shouting orders. Quinn swiftly peered through the crack again. Katov got up and looked over his shoulder. Guards were trudging through the snow and fanning out along the train with their rifles at the ready. Two of them approached the car, one with a crowbar in his hand. There was a splintering sound as the boards nailed over the doors were wrenched off. The doors slid open.

"Out! Everyone out!"

Quinn was banged in the back even before he had time to jump. He tumbled to the ground, and the surviving prisoners fell on top of him in their eagerness to gain the open air.

He finally extricated himself to see the man from Tompo adjusting the bag around his neck. "See what I mean, friend?" he said calmly.

Looking along the train, Quinn understood why it had stopped in open countryside. Prisoners were already hauling their dead companions out of the cattle cars up ahead.

Quinn was glad that he, Katov, and Tompo had been assigned to dig the mass grave rather than carry corpses. The guards had issued them spades and pickaxes and herded them a short way up the slope.

The fresh, loose snow on the surface was easy enough to shovel away, but the ground beneath was frozen. The armed guards had no need to shout or threaten. Weak as they were, the prisoners worked like men possessed because the act of digging warmed them for the first time in hours. The work became easier after a while. The soil was heavy and full of roots but no longer rock hard.

"All right, that's deep enough!"

Quinn straightened up and leaned on his shovel, panting. Though exhausted he was feeling better and clearer-headed. He looked down at the train. The dead were laid out in a row on the embankment, having either suffocated in the over-crowded cars or simply died of cold and hunger.

From the head of the train came the monotonous hiss of the locomotive. Then a single shot rang out. A commissar was standing over one of the bodies on the ground, the heavy Mauser pistol still in his hand. He replaced it in the holster. He was wearing a fur hat and an ankle-length fur coat with the collar turned up. For a moment, Quinn thought it was Yanson.

Cold and hunger reasserted themselves. He glanced at Katov and Tompo. Katov was looking apathetic. The Sibiryak nodded at the corpses and spit in the snow. "Now or later," he said without a trace of expression. "What difference does it make?"

It had started to snow again. The guards beside the train shouted an order and the prisoners in the other party set to work. Two by two they carried the bodies up the slope, making heavy weather of the knee-deep snow. When the first pair reached the grave they paused for a moment. Even the guards allowed them a brief respite and averted their eyes as they pitched their burden over the edge.

Quinn edged closer to Tompo and glanced meaningfully at the wooded crest. "Don't be a fool! Run with me—we could make it to those trees!" he whispered.

Tompo briefly turned his head to look. He seemed to be gauging the distance. "I'd stop a bullet before I got there."

"The guards are just as cold and stiff as we are," Quinn said. "Give yourself the chance!"

"They'd blaze away, friend, if only because they're scared of the commissar."

Quinn persisted. Tompo's participation would not guarantee their escape, but three had a better chance than two or one. Besides, the Sibiryak was in much better shape. He had a store of bread and was inured to the cold. He could help them immeasurably, if only the man weren't paralyzed with apathy.

"There are only five of them," Quinn said in a low voice. "We'll wait till we've filled in the grave."

The lean face with the prominent cheekbones remained expressionless. "The grave? You won't even have one—they'll leave you lying out here in the snow."

"We'll make it with a bit of luck. You said so yourself: Now or later, what's the difference?"

"The difference is, I don't care. There's nothing left for me in this land. The war has taken everything from me."

"I'm a rich Englishman," Quinn said urgently. "Come with me, and if we escape I'll make you the richest man in the province!"

"I could leave Russia forever?"

Quinn nodded.

"All right then."

Tompo turned and looked up the hill again. When he turned back to Quinn there was a glint of amusement in his eyes. "We'll work up quite a sweat, friend."

Quinn, glowing with triumph, went over to Katov and explained his plan. "Can I count on you?"

Katov nodded. "Anything rather than another spell in that goddamned cattle car." He sounded mournful and unconvinced.

Without waiting for an order from the guards they started to fill in the grave as soon as the last of the bodies had been tossed into the trench. Quinn looked away whenever soil rained down on an upturned face. The trench filled rapidly.

"All right, that's enough! Back to the train!"

The members of the burial party were exhausted by their labors. They leaned on their shovels, breathing hard. Quinn exchanged a glance with Tompo, nodded to him and Katov, and was instantly fighting back panic. His weakened legs began to tremble so violently he was afraid he would fall over before he took a single step.

196

Tompo whispered something beside him. He dropped his pickax, crouched, and started running.

Tompo and Katov were faster on their feet—Quinn could see them a few yards ahead of him. He was vividly aware of the silence: the guards hadn't opened fire yet. His urge to pause and look back had become almost overpowering when he heard the first shouts, the first shots.

A bullet whistled past him. He ran on, eyes fixed on the wooded skyline. The snow was deeper than he'd thought; it clogged his shoes and added to their weight at every stride. More bullets kicked up the snow nearby, but his awareness of danger had vanished. There was room in his head for one thought only: Run!

The breath rasped in his throat, his lungs ached, his weary legs were dragging him down. Little fountains of snow sprang up around him as another volley rang out. He staggered on and fell, staggered on and fell, until it dawned on him that his feet were entangled in undergrowth. Looking up, he saw dark tree trunks and snowladen branches overhead, their evergreen foliage laden with snow. He scrambled to his feet and ran on, almost blinded by the white clouds that showered down on him from above.

The trees! He wasn't going to die after all! On he went, crawling now more than running. He'd lost sight of Tompo and Katov, and he needed the Sibiryak. But then, unexpectedly, all thought and feeling ceased: everything went black.

Someone shook him by the shoulder and rubbed his face with a handful of snow. He was sitting propped against a young fir tree with Tompo and Katov kneeling beside him. They were almost on the edge of a clearing. He started to say something, but the Sibiryak motioned him to be quiet.

He heard shouts some distance away, followed by silence. He waited, hardly breathing. Then came the sound of voices and a rustle of movement: some men were making their way through the undergrowth.

He raised his head and saw them moving among the trees—three of them. They reached the clearing and paused to confer before splitting up. Two of them walked off; the third didn't budge. He was only twenty yards away. They could see him silhouetted against the misty gray light: long greatcoat, fur hat, rifle with bayonet fixed. He had only to turn around to spot them.

More shots rang out in the distance. He hoped that meant other prisoners had made a run for it. The soldier in the clearing seemed to hesitate. Then he set off in the direction of the voices. It was absurd, but instead of feeling relieved Quinn wanted to throw up.

"Stay there!" Tompo rose and tiptoed off.

Quinn watched him go, suddenly worried that he might abandon them. He struggled to his feet and followed the Sibiryak with Katov at his heels.

Tompo had crawled to the edge of the wood by the time they caught him up. Soldiers could be seen descending the slope in single file. The train was still standing there, but the doors of the cattle cars had been nailed shut again. A perpendicular thread of vapor from the locomotive's smokestack was rising into the sky. The air was windless and absolutely still.

They withdrew into the trees without a word. Tompo shared out some of his bread. A minute or two later they heard the train resume its journey. They looked at each other until the sound faded, then made their way back to the edge of the wood.

The train had gone. All that could now be seen below was the single railroad track, the dark hummock of freshly turned soil that marked the mass grave, and the trampled snow around it. Quinn experienced a sudden sense of anticlimax. He turned to the Sibiryak.

"What now?"

Tompo shrugged. "Now we start walking."

"Which way?"

"East."

The Sibiryak took the lead as a matter of course. Katov went next and Quinn brought up the rear. He was even weaker than he'd thought.

East . . . Somewhere in that direction they ought to come across Czech units of the White Army, but the longer he trudged through the snow the more meaningless the idea seemed. Every step was torture. There were times when he forgot he was walking at all. He put one foot before the other because someone ahead of him did the same.

Lieutenant Ikonikov of the Second Siberian Corps was awakened by rifle fire—scattered shots only. He'd stretched out for a nap fully dressed, so all he had to do was pull on his boots and buckle on his pistol belt. Picking up his binoculars, he went outside.

The sky was clear, an evening sky in which the first stars were visible. The temperature had fallen still further, and the trampled mud of the village street was dotted with frozen puddles.

He paused for a moment beside the fence enclosing the front garden. Nemisorskoye was a village thirteen miles northwest of Perm, and his company had captured it only that day. The house in which he'd taken up his quarters was the last house in the street and the only one left intact. A smell of burning still hung in the air.

It hadn't been militarily essential to torch the village. They'd encountered little resistance from the garrison, a depleted company of Red Guards whose defense of the place had been only halfhearted. Most of them had been killed in the course of the fighting. The rest had surrendered and been summarily executed by Ikonikov's men. Neither side took prisoners in this war.

Again Ikonikov heard shots. They came from the direction of the two-man picket he'd posted on the outskirts of the village.

The sentries had installed themselves behind an overturned peasant sledge. Stretching away to their front was an expanse of flat, open terrain. The snow shone like a mirror in the bluish-white twilight.

Ikonikov came up behind the men. "Having fun?" he said.

One of the two, a pallid slip of a youth, looked up from his rifle. "It's wolves, Lieutenant," he said. "A whole pack of them."

"I hate the brutes!" the other one chimed in.

Ikonikov peered in the direction they indicated. Something was certainly moving out there. Three gray, indistinct shapes were crawling across the plain. He raised his binoculars. The snow dazzled him for a moment. Then he saw one of the shapes rear up, fall forward, and crawl on. Wolves they weren't, those squirming, writhing figures, but they didn't look human either. The sentries loosed off another couple of rounds. "Cease fire!" he yelled.

He came out from behind the sledge. Something inhibited him from using his binoculars again, so he stood there watching and waiting. The figures slowly approached, looking for all the world like gray, bedraggled animals as they crawled along on all fours. They tried to walk the last few yards, clothes hanging in tatters from their emaciated bodies, bloodstained rags wound around their feet.

When they finally reached him they sank down in the snow and lay there like three toppled scarecrows. A graveyard smell assailed his nostrils.

"Who are you?" he demanded.

200

No answer. The sentries, who were standing behind him at the ready, lowered their rifles. The elder of the two crossed himself. At long last, one of the scarecrows raised his head and looked up. The twilight lent his face the ashen pallor of a corpse despite his bushy beard and eyebrows. The skin was peeling off his cheeks in strips, the eyes were barely visible in their sockets, the cracked and bleeding lips strove to mouth some words. They emerged as a series of hoarse, unintelligible croaks. It wasn't until Ikonikov bent down that he grasped their meaning.

"Friends! Don't shoot!"

The telegraphist on board the Allied Mission's special train at Omsk was jolted awake when the Hughes printer started chattering. He made an entry in his log—January 3, 23:09—and waited for the message to end. Then he bent over the ticker-tape, read it, and swore aloud.

He hurried out of the section and into the corridor. The eaves visible through the windows were fringed with icicles. He opened the door, flinching at the bitter cold. The path between the tracks had been shoveled clear, but the snow piled up in the background was as deep as the train was high.

The two sentries on guard outside the blue palace car were wearing heavy sheepskin coats, felt boots, and fur hats. Their breath hung in the air like smoke.

"There's a message coming in from the headquarters of the Second Siberian Corps," the telegraphist told them. "Major's eyes only! Urgent!"

As soon as Fitzmaurice entered the section—coatless, in his immaculately tailored uniform—the telegraphist switched his machine to receive. He caught the tickertape as it emerged from the printer and read the text aloud. When the message

201

ended he tore off the narrow ribbon of paper and handed it to Fitzmaurice.

"Well I'm damned, sir," he said, "so they made it after all!"

Fitzmaurice gave him a coolly disapproving stare. "Not a word to anyone, Sergeant. That's an order!"

Back behind his desk in the palace car, Fitzmaurice reread the message carefully. Then, summoning Ivory, he told him to inform Hollis and make them some tea. Just as the Indian was turning to go, he pointed to the gaily decorated Christmas tree in the corner. The needles were already turning brown and dropping in the overheated atmosphere.

"How much longer must I put up with that confounded thing?" Fitzmaurice demanded.

"The tree was your idea, sahib," Ivory said serenely.

"I know it was. Make sure you get rid of it!"

Something in the major's voice told Ivory that he'd just received a welcome piece of news.

PART FOUR

PART FOUR

THE SENTINEL

T H E blizzard had caught Fyodor Nikulin unawares. It took him over three hours to reach the posthouse, not one, and he'd found neither message nor supplies awaiting him there. The wind had now dropped, but the ugly yellow sky told him that more snow was in the offing. It would be wise to make the most of his breather and then go back.

This was his third fruitless trip. The posthouse windows, which he could see through his binoculars, signaled that the coast was clear, so what could be keeping Govorov? Should he risk a trip to the valley? That he should even contemplate such an idea was an ominous sign: he was losing his objectivity. He rose, strapped on his snowshoes, and set off on the return journey.

Nikulin was a robust, vigorous man, but it couldn't be denied that the winter had sapped his stamina. Life in the mountains had been hard since the first heavy snows and the advent of subzero temperatures. He'd lost weight, and his war wounds troubled him more than usual in the bitter cold. His supplies, which had not allowed for such a lengthy stay in the mountains, were running low. He eked them out by setting traps, shooting lynx and badgers and the occasional rabbit, and using melted snow to make his tea. He never doubted that he would survive; what perturbed and enervated him were the moments when solitude blinded him to the purpose of his lonely vigil.

Snow went whirling into the air, propelled by the freshening wind. In many places the drifts were twenty feet deep, in others the blizzard had dispersed the snow and exposed the bare, frozen ground beneath.

It was late afternoon by the time he reached the hut, a log cabin faced with pine bark and largely concealed by an overhanging rock. It had originally been used as a hideout by Govorov. Together they'd made it winterproof and equipped it with all he would need to render him independent of the outside world: a stove, a kerosene lamp, blankets, furs, winter clothing, tools, arms, ammunition, and a substantial supply of food.

The blizzard had uprooted one of the pine trees that hid the cabin from the air, and the entrance was blocked by a sizable drift. He used one of his snowshoes to dig it clear. He was still at work when the storm broke once more, so violently that he felt as if he were standing waist-deep in a raging torrent. He was exhausted, frozen, and famished by the time he squeezed through the door.

It was, if possible, even colder inside than out. He never risked lighting a fire before nightfall because of the smoke, but this time he threw caution to the winds. He fetched some logs from his store of dry wood and stacked them in the stove. He filled the kettle with water. He paused before striking a match. It was an unequal contest: willpower versus fatigue, hunger, and an overpowering desire for hot tea. Nikulin abandoned the struggle and lit the fire. When he'd finished his tea he opened one of his last cans of meat and beans and devoured two pieces of hardtack as well.

Some of his composure returned. He realized that he couldn't go on like this indefinitely. It had to be admitted, from an objective point of view, that his comrades had let him down. The Red Guards were to launch an all-out attempt to recapture Karmel before the winter set in—that had always been the plan. Well, not only had they failed to return, but the Whites and the Czechs had gone over to the attack. The latest word from Govorov was that Perm had fallen. There was now only a remote prospect of Karmel's recapture.

To hell with the gold! Responsibility for it was like a noose. He found it harder and harder to understand why his friends, the comrades in Moscow, had gone to such lengths to acquire it in the first place. Pride alone prevented him from abandoning it: he would never leave it to the enemy. Better that it should remain forever in the bowels of the mountain where it now lay hidden. . . .

The idea smote him like a revelation. He broke out in a sudden sweat and removed his fur coat. Then, having lit the kerosene lamp and put it on the table, he went and knelt down beside two ammunition boxes in the corner of the cabin. Their metal casing was white with frost. He carefully scraped it off and wiped them over before opening the nearer of the two. Lined with hardwood, it contained numerous sticks of dynamite eight inches long and coated with a thin film of gold dust: He knelt there motionless, staring at them. Then he threw back his head and laughed with a sense of relief.

"Let the mountains have it!" he said aloud. It had been taken from the earth, all that gold. Rather than let anyone else lay hands on it, he would give it back.

He filled his rucksack with dynamite. It would mean two or three trips, but the prospect only spurred him on. He opened the second box, which was also lined with hardwood but contained black-powder detonators and coils of fuse. These he stowed in an ammunition pouch.

He put his head outside. It had stopped snowing, but the light was almost gone. He swore, so eager to get started that he longed to set off right away.

Nikulin never got undressed at night—removing his boots was his sole concession to bedtime. Stretching out on his bearskin coat, he pulled the blankets up to his chin and, for the first time in weeks, fell asleep at once.

He awoke at first light. Impatient to put his plan into effect, he dispensed with breakfast and finished off the dregs of last night's strong black tea. Then he shouldered the rucksack, threaded the ammunition pouch onto his belt, and picked up his binoculars and rifle.

The temperature had dropped still further now that the storm was over. Absolute silence reigned. The sun, just visible behind the mountain peaks, was climbing into a crystalline sky.

Deep snowdrifts had blocked the old road to the pass, so Nikulin found the going hard. Ahead of him, on either side of the pass, two peaks of unequal height loomed above the rugged skyline. A little to the right of the larger one stood a trio of pitch pines, so tall that they were visible to the naked eye from a long way off. They were old trees with gray, lichen-encrusted trunks, and their crowns had been snapped off by the gales that so often raged at that altitude. Their few remaining branches projected from the trunks like naked, helpless arms—hence the name given them by the coachmen and wagoners who had used the road in former times: "The Three Crosses."

27

THE railroad station was almost hidden from view by clouds of dry snow sent whirling into the air by the wind. Inside, a powdery layer had crept beneath the door and covered the plank floor. The big iron stove in the corner was burning fiercely—Quinn could hear the lid of the saucepan rattle as the water seethed and bubbled, but he would have liked to move the chair still closer. All he said as he sat down was, "Go easier on me than you did yesterday."

Georgy Ivanov shrugged his shoulders. "No sensible man shaves in weather as cold as this." Sovna's ex-stationmaster had taken up barbering since the trains stopped running.

Quinn sat back. His face tingled as Ivanov wielded the shaving brush. The abrasions on his cheeks had healed, but the new skin was pink and sensitive. He shut his eyes and surrendered himself to the razor. Every now and then Ivanov broke off and turned away, convulsed by a racking cough. He'd finished one side when the telegraph in the next room started ticking away.

Quinn sat up. "Go and see what it is!"

The stationmaster returned wearing a puzzled frown. "You were right, there's a train coming. It's already passed Kargino. That's a two-hour run in normal times, but God knows when it really will get here."

Quinn rose hurriedly as soon as he was shaved and Ivanov helped him on with his coat. His frostbitten fingers found the buttons difficult as usual. He picked up his fur hat and gloves while Ivanov bustled around him, all obsequious civility. "Just fancy, a train!" he exclaimed. "I honestly thought you were pulling my leg."

Quinn said nothing. He turned up his coat collar and went outside. The icy wind blowing from the plain had swept the single railroad track clear of snow. It stretched away to the horizon, so straight that it might have been drawn with a ruler.

Opposite the station were some buildings that dated from the time before the railroad existed and Sovna was just a staging post on the mail-coach route between Perm and Ekaterinburg, which ran south of Karmel through the foothills of the Urals. Smoke was rising from the chimney of the former posthouse. Quinn could smell it as he crossed the track. The numbness that persisted in his extremities seemed to have been offset by greater sensitivity in other respects.

He entered the timber-built posthouse, a single room with crude bunks lining the walls, a central table flanked by a couple of benches, and an open fireplace.

Tompo was crouching in front of the hearth making breakfast. He filled a pan with strips of fat bacon, fried them crisp, and poured a bowl of beaten egg over them. His movements were slow and deliberate. Quinn couldn't help remembering their long trek and the hunger that had gnawed at his vitals. He'd soon ceased to feel the cold and become immune to pain. All that remained in the way of sensation—his sole source of strength and vestige of the will to survive—had been his feverish delusions about food.

Tompo held out the brimming plate. "Good God," said Quinn. "How can a person keep eating so much?"

"A man eats when the food's there and goes hungry when it isn't—that's how I was brought up." The Sibiryak's face was as expressionless as ever. "Besides, you're still only skin and bone."

He made a second omelet and poured out two mugs of tea. They sat down at the table and ate in silence. Eventually, Quinn said, "They're coming—the message just came through." He went over to his bunk and started to roll up the blankets.

Smoke appeared on the horizon. Like a ship steaming across an ocean of snow, the train crept slowly nearer down an avenue of telegraph poles blown askew by the wind. Tompo had saddled their mounts and the packhorse. They were Siberian ponies with long, shaggy manes. Quinn was holding his by the reins. The beasts' steaming breath and the crunch of their hooves in the snow were eloquent of the intense cold.

Georgy Ivanov had donned his stationmaster's finery, a black uniform with red piping, and was waiting beneath the overhanging roof. Although it was noon, a strange twilight prevailed. The sun was just a milky white disk in a gray, overcast sky.

The train, trailing a plume of snow, grew bigger and could now be seen more clearly. The Baldwin locomotive, which was hauling a dozen cattle cars and four passenger cars, crawled into the station and came to rest. The windows of the passenger cars were encrusted with ice and snow.

Quinn, standing motionless and outwardly calm on the posthouse side of the track, heard a slamming of doors and a babble of voices—English voices. Handing the halter to Tompo, he made his way around the front of the train. The platform was crowded with British soldiers in voluminous greatcoats, stout, knee-length boots, and fur caps with long earflaps. Their uniforms were brand-new. Georgy Ivanov was in conversation with an officer who topped him by at least a head.

They broke off and turned toward him as he approached. Quinn stopped short, staring in surprise at the snub nose, rosebud mouth, and boyish eyes.

Hollis advanced on him with his arms outstretched, then lowered them in sudden embarrassment. "Hello, Oliver," he said.

Quinn still hadn't recovered from his surprise. "What made him send you?"

"Fitzmaurice? He said you'd asked for me."

"I still marvel at the way you lied to me, the two of you."

"I tried to warn you off. Fitzmaurice . . ."

Quinn broke in with a dismissive gesture. "Tell me something. What's the latest word you have from Karmel? Is Moura Toumanova still there?"

"I haven't heard anything." Hollis fidgeted with the flap of his holster. "How are you feeling? What happened to your face?"

Quinn involuntarily felt the scar tissue on his cheek, then

211

was annoyed with himself for reacting at all. "Get the men ready to move out."

"How's Katov?" Hollis persisted.

"They had to amputate three frostbitten toes, but they saved the leg," Quinn said impassively. "They're sending him back to Omsk in a week's time." He looked down at the platform. "How many men did you bring?"

"A full-strength company." Hollis evidently found the change of subject a relief. "They're Hampshires—seasoned troops in first-class shape. Versatile, too. They may be infantry, but they can sit a horse if they have to." He looked inquiringly. "Why did you send for them?"

"Because I'm taking no more chances," Quinn said curtly. "What about Wajda—is he still at Karmel?"

Hollis patted his breast pocket. I've got what you asked for—Fitzmaurice pulled a few strings. Rudolf Wajda has been relieved of his command and reduced to the ranks."

"And Scala?"

Hollis shook his head. "Fitzmaurice urged the Yanks to relieve him, too, but they wouldn't play. He must have friends in high places."

"So Scala will be responsible for shipping the stuff out?"

"The Yanks want to be in control."

Quinn paused. "Assuming we find the gold, what are Fitzmaurice's orders?"

"We're to transport it to Omsk."

"And hand it over to the Whites?"

"I imagine so."

"Is that his intention?"

"Hell's teeth, Oliver, how should I know what arrangement he's come to with the Whites! I only know we're to get it to Omsk—*when* we find it."

"And Moura Toumanova? Does Fitzmaurice's promise to her still hold good? Papers, money, safe passage out of the country?"

"Of course." Hollis paused and studied Quinn. "That gold—are you sure it's still in the Karmel area?"

"Don't worry," Quinn said, "I'll find it." He might have been speaking to himself.

The four of them rode at the head of the column, Quinn beside Tompo, Hollis beside Captain Wade, the Hampshires' company commander. Then came the leading platoon, then a dozen horse-drawn sledges laden with supplies and equipment, then the fifty mules Quinn had asked for, and finally the two remaining platoons.

The ride had taken longer than Quinn had reckoned. Snowdrifts compelled them to make detours and trees overburdened with snow had fallen and blocked their route. They crossed the frozen river at the spot where Cutter had demolished the railroad bridge. Later they rode through a deserted village whose blackened ruins lay half-buried in snow. The mist that enveloped them was scarcely distinguishable from the gray sky above, but at last the clouds lifted and the valleys and mountains beyond Karmel showed up ahead of them.

Quinn reined in at the mouth of the bridge leading to the lower part of the town. The watchtowers on the near side of the river were unmanned. He looked up at the jagged, snowy peaks, which were flushed with the last rays of the setting sun.

Hollis spurred his horse forward. "Is this it? Karmel?"

Quinn nodded.

"Looks peaceful enough," Hollis said, but he sounded edgy.

The road beyond was bordered by towering walls of cleared snow with cavernous passages leading through them to the houses on either side. The snow on the roadway itself was frozen hard, and the horses' hooves made a crisp, metallic sound that intruded on the general hush. The few people they passed turned to watch the mounted column in mute surprise.

The station was deserted and the Czech troops' tents on the level ground beyond it were gone. The blue baggage cars were still standing in the siding, one of the two locomotives with steam up. A machine gun was mounted on a flatcar at the rear of the stationary train.

Quinn slid from the saddle and handed his horse to Tompo. Hollis dismounted too and followed him over. A sentry barred their path, a man with a clipped mustache iced over by his own frozen breath. He ported his rifle.

"Halt!"

"Out of my way!" Quinn swore at him.

Hollis stepped forward. "Easy, Oliver, the man's got his orders." He turned to the sentry. "We have to speak with the train commander."

The sentry eyed their new boots, fur-lined greatcoats and fur caps. "Americans?" he said.

"British," said Hollis. "We're taking over here."

The man gave them another stare, then turned and set off down the platform. They passed some more Czech soldiers clustered around a fire whose flames were reflected in the cars' gleaming blue paintwork.

They had reached the dining and Pullman cars toward the front of the train, immediately behind the tender of the locomotive with steam up. The snow on its roof had melted and the misted windows indicated that it was well heated. Voices and laughter could be heard.

The sentry climbed aboard and went inside. The voices died away. A curtain was drawn aside, a hand rubbed a peephole in the condensation, and a face appeared: the plump, rosy face of Lieutenant Scala.

Scala descended from the car with his fur coat draped around his shoulders like a Civil War general's cloak. "I knew I'd see you again, Quinn." He chuckled. "Hey, what'd you do to your face?" He bent forward and peered along the platform at the station, where Captain Wade was dividing his company

214

into detachments. "Brought your private army along or something?"

"Why have you got steam up?" Quinn demanded.

"The Yurovsky place is unheatable in this weather, so I moved in here. Look, do we have to stand around yakking in the cold?"

Quinn indicated Hollis. "Captain Hollis is taking over command here."

Scala looked from one to the other. "How will that appeal to General Wajda's people?"

"That's not your problem," Quinn said impatiently. "Just move out and dismiss those sentries."

A telephone started ringing inside the car. Scala turned to go, but Quinn checked him with a gesture.

The phone continued to ring. No one answered it. Scala's eyes twinkled slyly. "That suit you, Quinn?"

Quinn ignored him and turned to Hollis. "I wouldn't trust Mr. Scala too far if I were you—in fact I'd feel happier if you placed him under arrest, but that's your business. Just make sure he doesn't warn anyone."

He walked off before Hollis could utter a word. Tompo, who was waiting outside the station, handed him the reins. He mounted up, wheeled his horse, and rode off in the direction of the miners' village with the Sibiryak trotting along behind.

28

T H E light was fading fast now. The mountains were crisply silhouetted against a deep violet sky in which the first stars could be seen. Quinn followed the road beside the river, most of whose frozen surface was covered with snow. He reined in when they reached the village square. Standing in his stirrups, he looked across at the hotel. The chimneys stood out against

215

the sky as clearly as the mountains, but he could see no smoke.

He shook the reins and kicked his horse into a gallop, every other thought banished by the prospect of seeing Moura. His visions of her had literally kept him alive in prison.

No lights were visible inside the hotel. The veranda was choked with snow piled high by the wind, but footprints could be seen on the steps and the door stood ajar.

He dismounted and hurried up the steps. Tompo, following close behind, dismounted too and tethered their horses to a post. Quinn turned to him.

"Try the stable. She had a horse—a chestnut. See if it's there, but hand me one of those torches first."

He lit the pitch-pine torch and waited for it to stop smoking. Then, pushing the door wide open, he went in. The barroom was as bleak and cheerless as ever. He made for the inner door and peered down the passage beyond.

"Moura?"

He listened, already discounting the possibility of a reply.

"Moura? Moura!" The thought that he might be too late seemed unendurable. He hurried to the door at the end of the passage, which was also ajar. Memories overwhelmed him.

Once inside the room he stopped short, appalled by the scene of destruction he found. The low table had been upended and broken, the samovar and tea things smashed, the ottomans and cushions slit open.

Quinn stood rooted to the spot, thinking that taking another step might confront him with the sight of Moura's dead body. Involuntarily he recalled the scent of her hair when they'd stood so close together that their bodies and faces almost touched. Now, the room smelled of nothing but the kerosene seeping from the broken lamp.

"*Anglichanin!*"

He hadn't heard the footsteps in the passage.

216

"Come, I've something to show you." Tompo laid a hand on his shoulder.

The room was swimming before Quinn's eyes. He had a sense of déjà vu: he was standing at Catherine's bedside in the hospital at Hemlo, having hurried there in response to Cutter's telegram. Then, too, he'd arrived too late and found nothing but a woman's broken body. . . .

The Sibiryak had gone on ahead and was waiting at the foot of the veranda steps. The mountains were a dark mass now. Only a vestige of daylight clung to the very highest peaks.

"Give me that torch." Tompo put out his hand and Quinn, still dazed, relinquished it. The Sibiryak turned and led the way over to the coach house. The horses, which he'd tethered to a post, tossed their heads and whinnied at his approach.

Tompo lowered the torch and pointed to some footprints in the snow. He followed them around the back of the building.

Wind had piled the snow against the wooden wall. After a few yards Tompo came to a halt and stepped aside. He held the torch so that its light fell on one of the deepest drifts.

"The horses shied or I might have missed it," he said. "I haven't touched anything. . . ."

There was an arm protruding from the snow. Tompo returned the torch. Numbly, Quinn took it and looked on while the Sibiryak proceeded to scoop the snow away with both hands. The clothes that came to light were torn and blood-stained. Then came the face.

It was Timur. Quinn looked at the Mongol's close-cropped bullet-head. The eyes were closed, but the face itself was contorted with pain, even in death. The ears had been cut off and the throat was slit from ear to ear—hence the abundance of blood. Quinn straightened up and averted his eyes.

"Shall I bury him?"

"What?" Quinn's stomach was rebelling, but his compan-

217

ion's imperturbability was a help. "How long has he been dead?"

Tompo bent over the body. "Hard to tell in this temperature. Half a day, perhaps . . ."

The brutality of the murder implied only one thing: they'd tried to get the Mongol to talk. Moura had probably been forced to look on while he was tortured. Quinn experienced another wave of nausea.

Tompo relieved him of the torch and doused it in the snow. The darkness was a relief.

"You knew him?"

"Yes."

"There were several of them," Tompo said. "No one could have tackled him single-handed, not a man like that. Any idea who they were?"

"Possibly."

"Don't you want me to bury him?"

"Later. I'll send a couple of men."

They made their way back to the horses, boots crunching in the snow. Quinn looked up at the sky. The stars were shining with a brilliance that foretold a further drop in temperature. Unhitching his horse, he held it with one hand and patted it with the other. Moura's wagon and sleigh were still standing under the overhanging roof of the coach house.

"Is her chestnut in the stable?"

Tompo pointed to some tracks in the snow. "Gone. Three of them rode out from Karmel. There were four when they left." He pointed toward the mountains. "They also took some mules along."

"Think we could trail them?"

"Tomorrow, yes—if it doesn't snow in the night."

Quinn climbed into the saddle and rode out from under the coach house roof, then reined in and looked across at the dark, silent, deserted hotel.

She's alive, he told himself—they need her alive. But he

could not get rid of the thought that she was dead in the snow somewhere like her Mongol.

He wheeled his horse and set off for Karmel at a gallop. The beast was tired, but he spurred it on mercilessly. Before long the lights of the town showed up ahead like a mirror image of the star-spangled sky. He hated the beauty of the evening.

29

H A M P S H I R E S were guarding the gates, drive, and main entrance of the Diatsaro mansion. A dozen of them were drawn up in front of the portico when Quinn and Tompo got there. Sergeant Reid, a man in his forties with an unruly mustache, who did not look anything like a soldier, stepped up to Quinn and saluted.

"Everything's under control. Luckily, the Czechs were more scared of us than we were of them."

"Where's Captain Hollis?"

"In there, sir." The sergeant gestured at the house with its blue and gold colonnades. "Quite a place. These Russians are crazy people!"

Quinn turned to Tompo. "Get someone to look after the horses, then join me inside."

He made his way into the entrance hall. Some Czech soldiers were descending the marble staircase, two with a cabin trunk between them, the rest toting leather suitcases—Prince Diatsaro's, judging by their array of colorful stickers from all the best hotels in Europe. Hollis was in the gallery with Aina Diatsaro, a fur-coated figure with a fur pillbox on her head and a muff dangling from her neck. The prince's daughter was talking earnestly.

Quinn waited for them at the foot of the stairs. Hollis, whose eyes were glued to the girl at his side, didn't notice him until she came to a sudden stop. He cleared his throat in some embarrassment. "I think you've already met. . . ."

Quinn nodded. His reappearance was clearly unwelcome to Aina, who ignored him and swept on. Hollis took her arm.

"I'll see you out—"

"Don't trouble," she retorted. "I know my way."

Undeterred, Hollis escorted her to the door and held it open for her before rejoining Quinn.

"What was all that about? Has she got something against you?"

"I obviously turned up at the wrong moment, that's all."

Hollis looked puzzled. Then he blushed. "I didn't expect you back so soon."

"There wasn't any point in staying," Quinn said brusquely. "All I found was a dead body."

"Oh, God!" Hollis exclaimed. "Not the Toumanova woman?"

"No, but why the hell should you care? You and Fitzmaurice didn't give a damn about her!"

They both fell silent. More soldiers came trooping downstairs laden with suitcases and added them to the rest of the baggage on the marble floor. "Wajda's stuff?" Quinn asked.

"Yes. He took his dismissal surprisingly calmly."

"What about Ryazanov?"

"Ryazanov left here yesterday," Hollis said. "According to Wajda."

Quinn started up the stairs. "Don't forget," Hollis said, trailing after him, "my orders are to get Wajda back to Omsk. He'll have to justify his actions there, so go easy on him."

The bedroom, a semicircular room with lofty windows and brocade curtains, was vast enough to have served as a ballroom. The chandelier in the center of the stucco ceiling cast a subdued glow over the oak paneling, plush chairs, and ornate four-poster.

Visible through an open door in the corner was a marble bathroom with gold-plated fittings. Rudolf Wajda was standing in front of a mirror, shaving. He paused when they entered, glanced over his shoulder, and said something in Czech.

A soldier emerged from the bathroom and shut the door behind him—a barrel-chested Czech with mean little eyes. "Out!" he said. His fingers closed around the gun in the holster at his side.

Something snapped inside Quinn's head. He stepped forward and drove his fist into the pit of the man's stomach. The Czech gave a grunt and doubled up, the gun clattered to the floor. As he reached for it, Quinn punched him again.

The gun was a Nagant service revolver. Quinn picked it up. "Get out," he said.

The Czech staggered to the door and disappeared.

"Calm down, Oliver," Hollis said. "What's wrong with you?"

Quinn stuffed the gun into his waistband. Hearing a sound behind him, he turned to see Wajda standing in the bathroom doorway. Wajda's pale, bland face was expressionless. A scent of eau de cologne hung in the air.

Wajda closed the door behind him. He was wearing a white shirt and uniform trousers. His jacket, still adorned with a general's shoulder boards, was hanging on a chair. He put it on and did up the buttons one by one, deliberately ignoring Quinn. "I thought we'd discussed everything," he said to Hollis.

"Where's Moura Toumanova?" Quinn demanded.

Wajda produced a clean handkerchief from his pocket. The scent of eau de cologne grew stronger. He held the handkerchief to his cheek as if he'd cut himself while shaving. His brown eyes transferred their long-lashed gaze to Quinn. "So

221

you're behind all this, eh? I see now I was a fool to let you walk out of here."

"You mean you should have handed me over to Ryazanov's mercies?" Quinn replied. "Well, it's too late for that."

Again Wajda raised the handkerchief and pressed it to his cheek. He turned to Hollis: "Do I have to put up with this?" he asked.

"Everything would be far simpler if we could have a word with Ryazanov," Hollis said mildly.

"I already told you—he left here and I've no idea where he went." Wajda lowered the handkerchief, and Quinn saw that he really had cut himself shaving. There was a small red blemish on his pallid cheek.

Wajda continued to address Hollis. "I didn't argue when you relieved me of my command and I instructed my men to obey your orders. You tell me I'm to come to Omsk for questioning. Well, I'm still prepared to do that, but I refuse to be browbeaten by this individual." He headed for the door. Quinn made no move to stop him. Hollis breathed a sigh of relief.

The Czech reached the door and opened it. Tompo was standing outside with his arms folded. Wajda froze.

"Come in and shut the door, Tompo," Quinn said quietly.

Wajda backed away as Tompo complied, moving in his usual lithe, unhurried manner. Tompo scrutinized him closely. Then his lean face broke into a smile.

"I think he'll talk, *Anglichanin*," he said. "He isn't the type to stand pain for long."

Wajda retraced his steps with obvious reluctance. "Well," he said dully, "what do you want?"

"You knew what Ryazanov was," Quinn said calmly. "You knew he was the political commissar responsible for the train . . ."

"My job was to secure the bullion," Wajda said, "—that's why I needed him. Omsk wanted it and Fitzmaurice didn't

222

mind what I did to get hold of it. He gave me an entirely free hand."

"You knew when you spoke with me that the gold had never left this area, and you knew about Fyodor Nikulin, the train commander. You knew Nikulin transferred it. Where to?"

"We never found out."

Quinn glared at him, then looked at Tompo.

"It's the truth!" Wajda protested. "Nikulin removed it from the Xenia Mine without Ryazanov's knowledge. Only he knew its new location and he refused to divulge it."

"When did you last see Ryazanov?"

"Yesterday evening. We'd been warned by Dexter Scala that British troops were on the way here. Ryazanov wanted to make a final attempt to bargain with Nikulin. The man's position was hopeless, and Ryazanov thought he might be able to talk him around: safe passage for him and Moura Toumanova plus a share of the gold . . ."

Quinn's breathing had quickened. "Except that Moura Toumanova would have rejected such an offer."

"Really?" sneered Wajda. "You obviously know her better than I do."

"And, because she rejected it, Ryazanov killed her body-guard."

Wajda's eyes widened. "What is this, another of your fairy tales? It was Ryazanov who picked the Mongol to guard her. Why should he kill him?"

"He's dead," Quinn said, "like all the rest." He paused. "When did Ryazanov get back?"

"I already told you," Wajda said, "I haven't seen him since last night."

"Where has he taken her?"

Wajda tugged his uniform jacket straight. "You know what really amuses me, Quinn? You've made no progress at all. Cutter never found that gold and neither will you!"

"Where has he taken her?" Quinn repeated.

"You see?" Wajda said with a laugh, turning to Hollis. "All that really interests your friend is a redheaded whore!"

Quinn slapped him in the face backhanded. It wasn't a hard blow, but Wajda's jaw dropped. "A redheaded whore!" he yelled.

This time Quinn slapped him as hard as he could. Wajda put a hand to his cheek and glared at Quinn with unadulterated loathing. Quinn's fingers had raised four red welts.

"You'd better pray that I find her alive," Quinn whispered hoarsely. "If I don't, I'll kill you, I swear it!"

He went over to Tompo and handed him the Czech orderly's gun. "There's a prison here—the former Cheka headquarters. Lock him up in a cell. No blankets or food."

He went to the door, opened it, and strode off down the passage without waiting to see if Hollis was following.

30

THE majordomo had opened the door and ushered them inside. The big entrance hall with the paneled ceiling and the clutter of armchairs and sofas was deserted. A couple of oil lamps were burning on small tables.

"Don't disturb him at dinner," Quinn said. "We can wait."

The scrawny manservant in the striped vest smiled. "His Excellency will be grateful for any excuse. Besides, they've almost finished."

He went over to the double doors and slid them apart. The voices beyond swelled in volume. A good twenty people were seated around a table under a chandelier laden with candles. A Christmas tree was standing in one corner, its branches sprayed with a silvery solution to simulate hoarfrost.

Quinn turned away and walked over to the open fireplace. The fire was burning low, but there was a stack of cut logs

224

beside it. Quinn resisted the temptation to pick some up and stoke the embers. Hollis was standing beside him, still looking nonplussed. He hadn't spoken a word on the way to the hunting lodge. All he said now was, "Fancy slapping him in the face like that! It wasn't like you, Oliver."

Quinn turned and stood with his back to the fire. The hubbub of conversation in the dining room died away, then resumed as Sergei Diatsaro emerged, so tall that his head almost brushed the top of the doorframe. He was wearing a tuxedo.

"Sorry to interrupt your dinner," Quinn said.

"Nonsense! The less there is on the plates the more the meals drag on. As for the names our chef dreams up . . . Tonight's dessert was *Merveille de pommes meringuées*—it turned out to be plain baked apples." Diatsaro shook hands. "I heard you were back. Karmel must hold some mysterious attraction for you."

Quinn indicated Hollis. "This is Captain Hollis," he said.

Hollis stiffly inclined his head. "Cloudesley Hollis," he said, "Royal Engineers."

"Royal, eh? You must meet my mother—she adores anything to do with royalty." Diatsaro laughed. "Take care, though—she's bound to ask you why your king didn't lift a finger to save his cousin the czar."

"I'm afraid I couldn't hope to explain," Hollis said, rather shamefaced.

"Just pretend to have a bad conscience and you'll win her heart," Diatsaro told him. "That's another of her great loves, men with bad consciences."

There was a scraping of chairs from the adjoining room and the diners started filing out. Aina Diatsaro appeared arm in arm with a white-haired old lady as gaunt and bony as her son.

The prince turned. "Aina, over here, please."

Aina, who had changed into an evening gown and was wearing her long, wavy hair loose on the shoulders, moved with the serene self-assurance of a young woman confident of her effect on the opposite sex. She greeted Hollis with a nod and a sparkle in her vivid, gray-blue eyes.

"Be good enough to introduce Captain Hollis to your grandmother," Diatsaro said. "Captain Hollis of the *Royal Engineers*," he added.

Aina eyed her father coolly. "You're impossible," she said. She took Hollis's arm. "I'm sorry you couldn't make dinner," she told him, "but now that you're here I forgive you."

Whether because of the peaceful atmosphere or Sergei Diatsaro's company or both, Quinn felt calmer once they were closeted in the gun room and the majordomo had served tea. There was a chessboard on the desk with the beginnings of a game on it. Diatsaro began to set out the pieces afresh. "Do you have time for a game?"

"I haven't played for ages."

"You can be white."

Quinn led off. "General Wajda has been relieved of his command, did your daughter tell you?"

"Yes. Aina's an amazingly perceptive girl. Their . . . liaison was already turning sour, I think, but nothing kills romance for a Diatsaro woman like professional disgrace." He smiled to himself. "She's an amazing girl, really. . . . Incidentally, is Captain Hollis married?"

"No."

"Ah . . ."

They played on, but Quinn was incapable of concentrating. He lost several pieces in short order. The second time Diatsaro called check he resigned.

"Your thoughts are elsewhere, my friend. I do hope for your sake they're not with my daughter."

"That woman at the miners' village, Moura Toumanova," Quinn corrected. "I need to find her."

"Something tells me there's more to this than lust," Diatsaro said.

"She's disappeared." Quinn reached across the chessboard and closed his fist around Diatsaro's queen. "I'm looking for a place in the mountains—a place where she could be detained under guard. A hunter's cabin, a derelict mining camp—somewhere like that. Do you have a map of the area?"

The prince rose and went over to a built-in closet with shelves at the top and drawers at the bottom. The shelves held a collection of rock samples. He opened one of the drawers and took out some rolled-up maps gray with dust. "They're pretty old," he said, undoing the string that held them together.

"Is there a geological map among them?"

Diatsaro handed over the entire bundle and cleared away the chess set. Quinn leafed through the maps, selected one, and spread it out on the table. The prince produced two rock samples, coarse-grained lumps of gneiss, for use as paperweights.

Quinn studied the marks that recorded the results of geological tests. One spot was marked with the "Au" that symbolized gold. He pointed to it. "That's where the gold was hidden when it arrived here, in the Xenia Mine itself."

"So it really did exist?" Diatsaro emitted a grunt of surprise.

"Yes. But they'd already moved it somewhere else." Quinn drew a circle on the map with his forefinger. "It's somewhere in this area."

Diatsaro glanced dubiously at the map.

"They didn't have the time to prepare a special hiding place," Quinn went on. "That means they must have used an existing mine."

"Once gold had been found at the Xenia," Diatsaro said, "people went rooting around all over the place."

"No, I don't mean an abandoned claim. It would have to be

227

an excavation at least as big as the Xenia, complete with shafts that haven't collapsed and some means of mechanical transportation. A conveyor belt, an elevator—something of the kind. You've hunted this district for years. Think hard—it may have been Govorov who suggested the place."

Diatsaro bent over the map. He pondered awhile, then pointed to a line that began at the miners' village and wound its way up into the mountains. "That's the old pass road," he said, "and that's the former posthouse. The coachmen used to change horses there before tackling the final ascent to the pass, which was very steep. The posthouse keeper was a woman. Everyone called her 'Red Dora' on account of her hair."

"Dora Nikulin?"

"Nikulin?" Diatsaro looked mystified.

"Was she married?"

"I never saw any sign of a husband. She had two children, though—a boy and a girl."

"Was the girl's name Moura?"

"I wouldn't know."

"Do you know what became of them?"

"The posthouse closed down when the old road was abandoned. The family must have left Karmel. The posthouse itself has been derelict for twenty years." Diatsaro pointed to the map again. "The road had a sinister reputation, especially the final stretch. There were stones and crosses every few hundred yards, marking where people had fallen to their deaths."

"It was superseded by the new road running parallel to the Trans-Siberian?"

"Yes, and not a day too soon. It had tight hairpin bends with sheer walls of rock on one side and precipices on the other. It was impassable for most of the winter months and dangerous even in summer. There are very few windless days up there. The brakes weren't strong enough, so the coachmen used to reinforce them by towing tree trunks on chains, but

228

not even that was a guarantee of safety. Accidents were reported after every storm—one gust could send a wagon or a coach toppling over the edge in seconds. See this gorge here? It's still called the Horses' Graveyard on account of all the bones and debris lying at the bottom."

Quinn pointed to another spot on the map. "This is the summit of the pass?"

"Yes, flanked by 'The Brothers,' two peaks of unequal height."

"What about this line branching off it?" Quinn indicated a symbol east of the pass, a "K" in a circle. "That must stand for potassium."

Diatsaro threw back his head and laughed. "Potassium indeed! That mine ruined another Karmel family," he said, "—the Rothsteins."

"So it *was* mined?"

"Nikolai Rothstein had made a lot of money out of manufacturing gunpowder. His factories in Perm used to import saltpeter from abroad. When deposits of potassium nitrate were found near Karmel he thought he could get rich even quicker by mining the stuff himself, but there were difficulties from the outset. The shafts cost a fortune to sink and kept on flooding. Transportation was another problem. Rothstein abandoned the mine in the end, but by then it was too late." Diatsaro shook his head as he recalled what happened. "My mother's sister was going to marry one of Rothstein's sons. They were already engaged, but the engagement was broken off when it became known that Nikolai Rothstein had gone bankrupt."

He fell silent. Then he said, "You think they could have hidden it there?"

Quinn didn't reply at once. An abandoned potassium mine . . . He knew he was on the track of something important, and he had no wish to share his discovery with anyone, not even Diatsaro. "Anything's possible," he said, rolling up the map. "May I make a copy of this?"

"Keep it." Diatsaro replaced the rock samples and the rest of the maps in the cupboard. "Got time for another?" he asked, nodding at the chessboard.

"If you like."

Diatsaro concealed two pawns in his hands and held them out. Quinn drew white again, but he was just as preoccupied as before and soon lost the initiative. Although an exchange of queens made it seem possible that he might at least achieve a draw, a stupid blunder finally cost him the game.

The prince eyed him thoughtfully. "You weren't at your best that time, either. I could tell. What were you thinking about?"

"All I need is some sleep," Quinn said evasively. "I was wondering, where's your dog?"

"I had to shoot him." Diatsaro scooped the chessmen into their box. "Shall we go and see how your friend's getting on?"

They were playing poker at a table in the corner of the hall: three elderly ladies, one elderly man in a bemedaled uniform, and Hollis. They were playing for money, too, to judge by the chips in front of them. The biggest pile reposed in front of Xenia Diatsaro, who was sitting ramrod straight in a nest of cushions, her hair and cheeks so liberally powdered that they were almost indistinguishable in color.

Aina Diatsaro, who wasn't playing, had installed herself in a chair behind Hollis. He'd obviously been losing, because she laid a hand on his arm as he pushed the last of his chips across the table and said, "I warned you!"

The old princess glared at him. "You're not giving up, surely?"

Hollis reached for a pencil and a piece of paper. "You'll have to take another IOU, I'm afraid."

230

"We can always increase the stakes," she suggested. "That way you can recoup your losses more quickly."

Hollis jotted down a figure, added his signature, and handed her the slip. She glanced at it, smiled, and said, "That's the spirit." Then she counted out some chips and pushed them across. Then Quinn and her son walked up to the table, and her expression became frigid and aloof.

Hollis swiveled in his chair and looked up at Quinn. "Mind if I play on for a bit?"

"Don't let me disturb you."

"Right!" Impatiently, Xenia Diatsaro thrust the deck at the old lady beside her. "Hurry up and deal."

Quinn opened his eyes. The blind over the window had a faintly translucent look. He got up, raised it an inch or two, and peered out. A wave of cold air smote his cheek. There was no daylight yet, just a gray penumbra.

He got dressed. Nothing was stirring next door in Hollis's section. By the time he emerged from the car, the first mountain peaks were beginning to etch themselves on the eastern sky.

He walked down the train. The baggage cars' double doors were open, and the Hampshires had rigged up their tents inside because of the cold. Tompo was in the last car, asleep under a blanket in the straw with his saddle for a pillow. Quinn woke him.

"We move out an hour from now."

The dining car was a strange blend of the luxurious and the functional. Half of it was a communications center full of cables and apparatus; the other half boasted wall-to-wall carpeting and tables draped in white damask. Quinn had only just sat down to breakfast when Hollis appeared wearing an army greatcoat over his pajamas. "Morning," he said. "You're up early."

231

"I'm planning to make an early start."

Hollis said no more until breakfast had been served: tea with condensed milk, toast, canned butter and marmalade. He didn't touch any food, just sipped his tea. "I knocked on your door when I got back," he said eventually.

"I must have slept deeply."

"Well," Hollis said, "did Sergei Diatsaro prove informative?"

"How much did you lose last night?" Quinn asked.

Hollis stared at him, then ran his hand through his hair in a look of total befuddlement. "I've never known such a woman—she's an absolute demon." He stopped then, remembering something. "Look, Oliver, what are you keeping from me?"

"I'm keeping nothing from you," Quinn replied. "All I know is that they're holding Moura Toumanova somewhere in the mountains. If I'm lucky I'll pick up their trail."

"Why this preoccupation with a common prostitute?" Hollis asked. "Has it ever occurred to you that she may even have been responsible for Cutter's death? She was the last person to see him alive."

"So what?" Quinn rose angrily. "That's none of your concern. The gold's all that matters to you—or has Fitzmaurice abandoned the hunt?"

Hollis sighed. "Look, if you must be this way, at least use a little good sense. Don't go after them alone. Take a platoon along with you."

"No point—they'd see us coming a mile off."

The Sibiryak was waiting with the horses already saddled and a pack mule on a leading rein.

Hollis stood watching at the open window of the dining car as they led their animals along the platform to the head of the train. He looked down at them and their heavy-laden mule,

232

shaking his head. "You ought to see yourselves," he said with a nervous laugh. "You look like a couple of forty-niners."

They crossed the track and mounted up. Day was breaking, but the sun was visible only as a pale glow filtering through the morning.

"Very appropriate . . ."

Quinn wasn't aware of having uttered the words aloud. All he knew was that his mood had changed. Now that they were actually on the move he felt a lightening of the heart.

31

T H E wind was blowing straight at them, and blowing so hard that making progress against it was like wading up a river in flood. At the end of the gorge Quinn paused briefly to look up at the heights above. He was tired to the point of exhaustion, but memories of his days as a fugitive with Tompo and Katov drove him on. Almost as if he were punishing himself for his momentary distractedness, he set off up the precipitous slope.

His calculations had been wrong. Deep snow and numerous drifts compelled them to make such lengthy detours that the climb took all day. The sun had gone down behind the mountains by the time Quinn reached the crest. He waited to catch his breath before surveying his surroundings.

He had a panoramic view of the snow-covered hills and valleys. The old road zigzagged upward and disappeared between two jagged peaks of unequal height, which still stood out clearly against the evening sky. The former staging post was situated on the side of a hill separated from him by a sizable dip in the ground. The scattered buildings were only dimly visible in the dusk.

He removed his gloves, unbuttoned his coat, took out his binoculars, and dried the lenses. It took him a few moments to distinguish the posthouse itself from the tumbledown out-buildings: a smithy, a saddlery, a garage, a stable. The sloping roof was covered with snow, the eaves on the south side fringed with icicles. He could detect no lights, no smoke. The whole place looked deserted, derelict.

He lowered the binoculars. Should he turn back and use the last of the fading light to rejoin Tompo at the rendezvous? The Sibiryak would have pitched their tent and prepared supper by now. Tired and hungry though he was, he waited. A sprinkling of stars appeared. The sky became even clearer, the cold more intense. The wind veered and moderated to a steady evening breeze. And then, quite suddenly, he caught a whiff of something in the air.

He raised the binoculars again: sure enough, smoke was curling upward from the posthouse chimney. So they'd only been waiting for nightfall. . . .

He replaced the binoculars beneath his coat, buttoned it up, and pulled his gloves on. With a last glance across the dip, he reluctantly abandoned his vantage point and set off down the mountainside.

The evening meal—canned meat and beans and canned suet pudding washed down with tea—was over. Tompo had scraped away the snow and pitched their tent below the timberline.

They were sitting side by side with their backs against the mule's load. The little kerosene stove gave off a modicum of heat. The animals, tethered nearby, were stirring restlessly.

"They're nervous," Tompo said. "Their first time in the mountains, probably."

Quinn drew his rucksack toward him. He took out the reserve magazine for his rifle and slipped it into the side pocket of his coat. He was itching to return to the staging post, but he told himself that it would be wiser to rest after such a tiring day. Besides, their chances of taking the opposition by surprise would be better if they waited till late at night to move.

"Let's get some sleep," he said.

Tompo extinguished the stove and they retired to the tent. The animals continued to stir uneasily. Once, when a night bird took wing, snow came pattering down on the canvas from the branches overhead.

"Five hours," Quinn told himself, already half asleep. "You'll wake up in five hours' time. . . ."

He would do so precisely five hours from now, he knew. It was a knack he'd developed many years ago, and he always found it oddly reassuring.

Daybreak was still a good two hours off, but Quinn covered the ground as fast as the deep snow permitted. They approached by way of a copse that extended to within a few yards of the old posthouse corral. Only the tips of the rotting fence posts protruded from the snow.

All he could see of the buildings from this angle were dilapidated walls and sagging roofs. The cluster of ruins made an even more deserted impression at close range, but appearances could be deceptive. He crept closer, every sense on the alert.

A stable loomed up ahead. Straining his eyes, he detected tracks in the snow. He stopped short: an almost imperceptible sound had come from inside the stable—a muffled snort. He glanced at Tompo.

"They must keep their horses in there," Tompo whispered. "Shall I see how many there are?"

"Not now." Looking around for cover, Quinn spotted a stone hut not far away. It turned out to be a kind of storeroom half sunk into the hillside. The door was missing, and the smell issuing from its dark interior suggested that some wild animal, possibly a bear, had recently bedded down there.

Their vantage point was less than fifty yards from the posthouse itself, but they could see no light or smoke. The windows had shutters. Snow had drifted up against the door, and beside it, ranged along the wall beneath the eaves, was a woodpile.

Quinn studied the building intently, surprised that no sentries had been posted. Did Ryazanov really feel so cocksure?

The cold was beginning to bite. His cheeks ached, his feet tingled in their felt boots, and his hands, which were holding the Nagant-Mosin rifle across his body, had grown numb. It was a relief when Tompo broke the silence. "I could take a closer look," he whispered.

"No, let's wait a bit longer."

Minutes went by. Then they heard a sound from inside the posthouse. A glimmer of light became visible: someone had lit a lamp. The door opened a crack and came to a stop, obstructed by snow. With a muffled curse, someone inside threw his weight against it.

The door opened at last and a figure stood outlined against the light. Quinn had never seen the man before. He was tall and thin, with dark, tousled hair and a long woolen scarf wound around his neck. No gun.

He lingered in the doorway for a moment, stretching as if he'd just woken up, then coughed until his shoulders shook. A voice from inside the posthouse called something. The man in the doorway went to the woodpile and collected an armful of logs. His scarf had come unwound while he was bending down, and he almost tripped over it on the way back.

He left the door ajar, presumably intending to fetch some more wood. Quinn, who hadn't taken his eyes off the man, became aware that Tompo had drawn his knife. "I'll get him when he comes out again," Tompo whispered. "He'll have his hands full—it'll be child's play, believe me."

236

"We don't know how many there are," Quinn whispered back.

"They'll come looking for him when he doesn't return. We'll pick them off one by one."

"First let's find the woman—" Quinn broke off because the man had reappeared. He fetched another armful of wood from the pile and carried it inside. A moment later the door closed behind him.

They waited. Smoke began to rise from the chimney. Quinn handed Tompo his rifle. "Cover me."

He crept up to the posthouse and put his ear to the door. Not a sound. Edging sideways, he paused in front of the first shuttered window but could still hear nothing. Noiselessly, step by step, he made his way over to the other side of the door.

Suddenly he stiffened. A thin shaft of light was escaping through a crack in a shutter. Voices could be heard—two of them, both male, one interrupted by periodic fits of coughing.

Quinn applied his eye to the shutter. He was looking into a room with a high ceiling and walls of natural stone. The light, which came from a kerosene lamp and a fire burning on the open hearth, was not very strong, and the windowpane was so grimy that it shrouded everything in a kind of mist. One of the men he'd already seen fetching wood; the other, a thickset fellow with a heavy Mauser pistol in his belt, was standing in front of the fire with his legs apart. Although he had his back to Quinn, his muscular build and white-blond hair seemed familiar.

In any case, neither man was Viktor Ryazanov, and there was no sign of Moura, either.

The man with the scarf took a steaming saucepan off the fire, filled two mugs, and handed one to his companion. When the other man turned to take it from him Quinn recognized him as Budyek, the Czech sergeant who had met him at Karmel station with Scala.

Budyek sat down beside the fire on an upended log. The man with the scarf put his own mug down, poured a third, and walked off with it. When he reentered Quinn's field of vision his hands were empty.

Quinn straightened up, frozen stiff in spite of his sheepskin coat and felt boots. From close at hand came the plaintive hoot of an owl. He turned and looked back at Tompo, who gestured at him reassuringly.

When he bent to look through the crack again, Moura was standing near the fire. Her wrists were bound, but not behind her, so she was able to hold her mug and drink from it. She was wearing a man's shirt and a long skirt over her riding boots. Quinn gazed at her with an unexpected surge of naked physical desire. It was as if he could feel the warmth of her body, smell the scent of her hair. His desire was so powerful he felt she would sense it and would turn to look.

She said something, and the thin man relieved her of her mug. Then she raised her bound hands and said something else. The thin man appealed to Budyek, or so it seemed, but the sergeant cut him short. With a toss of her head, Moura disappeared from view once more.

Quinn abandoned his post at the window, relieved that he had not been heard or seen by the men, but almost disappointed that she hadn't sensed his presence.

"How many are there?" Tompo asked.

"Two, from the look of it."

He picked up his rifle again and pointed to the stable. "Untether one of the horses and frighten it. Sooner or later they'll hear and come to investigate."

"Why not do that yourself and leave the rest to me?" Tompo had drawn his knife again.

"Because I want to get one of them to talk, if I can. Go on, move!"

Quinn made his way back to the posthouse and secreted himself near the door. Moura's captors had cleared a path to the stable. Tompo tiptoed along it and disappeared inside.

The silence persisted. Quinn could hear nothing but his own subdued breathing. He propped the rifle against the wall and unbuttoned his coat. Cocking his pistol and sticking it in his belt so that he could draw it in a hurry, he waited and listened. After what seemed an eternity he heard horses whinnying, hooves clattering around on a cobbled floor.

He focused his attention on the posthouse door, his heart thudding. Finally the noises from the stable grew louder as the frightened horses continued to stamp and whinny.

All at once the door burst open and a shaft of light slanted across the snow. The thin man emerged and stared in the direction of the stable. Pausing to recover from a fit of coughing, he wound the scarf more tightly around his neck and set off. He ran the last few yards, and Quinn saw the stable door close behind him.

The noises from the stable redoubled—the horses sounded as if they were galloping around inside, panic-stricken—but nothing else happened. Then Quinn heard footsteps approach the open door of the posthouse and Budyek appeared. He wasn't alone: he was holding the Mauser in one hand and gripping Moura's arm with the other.

Quinn flattened himself against the wall. They were standing with their backs to him only a few yards away. Budyek drew the girl closer.

"Malkin? Hey, Malkin!" he called. "What's up?"

His tone was unperturbed. When he got no answer he set off for the stable with one arm firmly clasping Moura's waist.

Quinn reached for his pistol but decided against it for fear of hitting her in the dark. They were halfway to the stable by now. He couldn't wait any longer. Without stopping to think, he sprinted after them. When he was only a few yards away he shouted, "Moura, run!"

239

He reached Budyek just as the Czech turned, letting go of Moura. Counting on surprise, he sprang at him and fastened his hands around his wrist, forcing the Mauser down toward the ground.

Budyek must have brought his other arm up, because something hard hit him in the face and a fireball of pain exploded in his head. He got one hand under Budyek's chin and began to drive his fingers into the muscular throat until Budyek hit him again, harder. He grasped at something, dug his fingers into it, and realized he had fallen face down into the snow.

"On your feet!"

Opening his eyes, he saw a pair of boots beside him. He tried to grab them, but a kick sent him flying.

"On your feet, I said!"

He struggled to his knees and stood up. The pain in his head became more agonizing still and the figure in front of him seemed to lurch and sway. There was a gun in its right hand. In the left hand was a spare clip of bullets—the heavy metal object Budyek had pulled from a coat pocket to hit him with.

"Good." Budyek gestured toward the posthouse with his automatic. "Now move! I want a little talk with you."

Quinn almost swung at him again, but he'd spotted a movement behind the Czech's back. He racked his brains for some way of distracting him. "Still doing other people's dirty work for them?" he said.

Budyek guffawed. "Your friend Davis died much too quick. With you I'll take my time. . . ."

He stiffened suddenly and was about to turn when Quinn spit in his face. Budyek swore violently but never completed the sentence. His upraised arm froze in midair, then slowly descended. He had realized the danger behind him too late.

An arm wrapped around his throat. He struggled, gasping for breath. Then a gurgling sound came out of his lips and a tremor ran through his body. His hand went limp and the gun slipped from his fingers into the snow.

The imprisoning arm withdrew. The heavy body swayed, then crashed to the ground. Quinn stepped back just in time to avoid it. The whole sequence of events was so quick that he didn't grasp exactly what had happened until he saw Tompo bend over the prone form and tug his knife out of its back.

"Maybe next time you'll listen to me," the Sibiryak said coolly.

Quinn nodded. "I stand corrected." He looked around. Moura had run back to the posthouse and was standing stiffly in the doorway, watching. He turned back to Tompo. "What about the other man?"

"No need to worry about him anymore." Tompo bent over the corpse, grasped it under the arms, and hauled it through the snow to the stable.

Quinn made his way back to the posthouse. A plaid shawl was lying on the path. He picked it up and walked on. Another few steps and he was beside her. He restrained an impulse to put his arm around her, deterred by the memory of Budyek doing likewise. All he said was, "It's over now." He held out the shawl.

She stood rooted to the spot, dazed and trembling. He draped the shawl around her shoulders. He'd forgotten that her hands were still bound, and the wrap slipped to the ground. He retrieved it and put his arm around her, but at the first touch she started and shrank away.

"Let's go inside," he said.

She hadn't even looked at him yet; she was staring past him at the stable, into which Tompo had just dragged the body. Now she turned and gazed at Quinn with an air of bewilderment, as if she still hadn't recognized him.

"Moura," he said.

She seemed startled by the sound of her own name. "*Anglichanin*," she murmured.

He put his arm around her once more. She didn't resist this

241

time, and he felt her relax as he led her inside. She nestled against him with her head on his shoulder. It was such an uncharacteristic gesture that he could only attribute it to the lingering effects of shock. He liked the feel of her body in his arms, shivering with cold but very much alive.

32

ALTHOUGH the posthouse contained no relics of the old days, Quinn could picture it thronged with travelers who had hurried inside to warm their frozen limbs beside the fire and drink tea while waiting for a storm to blow over or the coachman to change horses.

Moura had drawn her chair up to the hearth and was sitting there with her hands side by side on her lap as if still unused to the absence of the rope that had bound her wrists together.

Neither of them had yet exchanged a word. Not even the crackle of the logs in the fireplace could dispel the silence that reigned in the room.

Quinn saw now in the firelight how much Moura had changed. Her face was thinner, and there were shadows beneath her eyes and lines around her mouth that hadn't been there before. Quinn had once fancied that her face would never age. He had been wrong, but that merely made her more real to him and intensified his desire for her. It dominated him completely, this insane pull toward a woman in wartime. He longed to touch her, embrace her, possess her. Everything else had become meaningless.

She raised her head and gave him a puzzled look. Her face, almost stony till now, underwent a transformation. The expression in her eyes seemed to say that she had read his mind. Then her face grew serious again. She got up, retired to the room next door, and returned with some white cloths in her hand. For want of anything better, she moistened them with tea from the saucepan.

"Let me clean the wound for you."

His throat tightened. "Not yet," he said hoarsely.

She stood there and waited until he complied. He felt a stab of pain as she gently swabbed the wound where Budyek had clubbed him. The magazine from the Mauser had caught him on the cheek, lacerating the new skin and inflicting a deep, jagged gash.

"Keep still." She wiped away the blood, threw the first cloth into the fire, and set to work with another. "Does it hurt?"

"Does what hurt?"

Her face broke into a smile. It was almost her old smile, except that it remained on the surface and failed to hide her latent fear. "Would you like some tea?"

"For God's sake!" Quinn protested. "Stop treating me like a stranger. It's me. Oliver Quinn—don't you recognize me?"

"It's still hot," she said calmly.

She filled a mug and handed it to him, then perched on the edge of the raised hearth. The fire had burned low. Again they withdrew into their own, separate realms of silence. They might indeed have been strangers, Quinn reflected: travelers who had met on board a mail coach and could think of nothing to say to each other. He sipped his tea. It was strong and bitter.

Moura ran a hand through her hair. "When did you get back?" she asked at length.

"The day before yesterday."

She edged nearer the fire. "Did you—"

"Yes," he said. "I'm afraid so. We found him by the stable."

"Poor Timur—he tried to fight them off, but there were three of them. . . ."

"Was Ryazanov the third man?"

243

"Yes . . . I warned you about him, remember?"

She shivered, though it might have been the cold. The fire was on the verge of going out. Quinn fed it with the last of the logs and went outside to fetch some more.

Nothing was stirring in the stable; the door was shut and the horses had quieted. There was no sign of Tompo, and he wondered what was keeping him. The sky was clear and frosty. He peered at his watch. First light was less than an hour away.

He collected an armful of wood from the pile and made up the fire again. The shawl was lying on the floor. He picked it up and replaced it around her shoulders. It was only when she thanked him that he noticed she was still wearing the gold chain around her neck. Abruptly convinced that it was a gift from Cutter, he was overcome with jealousy as fierce as that which had gripped him long ago, when another woman was involved. . . .

"That man you came with," she said, "—who is he?" Her tone was almost conversational. "He . . . he killed that Czech without a moment's hesitation."

Quinn returned to the present with an effort. "His name is Tompo," he said eventually. "He's a Sibiryak—we were in prison together at Perm."

She looked at him. "You really went there? I did my best to talk you out of it."

"You'd have done better to tell me the truth."

"You know I wasn't free to speak."

"You were happy enough to confide in Tom Cutter."

She made an attempt at one of her old, seductive smiles. "You were glad to see me just now."

"Fyodor Nikulin is your brother."

She looked at him in surprise. "How did you find out?"

"I came across a Cheka commissar in Perm who used to know him."

244

She gazed into the fire for a moment, lost in thought. Then she said quietly, "I'm glad you know."

"When did he take you into his confidence?"

"Fyodor? Back in Moscow. He'd been recalled from the front and offered this new command, but he wanted nothing to do with it. Fyodor was a soldier all his life. A revolutionary fighting for a world in which gold would mean nothing anymore. They tried to tempt him—they promised to convert the train into an armored train and put him in command of it when the job was done, but he still said no. Even when he was ordered to accept he did so against his better judgment."

"So you accompanied him to Karmel," he said.

She nodded. "It was his idea. My husband had been killed eight months earlier. It brought Fyodor and me closer together, because he had fought in his unit."

"And you had a way of getting in touch with your brother?"

"I haven't seen him for months." Moura looked up at him. "Everyone had given up on Fyodor!" she added angrily. "The Red Guards promised to recapture Karmel and did nothing. Ryazanov deserted to the Czechs. Fyodor's helpers were murdered—liquidated . . . I tried to talk him into making a deal while he could still negotiate his terms."

"A deal with Cutter?"

"Fyodor's life was on the line—mine too!" she added sharply. "I tried to convince him. Let's go, I said—let's go right now. You aren't interested in the gold. You want to survive, don't you? Well, if you don't, I damn well do!" She fell silent, exhausted. "But I wasn't talking to the same man," she continued. "Do you see? Fyodor Nikulin, my own brother, simply wouldn't listen to me. Then I began to understand: the gold! The gold had suddenly become important to him—more important to him than me—or anything else in the world."

"We need to get in touch with him," Quinn said.

"It's pointless."

A log disintegrated. Moura leaned forward and thrust the embers back into the fire with another log, then added it to the blaze, her hair shining beautifully in its reflected glow. "Here, some more tea," she said. He held out his mug and she refilled it. "How on earth did you find me?"

"Someone told me about the posthouse keeper, a woman known as 'Red Dora.' " He touched her hair. "I assume she was your mother."

Moura looked around the room with a wry smile. "Everyone in Karmel thought she was wonderful. What a courageous woman, they said, bringing up her children alone in the wilds. . . . But you know, I detested her. My one aim in life was not to grow up like her. I still can't bring myself to do any of the things that made her so special. I neither inherited her practical nature, nor did I inherit her hatred of all men. . . ."

She pointed to the back door. "Before the coaches arrived she used to lock me up in a barn behind the house. I was only a child, but no one was allowed to set eyes on me. She kept me locked up till the horses had been changed and everyone had gone. Why? To shield me from lecherous glances!" Moura laughed bitterly. "I hated my mother and I hated this place. When I left here I swore I'd never return. The first thing I did was dye my hair black, but the red showed through."

"Surely your father treated you better," said Quinn recalling what she'd told him at the miners' village.

"My father was different. I adored him, but he was never around. Alexis Nikulin was a prospector—he spent his life looking for gold all over Russia, but he never found enough. Her voice took on a soft affectionate note. "Every now and then he would reappear, sometimes for a whole week, sometimes only for an hour or two. He always brought the oddest presents with him—kites too flimsy for the mountain winds, Chinese silk slippers that didn't fit anyone, Japanese kimonos, ostrich feathers from South Africa, strings of beads, colored

246

stones—and every present had a story. Later on I came to suspect that he'd bought the things in some bazaar and made up the stories to go with them, but it didn't matter. My father was a captivating man. . . ." Moura looked at Quinn. "You know, the first time I saw you, you reminded me of him. . . ."

Quinn forced himself to ask: "What became of your parents?"

"My mother's still alive. She married a senior Party official in Kazan, where she has a monopoly of all the droshkies in the city—the Cab Queen, they call her. My father's dead—killed during a brawl in the Kolyma goldfields. That was one of the reasons why Fyodor hated everything to do with gold—why he originally turned the assignment down. That was in Moscow, though. He's a different person these days. . . ."

"He may have changed again since you saw him last." Quinn thought of his spell in "the Box" at Perm. "Alone in the mountains in this weather? Solitude and hardship can wear a man down in the end."

"The gold, that's all you're interested in! Fyodor, Cutter, and now you, too, *Anglichanin* . . ." She gave a sharp, unnatural laugh. "What will you give me if I tell you where it is? How about saying you love me—would that be so hard? One little lie in exchange for a fortune? No! Don't say it—I don't want to hear. I wouldn't believe you anyway."

He laid a hand on her arm. It was a gesture that conveyed more of his emotions than any embrace. "When this is over," he said, "I'll tell you what you want to hear."

"When this is over, we won't know each other anymore."

He began gently toying with the gold chain at her throat.

"Yes?" she asked.

Quinn bent forward to kiss her neck, but just as he was about to he caught sight of the chain. Attached to it was a gold charm in the shape of a four-leaf clover. He stared at it. The touch of the yellow metal seemed to sear his flesh. Tom Cutter! She'd been wearing his charm next to her skin. . . .

247

He wrenched the chain from her neck. He drew back and looked at her. All the color had drained from her cheeks. She clasped her neck with one hand and held out the other for the chain.

"Why did you do that?" she asked. "Are you really so jealous of a dead man?"

"You slept with him?"

"What a stupid question! You of all people should know that it was gold that brought Tom Cutter to Karmel, not women. He put on an act with me, just like you do now—pretending I'm the kind of woman a man could fall in love with." She rubbed her neck, the weariness and pain now unmistakably carved into her once beautiful face. "He was more barefaced than you, that's the only difference. Lying came easier to him."

"Stop it." Quinn dropped the broken chain into her outstretched hand.

"When he saw it wasn't necessary to pretend to me any longer," she went on, "he suggested a deal: ten percent of the gold for Fyodor and me . . . but by then I knew I'd become involved in something that was getting out of hand. All the same, I told Fyodor about Cutter's proposition at our next rendezvous. He took it surprisingly calmly and agreed to meet with him. That should have aroused my suspicions, I suppose. But all I wanted was to end this nightmare. . . ."

That, Quinn realized, must have been when Cutter sent his message to Omsk.

"I don't know what happened," Moura said. "I really don't, believe me. I waited for Cutter to return but he never did."

Quinn said, "Have you seen your brother since then?"

"Yes, once. He didn't say a word about the meeting and I couldn't bring myself to ask him about it. His manner was much the same as usual, but I'm convinced he killed Cutter." Her voice rose. "And he won't hesitate to kill again. He'd even kill me if he knew I'd given him away." She sighed and inspected the broken chain. "So you see, the truth does neither of us any good."

"But it does," Quinn said. "We know now at least that we have been honest with each other."

The fire had burned low and the logs had run out again. Either they must have been air-dried for months, Quinn thought, or he'd lost his sense of time.

He got up, opened a window, and pushed the shutters back. Cold air came streaming in. All that marked the route of the old pass road were some crooked posts protruding from the snow. The stars had faded; the mountains were still in darkness, but the sky beyond the wooded hills on the Karmel side was faintly streaked with gray.

He strove to recall the self-confident mood in which he'd awoken in his section on board the train only twenty-four hours earlier. He'd kept Hollis guessing and insisted on acting independently. The best thing he could do now was return to Karmel and leave the rest to Hollis. He could dispatch a platoon into the mountains. It didn't matter if the gold was hidden in the potassium mine or somewhere else. They'd find it sooner or later—it and the man who was guarding it.

He shut the window and rejoined Moura beside the fire. "What if we go back to Karmel?" he said at length. She looked at him questioningly. "Would you help us?" he added.

"In what way?"

"By telling us everything you know?"

"I already have," she said, bristling.

"We haven't talked about the mine. The one where they've hidden the gold."

"I know nothing of that. Fyodor trusted no one with such secrets, not even me."

"What about Govorov?"

249

"Pavel Pavlovich would never betray Fyodor."

Quinn gestured at their surroundings. "I assume he once used this place as a hideout. Where is he now?"

"Ryazanov forced him to go with him." She turned, annoyed, as the door behind them opened. A wave of cold air accompanied Tompo inside.

He deposited Budyek's belt and automatic on the edge of the raised hearth. Moura filled the remaining mug with tea and held it out, but Tompo shook his head.

"*Anglichanin*," he said, "I brought our animals up from the bivouac. But come, please, I've something to show you."

"What is it?"

"Come outside a minute."

When Moura started to follow the Sibiryak paused and shook his head. "Not you," he said.

It was a request, not an order. Quinn had never heard the big man speak so gently.

Tompo led the way. The sky was gradually paling, and the stable, starkly outlined against it in the half-light, looked bigger than it had at night.

Tompo paused at the door and turned. Moura, reluctant to be left alone, had ignored his request. "Don't come in," he said, and this time he sounded almost imploring.

Quinn looked at him. "What is it?"

"Something she shouldn't see."

Moura turned to Quinn. "What does he mean?" she protested. "Who does he think I am?"

The ramshackle door was ajar. Tompo hesitated, then went inside. Quinn put an arm around Moura and followed him in. A strong smell of hay and horse dung came to meet them, and they could hear the animals stirring uneasily.

Quinn's eyes took a little while to get used to the gloom. Then he made out a figure standing at the back of the stable.

* * *

There was an interval of several seconds before his surprise at
seeing Govorov gave way to shock. He stared at the figure
until the truth sank in: Govorov wasn't standing at all. The
tips of his toes were only just touching the ground, but he
wasn't hanging by the neck. Ryazanov had wanted to get him
to talk, and so Govorov had been tortured, had been given the
"strappado": the rope had been tied to his wrists from behind
and thrown over a beam. They'd hoisted and dropped him,
hoisted and dropped him until his arms had been twisted
from the sockets. . . .

For an instant Quinn was conscious only of his own sheer
horror. Then he became aware that Moura had stiffened in his
arms. A sound escaped her lips—just a sound, not a cry. He
buried her face in his chest to spare her the sight. She tried to
free herself when he made to turn away, but he held her tight.

"You can't just leave him hanging there," she said hoarsely.

"Of course not," Quinn told her. "Tompo will do what has
to be done."

He led her out, still holding her close. Tompo and the
horses could be heard moving around inside the stable.

"I had no idea," he said. Had Govorov talked before his
death? Remembering his own experiences in Perm, he assumed Govorov had. "I'm sorry, Moura. Come back to the
house."

"What then?" She seemed a little calmer. "Will you take
me back to Karmel?"

He looked up. The sun was rising above the snow-capped
hills in the east. The light was almost white, and the cold,
instead of abating, seemed even more intense. The pass was
still swathed in a pall of mist from which only the peaks that
flanked it—The Brothers—reared their heads.

She must have followed the direction of his gaze, because he
heard her say, "What if I beg you, if I ask you not to go, if I

say I love you, *Anglichanin?* How often do you think I've told a man that?"

Quinn, transfixed by her dark, glowing eyes and pale face, thought how beautiful she was. "Scores of times," he said. He owed her that, he decided, much as it hurt: he owed her the truth.

"I hate you!" she cried. Then, from one moment to the next, she quieted. "I haven't slept all night. I'm too tired to go into the mountains."

"Tompo will escort you back to Karmel," he said.

"Alone?" She shook her head. "You still want the gold?"

"I can't turn back now," he said wearily. "Too much has happened. . . ."

"What can I say, what can I do, to dissuade you?" she asked. "How can I make you see the futility of your own greed?"

He didn't reply.

Finally, she said, "At least give me an hour before we leave. . . ."

33

ALTHOUGH Fyodor Nikulin had been awake for hours, he didn't get up as soon as dawn broke. Even he, with his iron constitution, was finding it harder and harder to sleep. Most of the time he lay there with his eyes open, immersed in a kind of torpor from which all sense of reality was absent—indeed, he often found it hard to remember why he was there at all. Getting up in the morning seemed an act that demanded almost superhuman willpower.

He rose in the end and pulled on his boots. It was so cold inside the cabin that frost had transformed the nails in the walls into little white cones. Everything was coated with rime. His stock of kerosene for the stove had run out days ago. He felt so dizzy when he went outside that he had to cling to the doorframe for support.

The sun had climbed above the mountains. He collected some wood and lit a fire—a risk he would never have taken until lately. He made tea and opened one of his last cans of meat. The tea he drank, but the meat he left untouched and munched some hardtack instead. Not even this meager breakfast improved his morale.

"You promised!"

He shook his head at the sound of his own voice. Then, hurrying back into the cabin, he knelt down and opened one of the boxes. His hands trembled as he took out the gold bar and polished it on his coat. Its weight and luster soothed him, but he couldn't recall exactly when he'd last gone to the mine. He knew only that he'd brought it back one day to convince himself that the gold was more than just a figment of his imagination.

He went outside again. The sky was cloudless, and the sunlit snow on the slopes below the massif dazzled him. Screwing up his eyes and wrinkling his brow, he squinted at the white waste in sudden alarm. Something was wrong.

He fetched his binoculars. The furrows in his brow deepened as he peered through them: there were footprints in the snow on the track leading to the potassium mine. His own, or had it snowed since his last visit? He followed them by eye to the spot where the track veered off and disappeared from view. Whose were they?

Quickly, he scrambled up the slope behind the cabin for a better look, but before he could reach the top his eye was caught by something else: some dark specks were visible in the valley far below. They were moving, but almost imperceptibly, like pieces of flotsam drifting on an ocean of snow.

He held his breath. Three figures were toiling up the old road to the pass. Still too far off for him to see their faces, they were wearing long coats and fur hats, and the last of the three was leading a mule.

Nikulin forgot about the footprints and stared at the figures incredulously, more curious and excited than alarmed. Then he slithered down the slope, kicked some snow over the fire, and hurried into the cabin, where he buckled on his snowshoes and picked up his rifle.

Outside once more, he set off down a snowy ravine with towering walls of rock on either side. Through some trees, across a stretch of level, open ground, and down another ravine. He was out of breath by the time he reached the wood. He paused for a moment, then disappeared among the firs.

34

QUINN had taken the lead. It was hard enough going on the flat, and they made even slower progress uphill. They'd already been en route for four hours, but he was too tensed-up to feel tired.

Ahead of them lay another uphill stretch flanked by a wood. A raucous cry stopped him in his tracks, and a bird skimmed the tops of the firs. The snow was so dazzling he could scarcely see it. The harsh note resembled that of a jay, but the bird itself was too big, with long, pointed wings—probably a bird of prey.

Moura had caught up and was staring, like him, at the bird circling the wood. Her weary face looked even wearier in the brilliant sunlight.

Tompo, leading the mule laden with their equipment, halted beside them. He unslung the canteen and handed it to Moura, then turned to Quinn. "Why not let her rest a little?" he suggested.

Quinn was reminded of Timur the Mongol. Tompo had adopted the same protective attitude toward her, and he couldn't help chuckling at the thought. "You see?" he said to Moura. "First Mongolia, now Siberia. You've conquered more provinces than Peter the Great!"

She smiled despite her exhaustion.

"Let her be!" Tompo said huffily.

Quinn paused for a few minutes before taking the lead again. The climb was a long one. The sun had melted the surface snow, but the layer beneath was smooth and slippery. He trod with care, concentrating hard. The birdcalls had ceased.

The old road curved sharply to the right when it breasted the summit of the rise and the fir trees ended. Quinn covered the last few yards at a brisker pace and was panting by the time he reached the summit. Then he froze.

The man was standing in the middle of the road not thirty feet away, holding a rifle. The spot was well chosen, not only because the trees had concealed him until the last moment, but because the sun was at his back. All that could be discerned was a gaunt, erect figure in a long fur coat and a fur hat.

Quinn heard Moura's exclamation as she reached his side. "Fyodor," she said in a low, almost inaudible voice.

The man in front of them hadn't moved. "Moura!" he called hoarsely.

"I'll speak to him," she whispered.

Quinn put his arm out, stopping her.

"Moura!" The man spoke haltingly, almost as if he had a speech impediment. "You . . . you shouldn't have come!"

"Fyodor, listen to me!"

The motionless figure came to life. Nikulin raised the rifle and cocked it. The click of the bolt sounded overloud in the stillness.

"Come here!" he called, still hoarsely but more articulately. "Come here—alone!"

Quinn gripped her by the arm and held her back.

Nikulin stared at them with the rifle still poised. "You

shouldn't have come!" he repeated. His voice had taken on a menacing note. "Goddamn you, why have you done this to me?"

Quinn, his whole attention focused on Nikulin, had forgotten all about Tompo, who was edging off to one side, hoping to spread out the target. Nikulin didn't hesitate for an instant. He fired one shot only, but its echoes filled the air like a series of thunderclaps.

Tompo stopped dead as if he'd run into a brick wall. He remained standing with his right hand outstretched. The knife he had been holding behind him slipped from his fingers. Then his legs folded and he sank to his knees.

Quinn had let go of Moura. He ran to Tompo and bent over him, supporting him by the shoulders. Tompo looked up. For a moment Quinn thought he was unhurt: there was no pain on the Sibiryak's face, just a look of surprise.

"*Anglichanin* . . ." Tompo fought for breath, smiling faintly.

Quinn knelt beside him in the snow. Tompo's shoulders started to tremble and his body slowly sagged forward. "Get up," Quinn urged him. "Come on, I'll help you!"

With an effort, Tompo raised his head once more. "Just a little rest, *Anglichanin*. . ."

"What the devil were you trying to do?"

"I wanted to get over to where I could get his attention and let you shoot him, or throw the knife. Where is my knife?"

"I'll find it later," Quinn said, but Tompo seemed to have forgotten it already. "Listen, you think she turned my head, but she didn't. You'll be all right. We'll go back to Karmel as soon as you're on your feet. Where are you hit?"

"*Anglichanin* . . . watch out for the sister . . ."

The last words were uttered in a groan. Tompo's body sagged; Quinn could scarcely hold him up. His head fell forward and his fur hat slid off, exposing the bristly crop of hair that had grown since his head was shaved in prison.

256

"Tompo!"

There was no answer. Quinn lowered him into the snow as gently as he could and stood up. Dazedly, he looked around. Moura was immobile, her face twitching.

Nikulin came toward them with his rifle at the ready. His snowshoes made a crunching noise in the snow. Quinn could see his face clearly now. The resemblance to Moura was striking. He had the same red hair and high cheekbones, but the deepset, red-rimmed eyes had a wild, hunted look.

Nikulin halted beside the body. He gave it only a cursory glance, then turned to them and said, "Come with me."

She shrank away from him and clung to Quinn. Her face was still twitching. "You saw me!" she shouted. "Don't you trust anyone anymore? He was a friend. You're insane!"

The sound of her voice was suddenly echoed from above. Quinn looked up. Several birds were now circling over the bleak, white waste, but he still couldn't identify them. He turned to look for the mule. It had galloped off at the sound of the shot, only to get stuck in a snowdrift. Ignoring Nikulin, he unstrapped the saddlebags and discarded them. Then he helped the beast to extricate itself and led it over to the spot where Tompo's body lay. It shied at the sight.

Moura joined him. "I'll hold it," she said.

He handed her the leading rein. Tompo's hands were clasped over his stomach, and it was only now, as Quinn hauled the body erect and the lifeless arms hung limp, that the blood-sodden patch on the coat came to light. Propping the Sibiryak against the mule's flank, he finally managed to get him across the saddle. All the time Moura had been speaking soothingly to the frightened animal. Quinn stooped to retrieve the fur hat and took the rein from Moura's hand. Her face was still a horrified mask. He put his arm around her and held her tight. "Speak to him," she murmured.

Quinn wasn't sure if that would make any difference. However, he took several steps toward Nikulin and said, "You can't shoot everyone that comes up here. By tomorrow there'll be a hundred men out looking for us."

Nikulin just stood there. Quinn wasn't even sure if he'd heard. "Govorov's dead," he went on.

The red-rimmed eyes swiveled in Moura's direction. "Is this true?" Nikulin asked her. "What happened?"

Quinn answered for her. "He didn't die as quickly as this man here. He died a slow, painful death. It gave him ample time to talk."

"Never," Nikulin said. "It isn't possible."

"Oh, yes," Quinn said angrily. "Govorov talked sure enough. . . . Instead of waylaying us here, you'd have done better to stop Ryazanov."

Slowly, Nikulin turned and looked over his shoulder at someplace in the mountains behind him. "What about Ryazanov?" he demanded.

"We've been here on the move for hours," Quinn said. "We can talk about Ryazanov, but not here."

Nikulin looked around, then gestured with his rifle at the tracks his snowshoes had left in the fresh snow. "You go first," he said, and stepped aside to let Quinn pass.

Quinn led the mule down the slope and away from the road. When he paused and looked back, Nikulin had shouldered his rifle and was following with Moura beside him. For just a moment he had thought Nikulin might shoot him in the back.

A cold wind had sprung up, sending spindrifts of fine snow whirling through the air. Unable to see more than a couple of yards ahead, he concentrated on Nikulin's tracks.

35

THE wind was a gale at this altitude. The rocks around the cabin formed a shield against it, but sporadic gusts would whip up the snow and bring clouds of it down on their heads.

Nikulin had built a fire outside the cabin and made tea for them. The climb had been too arduous for conversation, but now he glanced at the sky and said, "Another half-hour and the wind will drop."

Quinn groped in his pockets for a cigarette. Nikulin stared at the Players he produced with a look of undisguised longing on his hitherto impassive face. Seeing it, Quinn handed him the pack. Moura, too, must have noticed her brother's reaction. "At least there's something you miss," she said combatively.

Nikulin laid his rifle aside with an irritated glance. Quickly, he fingered a cigarette out of the pack and lit it with a smoldering twig from the fire, drawing in a lungful of smoke and exhaling it with relish. The edges of his lips were encrusted with raw, half-healed blisters. He gave another glance at the sky.

"You'd better be on your way," he said.

It was an unwelcome recall to reality. Quinn indicated the mule, which he'd tethered to a tree trunk. "Help me bury him first."

"There's no time."

"You buried Cutter, I presume?" Quinn said scathingly.

Nikulin frowned at Moura as if the name meant nothing to him, and she, unable to endure his playacting, looked away. "Don't pretend you didn't kill him!" she cried.

"I pretend nothing," he told her.

"You shot him down just as ruthlessly as you shot down the Sibiryak over there!"

259

Nikulin froze. "We're at war," he said. "People get killed."

"All you care about is the gold," she screamed at him. "The gold, the gold and nothing else!"

Nikulin turned to Quinn. "Did you know the *Anglichanin?*"

"I did," Quinn said cautiously.

"He was planning to kill me and lay hands on the gold," Nikulin said. "I got there first, that's all. There's no more to be said."

The cigarette had dwindled to a glowing butt between his fingers. Just as Quinn was wondering if the man was immune to pain, Nikulin winced and tossed it away.

"Everyone wants to survive, even in a war," Quinn said.

Nikulin seized the gun and leveled it at him. "*Akula!*" he growled. "*Prokliataya akula!*"

Quinn held his gaze. "Even if you kill me, too many people know the gold is still around. You can't hope to hold out much longer—you'll have to give it up in the end."

"Oh no. In the end the Red Guards will recapture Karmel and the gold will still be here!"

"Fyodor, listen to him!" Moura's tone was almost imploring.

Nikulin looked at her. "It's my responsibility," he muttered. "Can't you understand?"

"Look," Quinn said with studied calm, "Perm has fallen and Karmel's recapture is a pretty remote prospect, but even if it were recaptured, what would happen to you? The same as happened to your helpers: Fyodor Nikulin wouldn't be the man who saved and guarded the gold. He'd be the one who *lost* it! The officers who recapture Karmel are bound to claim all the credit and leave you out in the cold!"

A blazing log had rolled out of the fire. Nikulin shoved it back with the toe of his boot. Quinn caught a whiff of scorched leather. The Russian withdrew his foot, and for one brief moment his face made no secret of all he'd endured in the past few months.

"What do you suggest?" he asked dully.

How relieved Nikulin would be to rid himself of responsibility for the gold—Quinn clung to that thought. "As long as the cache isn't found you can dictate terms," he said.

Nikulin turned and disappeared into the cabin, to emerge with a gold bar in his hand. Even as they watched, he raised the slab of yellow metal above his head and hurled it into the fire. The embers disintegrated and a shower of sparks went up.

"I've been sitting on it all the time!" He emitted a short, sharp bark of laughter. "If I'd wanted the gold for myself I could have taken it and cleared out long ago." He retrieved his gun and leveled it at Quinn again. "Now get going, *Anglichanin!*"

"You're a fool to send me away," Quinn said. "I'll be back with a hundred well-rested, well-fed, well-armed British soldiers. They're only waiting for the word."

"They'll be too late."

The man's fanatical determination was almost palpable. Quinn fell silent to avoid provoking him further. He didn't move, didn't even dare to breathe until he saw him lower the rifle and turn to his sister. "Make up your mind," Nikulin said roughly. "Either stay or go with him."

"Give up, Fyodor! Please! He's giving you a way out."

Quinn went over to the tethered mule. The hungry beast had nibbled all the twigs it could reach. Tompo's body was stretched out in the snow where he'd left it, but there was no hope of digging a grave in the frozen ground without tools. He was about to hoist the corpse onto the mule again when he heard footsteps in the snow.

Moura halted beside him, her face pale and despairing. "For a moment I thought you'd talked some sense into him," she said.

"Hold the animal's head, would you? We're wasting time."

She took off her fur hat and shook out her hair. It was almost a re-creation of his very first sight of her, except that now she looked tense and shocked. "Why should I come with you? Give me one good reason."

If he forced her to come with him he would lose her as surely as he would if he left her behind. "It's up to you," he said, weary and suddenly resigned.

The hard line of her mouth softened in a smile—the old, seductive smile that came so easily to her. She thrust herself against him. "Say it!" she whispered.

The sound of the explosion came from far away. Gradually fading, its echoes rumbled around the mountains like the wheels of some gigantic juggernaut.

"What was that?"

Quinn looked up. The light had become less intense and the sun was temporarily veiled by a cloud of whirling snow. When it subsided the sun reappeared and the highland plateau regained its cool, virginal aspect.

"What was that?" she repeated.

They turned to see Nikulin scrambling up the slope, clutching a pair of binoculars. Quinn ran to follow.

Nikulin had reached the top and was looking up at the pass, seemingly unaware of anyone beside him. There was no expression on his face when he eventually lowered the binoculars and handed them over.

Quinn couldn't at first detect anything unusual. Then he made out the tracks in the snow leading to the foot of the mountain. They ended at the spot where the explosion had occurred: the snow there had vanished, disclosing a wall of bare rock and ice.

He lowered the binoculars, but Nikulin spoke before he could say a word. "Govorov . . . So he did betray me. . . ."

"There were three of them—they tortured him. I knew he'd talked as soon as I saw him, but they killed him anyway."

262

Nikulin looked dubious. "Did they all go up there?"

"Just Ryazanov with a string of mules, as far as I know."

"Much good it'll do him . . ."

Quinn barely caught the muttered words. The meaning of the explosion suddenly dawned on him. "You mined the approaches?"

Nikulin squared his shoulders. "No one will get at that gold—no one!" He laughed harshly. "It came out of the ground. Now it's going back."

He set off down the slope to the cabin. Moura, who had joined them, stayed put. "What did he mean?" she said.

"Did he have any dynamite with him when he left for the mountains?" Quinn asked.

"Dynamite? He had something with him—but really I'd no idea . . ."

"He's probably laid some charges in the mine itself."

They exchanged a glance, then returned to the cabin. Nikulin had disappeared inside, leaving his rifle propped against the wall—they could hear him moving around, apparently looking for something. Quinn stole over to the rifle, an imported Winchester, and picked it up. Moura watched him, frozen-faced.

Nikulin emerged with an armful of pitch-pine torches and a miner's safety lamp. He looked at Moura and Quinn as if wondering who they were and how they'd gotten there. The sight of the rifle in Quinn's hands seemed to perturb him for a moment. Then he threw back his head and laughed.

"You'd never get to see it without my help."

"We're coming with you," Quinn said.

"What? Just to see it—just to make sure it really exists?" Nikulin gave another laugh and walked over to the fire, which had burned low. He trampled the embers into the snow, then turned and strode off without a backward glance. He didn't seem to care if they followed him or not.

Moura gazed after him. "Has he lost his mind?" she whispered, looking mystified. "Why did he leave you the rifle?"

"You heard what he said. He's sure I won't use it because without him I'd never set eyes on the gold."

"And then, *Anglichanin*? What happens when you've seen it?"

Quinn touched her face and said nothing. Then, silently, they turned to follow Nikulin up the slope.

36

NIKULIN had maintained the same brisk pace all the way. Now he slowed and came to a halt. Whatever his reasons, Quinn was glad of the respite.

The wind had dropped just as Nikulin had predicted, and the sky was clear and cloudless. The sun was sinking below the crest ahead of them. Over two hours had passed since they left the cabin. The climb through deep powder snow had been strenuous enough, but here at the foot of the mountain the path that snaked around it was as smooth and slippery as ice.

"Look, one of the mules!" Nikulin exclaimed, pointing. There was a note of triumph in his voice.

The explosion had carried away part of the path. Quinn made out two bloody animal carcasses sprawled on the rocks lower down. There was a man, or what was left of one, a few yards farther down the mountain. He turned to warn Moura not to look.

"I already saw it," she said, sounding strangely calm.

The sun dipped below the crest. The light changed, bathing the twin peaks in a pastel pink glow, and the temperature dropped at once.

Nikulin set off again, even more slowly and gingerly than before. The narrow path was flanked on the right by a precipitous slope, on the left by an equally precipitous wall of rock.

After several hundred yards it came to a spur and swung sharply left around it.

Nikulin disappeared from view. Quinn and Moura followed his tracks in the snow, step by step. Beyond the bend the path abruptly widened out into sizable plateau. They found Nikulin standing beside a pair of mules, their muzzles frosted with condensation. Quinn figured they had escaped the blast and run ahead, up to the spot. Both animals wore packsaddles, and Nikulin had opened one of the saddlebags. He pulled out a Red Army map case and held it up. "Ryazanov's!" he said with another of his grating laughs.

Quinn surveyed the rock face in front of him. The pink light had changed to dull gray. Visible in the shadowy background was a cave hollowed out of an overhang. Somewhat higher up stood a trio of pitch pines. Their roots clung to the naked rock, their trunks were gray with lichen, their crowns had been snapped off by the wind. Bare branches projected from them like suppliant arms.

Nikulin replaced the map case in the saddlebag. He went over to the cave and stood there for a moment. He laughed again, and his laughter reechoed back.

"What's the matter, *Anglichanin?* I thought you were anxious to see it." He ducked beneath the overhang and disappeared.

Moura gripped Quinn's arm. "Do we have to follow him?"

"Wait here if you like," Quinn said. "I have to go in."

She thought about that as they made their way through a narrow cleft. As soon as they were inside the cave it opened out above and ahead of them. The far end was walled up, and standing ajar in the center of the wall was a rusty iron door.

Nikulin had hung the safety lamp around his neck and lit it. The door led to an inner chamber. The glare of the lamp revealed an elevator with two compartments, one above the other.

Quinn eyed the two rusty cables that supported the crude

contraption, neither of them thicker than a washing line. "Isn't there another shaft?" he asked.

Nikulin's face, lit from below by the lamp on his chest, registered impatience. He stepped into the elevator, which was enclosed by steel mesh, and they followed. There was just room for three inside. Nikulin pulled a lever and the cage began its rattling descent.

The walls of the shaft, which had been hewn out of the living rock, were so close that Quinn could have touched them. Illuminated by the glare of Nikulin's carbide lamp, the rock formations changed as they descended. They passed the first of the horizontal galleries. Quinn vainly tried to gauge the depth of the shaft by counting the seconds it took them to get to the bottom: three hundred feet, five hundred, a thousand? All he knew for sure was that Moura was clinging to him with her head against his chest and her hair brushing his cheek.

The elevator stopped with a jolt that sent echoes reverberating around the walls of the lofty chamber at the foot of the shaft. Nikulin got out first and lit one of the pitch-pine torches. Three tunnels led off the chamber, each high and wide enough to accommodate small tramways. Standing in the central gallery was a line of dump cars. The air was surprisingly fresh and slightly salty. Absolute silence reigned.

Nikulin set off as soon as the torch was properly alight. He ignored the three main tunnels in favor of a side gallery that sloped gently downhill. The roof was shored with pitprops and high enough for them to walk upright.

The torchlight played over walls of reddish rock salt veined with off-white deposits of kieserite. They passed galleries that had been exhausted and blocked off. Every now and then Quinn heard water dripping somewhere close at hand in the surrounding rock.

Nikulin behaved as if he were thoroughly at home in this

subterranean world. He never hesitated when he changed direction and always maintained a lead of several yards. Quinn imprinted the system of passages on his memory like a map. His misgivings diminished as he followed in Nikulin's footsteps. It was as if he were in the grip of some magnetic attraction. The underworld had cast its spell over him and aroused expectations quite unrelated to his reason for being there: he was in the magical realm of his boyhood dreams.

The air in the gallery became thinner, the sound of water louder. Nikulin had reached yet another intersection. He turned down a short passage so low that they had to proceed at a crouch. Quinn heard him cursing loudly a few yards ahead.

He was standing in a high, vaulted tunnel when they caught up with him. The torchlight disclosed the reason for his annoyance. Water trickling down the walls had formed a shallow stream in the middle of the gallery, and running along the water's edge was a length of fuse.

Nikulin had stooped to examine it. He straightened up. "Wait here," he said, and slowly waded on with the water lapping over his boots.

Quinn stared down the tunnel. Nikulin had halted and was standing there with the torch held aloft, peering ahead of him.

The shot rang out without warning. Nikulin let go of the torch and tried to catch it as it fell, but it hit the water and went out.

The echoes faded. As silence returned Quinn heard footsteps stumbling through the darkness toward him, then Nikulin's breathless voice.

"Another torch, quick, but back into the passage first!"

Quinn knew then that Ryazanov had brought a second man, the one who had caught the blast. Ryazanov and his two surviving mates must have been some yards behind when Nikulin's land mine went off.

He lit a second torch and Nikulin reached for it. His hand was wet with blood. Moura saw it and uttered a little cry.

"You're hurt!"

Nikulin looked at his hand for the first time. More blood was oozing from a bullet hole in his sleeve.

"Take it off," Moura told him.

"Later—it's just a nick," he said, but he let them help him out of his coat. As soon as Moura had knotted a handkerchief around the superficial wound in his forearm, he pulled it on again. He turned to Quinn. "Cover me," he said after a moment's hesitation.

"Watch out for Ryazanov," Quinn said. "There is no use dying down here. He has to come past us to get out."

"You want to see that gold, don't you?" Nikulin's face seemed to lose its rigidity at last; his expression was relaxed, almost cheerful. He chuckled. "We'd best make it quick, while it's still there."

Nikulin had extinguished the torch and was keeping to the right-hand side of the tunnel. All they had to guide them in the darkness was the sound of his stealthy footsteps. Rounding a bend, they saw a reddish glow some fifty yards ahead. Nikulin pointed to it and signaled to Moura to stay put, then turned to Quinn. "Ready?" he whispered.

The tunnel ended in an archway. Nikulin disappeared through it into the chamber beyond. A moment later Quinn heard his voice.

"Viktor?"

The chamber was a big one, judging by the echo. Quinn stepped forward, rifle in hand. The light came from two torches stuck in sconces. At the far end was another tunnel.

"Viktor? Viktor!"

Quinn couldn't see Nikulin, he could only hear his voice and the echoes rebounding from the rocky walls. Then he caught sight of Ryazanov emerging from the tunnel in the background with a saddlebag over his shoulder and a Mauser in his hand. His face looked white even in the reddish light of the torches. His dark, cruel eyes were darting in all directions.

"Fyodor? Is that you, Fyodor?"

"Were you expecting someone else?"

"I wasn't sure."

The echoes of the two voices intermingled.

"Tell me something, Viktor. Is there any good reason why I shouldn't treat you the way you treated Pavel Pavlovich?"

Ryazanov let the saddlebag slip from his shoulder. "Don't be a fool, Fyodor."

"What do you suggest, then?"

"We could talk it over sensibly . . . sensibly . . . sensibly . . ."

Quinn heard a movement. He turned his head and saw Nikulin ease forward out of the shadows. Ryazanov opened fire at once. Quinn dropped on one knee and opened fire himself. The crack of the Winchester added its echoes to those of the two automatics. He didn't know if he'd hit Ryazanov, but he saw him throw away his empty pistol and make a dash for the tunnel at the back of the chamber. He went on firing until the Winchester's magazine was empty.

All at once there was a blinding flash and the echoes were drowned by a thunderous detonation that seemed to come from everywhere at once. The rock quaked underfoot. Quinn was hurled to the ground by the shock wave.

It was hard to breathe in such a pall of acrid smoke and dust. Quinn struggled to his knees and crawled back on all fours. The darkness seemed inexplicable until he realized that the blast must have extinguished the torches on the wall.

"Moura? Moura?"

"Here . . ."

269

He stumbled through the darkness until he could make out her shape.

"What happened? Where's Fyodor?" Her voice was little more than a whisper.

"Can you light a torch?" he asked gently.

He saw the resinous wood catch fire. The smoke from the explosion was beginning to disperse. He took the torch and held it above his head.

Nikulin was lying not far away, face down, arms outstretched. There were no obvious injuries, and Quinn's first thought was that the explosion had simply knocked him out. It wasn't until he stooped and rolled him over on his back that he saw the bullet wounds in his chest.

Moura, who was kneeling beside her brother, looked up. "He's trying to say something."

Quinn bent down. Nikulin's eyes were open and staring. Although his gaunt face bore the marks of his months-long ordeal in the mountains, it wasn't that of a man in agony or afraid of death; the main impression was one of grim determination. Faint sounds were issuing from his lips. Quinn caught only snatches of what he was saying.

"Stop . . . him. . . . Don't . . . let . . . him . . ."

It wasn't clear for whom the words were intended. Who was to be stopped? Ryazanov? He himself? One thing was beyond question: Nikulin was referring to the gold. It would haunt him and dominate his thoughts to the last.

Quinn straightened up. There was nothing he could do for the dying man. He looked around. A big mound of rubble covered the spot where he'd last seen Ryazanov. Going closer, he saw a boot protruding from it, then a leg.

He unearthed one of the pitch-pine torches that had been mounted on the wall and lit it. Access to the tunnel at the back of the chamber was almost blocked by the debris that had buried Ryazanov. He scrambled over it and made his way along the gallery for about fifty yards. Running along the wall was a fuse, and inserted in boreholes drilled at ten-yard intervals were sticks of dynamite with blasting caps attached.

He retraced his steps until he found the place where the fuse had been cut. Only Ryazanov's foresight had prevented Nikulin's ingenious system of linked charges from going off and burying all four of them alive. He now realized what had set off the charge at the mouth of the tunnel: a last round from one of the two Russians' pistols must have detonated one of the blasting caps. . . .

Back he went to the end of the tunnel. It was sealed off by a brick wall with an inset steel door, but the door had been forced and was standing ajar.

The man-made cave beyond had been hewn out of dry rock salt. Quinn estimated that it was a hundred feet long, half as wide, and twelve feet high. Coughing because some of the smoke had penetrated the chamber and was catching in his throat, he raised the torch above his head.

Yes, there it was at last! The bars were stacked along the walls—thousands of them, together with something he hadn't expected. Ranged across the floor were hundreds of linen bags bulging with gold coin. He was looking at the gold reserves of the Imperial Bank of Russia—he had only to touch the bars to satisfy himself that it wasn't a dream.

It should have been a great moment, but all he felt was the pervasive chill and his own fatigue, not a hint of triumph.

He stood there, looking around, then finally picked up one of the bars. His only sensation was one of cold. The yellow metal seemed to freeze his fingers.

Moura was still kneeling beside her brother's body. Quinn stood over her, waiting. Eventually she looked up. Ignoring his outstretched hand, she rose to her feet and brushed the hair out of her eyes.

The silence persisted until he could stand it no longer. "Let's go," he said.

She glanced at the lifeless form on the ground. "I'll never forgive you," she said. "Never. Never!"

"It's all over," he said. "For him too. He can forget about the gold at last."

"Destroyer! I hate you!"

The walls around them echoed her words.

Her face was contorted—frightening to see. He loved her and longed to tell her so. He had missed his opportunity once already, but he knew this wasn't the right moment either, nor would it ever come again. . . .

37

IT started snowing the next day and continued to do so, heavily and without a break, for three whole days and nights. Karmel was engulfed by this fresh snow, which lay as much as twelve feet deep in the mountains. Now that Fyodor Nikulin was dead, nature seemed to have taken over his tutelary role.

Escorted by a platoon of Hampshires on muleback, Quinn and Hollis made the arduous trek into the mountains to recover Tompo's body before going on to the potassium mine, where they braved the nightmarish descent in the elevator to recover that of Nikulin. There could be no immediate prospect of removing the gold under present conditions, so a detachment was left to guard the mine. Karmel's civilian inhabitants were placed under curfew.

Ryazanov's corpse was left in the mine. Nikulin and Tompo were buried in the cemetery of the miners' village, where Timur had been laid to rest before them. Their graves were hacked out of the rock-hard ground by a burial party of Hampshires.

Quinn hadn't set eyes on Moura since their return to Karmel. There was no form of ceremony, and she only appeared at the last moment. She stood in the background like a casual onlooker, ignored Quinn when he went over to her, and walked off without a word as soon as the coffins had been lowered.

The snow was followed by a period of intense cold with temperatures as low as minus thirty. Fitzmaurice's telegrams from Omsk became increasingly brusque and his radiotelephone conversations consisted of tirades and injunctions to hurry. The Hampshires set to work. Simultaneously, a locomotive started to clear the track to the pass with a snowplow.

Teams of men and mules shuttled to and fro between the railroad station and the potassium mine no less than twenty-eight times, and it was late in January before all the bullion and specie had been loaded aboard the heavily guarded train.

The order to pull out was given as soon as the last consignment had arrived and been checked.

Quinn was sitting in his section when Hollis appeared in the doorway. In the weeks since the discovery of the gold, Hollis had changed. His face betrayed the fascination exerted on him by such a quantity of riches. He'd spent days adding up columns of figures and submitting progress reports to Fitzmaurice in Omsk. According to his final computations, the mine had yielded almost a hundred tons of bullion in bar and 1,100 bags of gold coins, each bag weighing sixty-six pounds.

He hovered now in the doorway with a sheepish expression on his face. "We'll be leaving in a couple of minutes." He cleared his throat. "You've got a visitor."

Quinn rose and looked out of the window. It had been a fine, cloudless day, but dusk was already falling. Beyond the bank of cleared snow on the far side of the track he made out the upper part of a sleigh and a figure muffled in furs. He tried to open the window, but it was frozen fast.

273

"How long has she been waiting there?"

"No idea." Hollis cleared his throat again. "I'm sorry Oliver, but I've strict orders from Omsk not to take any civilians with us. Even the Diatsaros have to take a later train. . . ."

Quinn elbowed him aside and hurried along the corridor. The cold was bitter, but he didn't trouble to go back for his coat. It was the same blue sleigh and the same horse she'd been using when he intercepted her on her way back from the mountains—light-years ago, or so it seemed.

When he reached the sleigh and looked up at her, her face was almost as it had been then: imbued with the perfection of a marble statue. There was a suitcase on the seat beside her.

"You're leaving Karmel?" he said at length.

"Yes. They lifted the curfew today."

"Forever?"

She did not seem to hear the question. She looked past him at the train. "What about you? Are you returning to Omsk?"

"Yes." He longed to see tears in her eyes—tears of sorrow or anger. Even a string of curses would have been better than nothing, but she merely looked down at him with a face like stone. "I don't have to take this train . . ." he began, but she leaned from the sleigh and held out her hand. There was something in the palm.

He took it from her. By the time he looked up again, having briefly glanced at the broken chain and the four-leaf clover, she'd whipped up her horse and driven off.

He stood there, straining his eyes until all he could see of her was a mane of red hair escaping from under a fur hat.

"Moura!"

He wanted to run after her, but he couldn't move.

EPILOGUE

Quinn spent the return journey typing up his report—sweating while the steam-heated train was on the move and shivering with cold whenever it stopped to pick up wood and water. He submitted his report to Major Fitzmaurice the day they reached Omsk. Fitzmaurice had left it to Quinn to get himself out of Russia. Quinn decided to stay.

Fitzmaurice, invoking orders from London, kept the gold train under guard inside the Allied Mission's compound. The Russians were quick to protest: Admiral Aleksandr Kolchak, Russia's self-styled "Supreme Ruler," demanded that it be handed over to him forthwith and bombarded London with telegrams for weeks on end. Fitzmaurice kept his men permanently on the alert, but it was Kolchak who eventually won the war of nerves by threatening—so malicious tongues alleged—to cease all operations against the Red Army. British troops were withdrawn and the Czech 6th Regiment assumed custody of the gold reserves.

Spring arrived, and still the civil war dragged on. White Russian troops scored few successes during 1919. The Red Army recaptured Perm and Karmel, penetrated the Urals, and thrust eastward along the Trans-Siberian Railroad. The

Whites retreated in total disorder. Streams of refugees reached the city of Omsk. Again and again, Quinn turned up in the camps, at the railroad station; kept on the lookout; asked after the same name.

Summer gave way to fall and winter. Red Guards were advancing on the headquarters at Omsk. As early as the beginning of November the weather turned so cold that the Om and the Irtysh froze over.

On November 14 the gold train, together with the special trains carrying Kolchak and the Allied Mission, pulled out of Omsk in an atmosphere of panic.

Their destination was Irkutsk, over two thousand miles away by rail. The Siberian steppe was deep in snow and lashed by icy winds that sent the temperature plummeting to thirty or forty degrees below zero. Some of the surrounding countryside was in Red hands. Thousands of soldiers and refugees struggled eastward along the rough, bumpy road that ran parallel to the Trans-Siberian. Quinn sat behind the window on that train, rubbed the ice away, stared outside. Did he expect a miracle?

All semblance of discipline had been lost. Cold, hunger, and typhus claimed countless victims. The main line was hopelessly clogged, but from time to time the unbelievable happened: White troops would manage to clear a stretch of track and trains sped past through refugee-clogged stations, their glowing windows misted with condensation. One of them was a train made up of fourteen blue cars hauled by two locomotives. The thousands of wretches on the road beside the track, foredoomed to freeze or starve to death, whispered the words as it rattled past. *"The gold train . . ."*

* * *

On January 15, 1920, the gold train and Kolchak's special train pulled into Irkutsk's Glazkov Station. The bullion was still being guarded by the same Czech unit, but the Czechs were now interested in one thing only: getting out of Russia.

Although the Red Army had yet to reach Irkutsk itself, the city was already in the hands of a revolutionary committee. The Czech commander struck a bargain with this "Political Center," as it was known: in return for a guarantee of safe passage and a train to transport them to Vladivostock, he and his men would withdraw.

Kolchak was dragged from his special train. After surviving for another three weeks, he was marched out of his cell at dawn and shot.

The gold train was back in Bolshevik hands. Only a few bars were missing from the original consignment of bullion, which was more than could be said of the gold coins: most of them had disappeared. . . .

The remaining actors in the drama were left with only one thing to do, and that was to save their skins. Two of them were already dead by this time. Sergei Diatsaro, who had left Karmel with his family, had succumbed to pneumonia on the way from Omsk to Irkutsk. Alexander Katov chose a more spectacular death. The day Omsk fell to the Reds he took off, machine-gunned one of their armored trains until his ammunition ran out, and nose-dived into the locomotive.

John Fitzmaurice, Oliver Quinn, Cloudesley Hollis, and the rest of the British Mission managed to bypass Irkutsk under cover of darkness and cross Lake Baikal, which was icebound, in company with Xenia Diatsaro and her granddaughter Aina, whom Hollis had married at Omsk. They were suffering from exposure by the time they reached Verchne-Udinsk but escaped to Vladivostock with a detachment of Japanese soldiers.

Dexter Scala and Rudolf Wajda, the American and the Czech, had never lost sight of the gold train. Scala retained responsibility for the consignment to the end, and Wajda, the ex-general, had friends among the soldiers guarding it. They sneaked out of Irkutsk equipped with sleighs, fresh horses, ample supplies of food, and a number of heavy chests, heading for the Mongolian border and Ulan Bator.

Theirs was a long and hazardous trek through country infested with bandits. The temperatures fell to minus forty degrees. It seems likely that they lost their horses and proceeded on foot, carrying as much of their loot as they could. Nobody knows for sure how far they got or if they ever reached Ulan Bator. But years later, some scattered bones and coins were discovered in the vicinity of their probable route.

As for Quinn, two images recurred to him over the years until they finally merged into one: Moura Toumanova's red hair streaming out from under her fur hat, and the rear lights of a train, a blue train speeding through the whiteness of the illimitable steppe.